MEET JERRY JEETER . . .

Financial reporter, liberal Democrat, and capitalist tool. In the cutthroat climate of shady corporate deals and hostile takeovers, Jeeter finds himself walking on a dangerous side of "the Street"—where economics and anarchy merge with deception . . . and murder!

FINAL OPTION

STEPHEN ROBINETT

AVON BOOKS ◆ NEW YORK

AVON BOOKS
A division of
The Hearst Corporation
105 Madison Avenue
New York, New York 10016

Copyright © 1990 by Stephen Robinett
Published by arrangement with the author
Library of Congress Catalog Card Number: 89-91362
ISBN: 0-380-75848-2

First Avon Books Printing: February 1990

AVON TRADEMARK REG. U.S. PAT. OFF. AND IN OTHER COUNTRIES, MARCA REGISTRADA, HECHO EN U.S.A.

Printed in the U.S.A.

RA 10 9 8 7 6 5 4 3 2 1

For My Parents

"He is in this [pursuing one's own self-interest], as in many other cases, led by an invisible hand to promote an end which was no part of his intention."

> Adam Smith, *The Wealth of Nations*, 1776

In the long run we're all dead.

> John Maynard Keynes, *The General Theory of Employment, Interest and Money*, 1936

Economics manipulates us all.

> Gerald Jeeter, "A Whiz-kid's Last Gasp," *Global Capitalism*, March 1989

Chapter One

Envy? Resentment? Greed? Or, as the police finally decided, self-defense? Do any of these words accurately describe why I did it? Perhaps. In all honesty, I have to say that much. At the time, I thought it had something to do with journalistic integrity and the truth. After all, if you can't trust the press, who can you trust?

For me, it started with Mr. Lusker, owner, publisher and principal personality behind *Global Capitalism*, a third-rate business and financial magazine and one of the few national magazines published from the West Coast, in our case, Los Angeles. With a circulation of only 70,000 and most of that in the United States, the magazine's name always struck me as pretentious. *Economic Imperialist* might have been a better name. Mr. Lusker's reactionary views—his "Publisher's Page" advocated Big Business, Big Bucks and the American Way—gave the magazine its quaint flavor.

Nevertheless, brokerage houses and investment bankers, our principal advertisers, found *Global Capitalism* useful. They supported the magazine. They supported me. They supported Mr. Lusker's twenty-acre estate in Palos Verdes and his avocational passion, ballooning. Everyone assumes Mr. Lusker took up ballooning to compete with another balloonist publisher on the East Coast, an accusation Mr. Lusker denies. He claims the hobby interested him from boyhood. Since no one can imagine Mr. Lusker actually having a boyhood, no one believes this.

Technically, my job was staff writer. Of the thirty-odd people it took to put out the magazine, only two or three wrote coherent English sentences. "By the staff of *Global Capitalism*" below an article usually meant me. I wrote everything from features to fillers. Occasionally, if Mr. Lusker was off ballooning or speaking to business groups—in either case, manipulating hot air—I even wrote his "Publisher's Page," an easy enough job. I just sat down at my computer, brought up the word processor and advocated everything I loathed for roughly a thousand words. Mr. Lusker often commented favorably on my efforts.

A "Publisher's Page" I wrote got me involved with Horton Queller's disappearance in the first place. We put *Global Capitalism* to bed around the tenth of each month. By the time copies hit mailboxes on the twenty-second and newsstands a few days later, I barely remember the contents. My attention is already on next month's deadline, sometimes a deadline two months out. Because the three-person art department needs as much time as possible to juggle photographs, illustrations, charts, graphs, ads and copy into a presentable package, we try to get copy finished as early as possible. Which meant I found myself working on the April "Publisher's Page" in late January. I thought I did a good job. Marv Walters, the usually sober editor of *Global Capitalism,* disagreed.

"Jeeter, Jeeter, Jeeter," he said on the phone, his voice weary with patient exasperation. "What are we going to do with you?"

"Fire me," I suggested, only half joking. With even the remotest prospect of another job, I would have encouraged the idea.

"Maybe," said Marv and let the word hang between us like something dead. He wanted to impress me with the seriousness of my crime. "I just read your April 'Publisher's Page.' "

"Pulitzer material, right?"

"He's going to shit bricks. You better come in here."

"I don't see the problem," I said, bewildered.

"*That's* the problem," he said and hung up. No good-byes. No jokes. Just click and a dead line. Definitely serious.

I retrieved a copy of my April "Publisher's Page" from the office file server, printed it out and reread it on the walk down the corridor to Marv's office. *Global Capitalism* occupies the second floor of a commercial building on Wilshire Boulevard, the address classy enough but the offices themselves wrong for a magazine. The private office design—mine a windowless cubicle with a desk and a computer—worked for a law office, the original tenants, but prevented the rapid interplay a magazine's staff needs to keep the presses rolling and advertisers happy. The more important offices—Mr. Lusker's, Marv's—are near the reception area. A long corridor connects them to what was generally called "the bowels," a collection of varying sized rooms for editorial personnel, a few artists, the ad staff and a bookkeeper—all of it linked by sophisticated telecommunications, a LAN network for computers, chirping featherweight phones for human beings, more of Mr. Lusker's toys. Since my office came only a few doors after Marv's, I occasionally felt as though four or five of us actually put out the magazine while everyone else hibernated in the rear of the building.

Still, the office setup gave me a chance to reread the April editorial before I confronted Marv. When I wrote it, the idea seemed reasonable enough. In a nutshell, it advocated privatizing the armed services and leasing them out to the highest bidder—the government, multinational corporations, foreign powers—to reduce the national debt, a logical extension of Mr. Lusker's general Weltanschauung.

Rose, the office receptionist and probably the most competent person in the building, saw me meandering down the corridor and glanced at the door to Marv's office, making a face like someone whistling silently.

"That bad?" I asked.

Rose nodded. A tall woman with a short haircut, she resembled a middle-aged and elongated pixie, an impression that more or less matched her personality. "He's steamed."

I walked over to Marv's door, hesitated a few seconds to get myself looking cheerful and went in.

I once read about some Jewish prisoners in Nazi concentration camps identifying so strongly with their captors that they tailored their prison uniforms to match those of their SS guards. Marv followed the same philosophy of interior design. He identified heavily with Mr. Lusker. He gave his office the same look as his captor's. A wall in Mr. Lusker's adjoining office displayed color blowups of hot air balloons along with a framed gun collection. The guns, Mr. Lusker liked to point out, had killed more than one good man, though why he liked the idea of killing good men I never understood. Marv's office wall displayed color blowups of sailboats in heavy seas and a framed coin collection. The coins, Marv liked to point out—especially when he found himself annoyed with Mr. Lusker and mimicking him—had bought more than one good man, presumably including Marv.

Even their desks matched. Marv's desk, smaller for his smaller office, occupied the room power-broker style, back to the plate-glass window overlooking Wilshire Boulevard, front to the office door, the same positioning Mr. Lusker used. There were minor differences. Mr. Lusker, a large man who sat erect behind his large desk, often looked like someone's idea of a nineteenth-century captain of industry. Marv, a small man with a tired face, usually looked like a burglar rifling the desk.

"You rang?" I said.

Marv, silhouetted by the morning glare from the window, looked at me across the piles of papers on his desk, his expression wearier than usual. "You've really done it this time, Jeeter. I hope you're prepared for the worst."

"What's the worst?"

Marv drew his index finger across his throat.

"I'll redo it."

"Too late," said Marv, shaking his head. A lock of gray hair fell across his forehead, the final touch in his disheveled look, itself the result of a two-hour head start on a full day of worrying. "At eight thirty-four this morning, he accessed the file server from the estate and pulled off this . . . this—" Marv slapped both hands down on his desk and stood up, beginning to pace. He made two complete passes in front of the leather couch beside his desk before he finished his sentence. "—whatever it is. This drivel. That's exactly what it is. Drivel."

"I'm glad you like it."

Marv glanced at me, disgusted. "Big joke, huh?"

"I guess you had to be there." I sat down on the corner of Marv's desk, positioning myself to watch his pacing exhibition.

"It's bullshit is what it is!" said Marv, glaring at me. *"And get off my desk!"*

I stood up. "Sorry."

Passing me, Marv snatched a printout of my "Publisher's Page" off his desk and shook it. *"Is* this a joke, Jeeter?"

I answered seriously. "I didn't think so at the time."

"You didn't *think* at the time."

I nodded, agreeing with him. I still needed a job. "You're right, Marv. Listen—"

"No, *you* listen. Two hours ago he got his hands on this drivel. God, I hate all this electronic crap! Computers, phones, voice mail, LAN networks! Back in the dinosaur days of typewriters, I always got my hands on everything *before* a publisher saw it. This sort of thing *never* happened. Maybe the next time I go out to the estate, I'll break his modem."

"That sounds like a good idea, Marv."

He glared at me again, his scowl deeper. "That wasn't serious."

"I know."

"What *is* serious is what I'm supposed to tell him today when he calls and reams me over this privatized army horseshit of yours. *That* is *very* serious."

"I could talk to him," I suggested. "I could say *mea culpa* five or six times and tell him I got it all wrong and that it was only a rough draft anyway and—"

"A rough draft?" interrupted Marv, stopping. "Of what? Your resignation?"

"Ahh . . ." I groped for a redeeming idea in the editorial and came up with the notion that started me in the first place. ". . . the post office. I'll tell him I really meant the post office. He did that piece last year on the virtues of private toll roads. I'll tell him it was an extension of that idea. That ought to do it."

"That ought to do it all right," said Marv, going back to pacing and looking disgusted. Before he could say anything else, the phone chirped. He glanced at it, noted the blinking light at the top of the display—Marv's private line, a number known only to Mr. Lusker—and walked over to his desk. "Shit! *Here* we go."

"You want me to leave?"

"Stay," he said, as though talking to a pet dog, visibly cheering up before he lifted the handset. "Good morning, sir . . . Yes, sir, I'm doing fine . . . It is good day for ballooning, sir, light wind and warm for January . . . That's one of the reasons I like California, too, sir. Is there anything in particular I can—" Marv looked at me and rolled his eyes. "Yes, sir, I've read Jeeter's April editorial."

Listening, I felt sure Mr. Lusker said "the" April editorial. Marv's echo, substituting my name for "the," shifted both the emphasis and the blame, positioning him further from ground zero in the event of an explosion. He listened a long time, probably alert for more opportunities to push everything onto my shoulders. When he found none, he went out of his way to make one, nodding, looking at me across his desk and, instead of answering Mr.

Lusker with a simple yes or no, adding, "Yes, sir, it's *all* Jeeter's work."

I felt like reaching across the desk and forcing Marv to eat his phone. With Mr. Lusker down on me, the rest of my career at *Global Capitalism* would last about thirty seconds.

"Marv," I said, reaching for the phone, "let me talk to him."

Marv waved me away and kept talking to Mr. Lusker. "No, sir. There's no one here. That was just someone out in the hall . . . Sure, if you give me a second, I'll close the door." Marv put Mr. Lusker on hold and shook his head, mystified. "I don't get it, Jeeter. He sounds weird."

"What do you mean, weird?"

"Weird," he said, as though repeating it would clarify it, "just weird."

"Can you give me a better hint?" I asked. "Weird's a little short on meaning."

Marv gestured toward the connecting door to Mr. Lusker's office. "This line comes up on his phone. Go in there and listen. I need some feedback on his thinking."

I followed orders, opening the connecting door to Mr. Lusker's office and walking to his desk. A solitary light blinked on the phone. I picked up the handset and glanced back through the doorway at Marv. He held up three fingers and started a countdown—three . . . two . . . one—we both pushed the button simultaneously.

I expected to hear an irate Mr. Lusker. Instead, he sounded cheerful. "Door closed, Marv?"

"Yes, sir."

"First, before I get to the real meat of this discussion, let me finish up on that 'Publisher's Page.' "

I shivered.

Marv temporized. "I can explain, sir—"

"Terrific, Marv. Absolutely terrific."

"Sir?"

"That Jeeter's got real wit. We should make more use of it. It doesn't show much in his other writing, but it certainly shows here. This is the best April Fool's send-up we've done in years." Mr. Lusker chuckled, a mirthful, snorting noise that made me hold the phone away from my ear. "Rent out the U.S. Army! I almost died laughing, Marv. That part about the troops singing 'The Battle Hymn of the Republic' as they marched off to war under the IBM logo had me in stitches, all wearing blue, of course, not gray. Gray's probably DEC or Amdahl. I had to stop reading and wipe the tears out of my eyes. We'll get mail, but that's exactly what *Global Capitalism* needs right now, mail, publicity, controversy—anything to get the right people talking about us. I want our circulation past a hundred K by the end of the year. One hundred thousand—that's the goal, Marv. Got it?"

"Yes, sir," answered Marv, the hollow tone in his voice indicating he probably wondered how a magazine that devoted most of its editorial space to the tedious activities of greedy people could generate anything more than boredom. "Controversy, sir. Right."

"As a matter of fact," said Mr. Lusker, anticipating Marv's next question on how to go about it, "I do have a few ideas on the best way to do it and I think Jeeter's our man."

"Jeeter," said Marv, looking at me through the open door, his voice sounding as though my name were an unfamiliar word in a foreign language.

"We'll make him a star," said Mr. Lusker and laughed at the idea. "It'll be his reward for this April Fool's joke. And while you're at it, we'll have him interview Madeline this afternoon. That, at least, he'll like. The story I want him to do is iffier."

"Iffier," echoed Marv. "What story would that be, sir?"

"Queller," said Mr. Lusker. "Does that name mean anything to you? Horton Queller."

Marv equivocated, uncertain whether he should play the name as obscure and praise Mr. Lusker for even knowing it or as a household word only an idiot would fail to recognize. "It sounds familiar, sir. Refresh my memory."

"Dead guy," said Mr. Lusker, recognizing and enjoying Marv's ignorance. "Missing anyway. He disappeared last June."

"Hmm," said Marv as though the information were in fact interesting, playing for time to think.

"Whiz-kid," added Mr. Lusker, dangling another clue.

"Ahh," said Marv, still in the dark.

"I keep a file on him in Stalag Seventeen," said Mr. Lusker, finally letting Marv off the hook. I looked across Mr. Lusker's office at the red file cabinet in the corner, Stalag Seventeen, named after an old movie, a place to keep enemies. And hobbyhorses. Clippings, tidbits of unsubstantiated gossip, probably an incriminating tape or two filled the cabinet. Each file tracked the sins of people Mr. Lusker considered out to emasculate capitalism, politicians in general, Commie Pinko Liberals in particular; in short, people more or less like me. Not that I give two hoots about communism or, for that matter, capitalism, as abstract ideas. I do vote for Democrats most of the time, probably enough of a crime in Mr. Lusker's eyes to get me my own manila folder in Stalag Seventeen.

Along with files on enemies, Mr. Lusker kept files on subjects he considered good story ideas, the hobbyhorses. Though an excellent businessman, Mr. Lusker seldom came up with anything close to a good story idea. Marv usually took the material, trashed most of it, worked up an entirely different story under the same title and thanked Mr. Lusker profusely for his hot tip.

"Give Jeeter a copy of the file," continued Mr. Lusker. "I'm sure the man has the talent to make this happen for us, don't you, Marv?"

Marv, either reluctant to give me an assignment that might raise my stock with Mr. Lusker or worried I would somehow screw it up, said, "I'm not sure, sir."

"Problem?" piped Mr. Lusker.

"Jerry's got a lot of work to do."

Now that I was a star, I was also "Jerry," not "Jeeter." Still, Marv had a point. My usual juggling act around the office always left me about to drop at least one ball, sometimes all of them. I seldom needed another assignment, especially one of Mr. Lusker's pet projects.

"I'm sure he'll find the time to do what I want done," said Mr. Lusker, ending the discussion.

"Yes, sir," said Marv and shrugged at me through the doorway, indicating he tried. "Anything else, sir?"

"You might like to know the reason I want us to do this Queller story," said Mr. Lusker, rebuking Marv.

Marv either failed to notice the rebuke or considered it politic to ignore it. "Yes, sir. I would like to know that."

"Some of my associates," began Mr. Lusker, a ploy he frequently used around the office to indicate that his well-connected sources of information were undoubtedly better than those of mere journalists, "have brought to my attention a new lead—no, two new leads in the disappearance of Horton Queller. I want them checked out."

"New leads, sir. That sounds promising."

"I'll fax them to you."

Almost before Mr. Lusker finished saying it, the fax machine in Marv's office beeped, an incoming transmission. While Marv and Mr. Lusker said their good-byes, I hung up, walked back into Marv's office and went over to the fax machine.

I tore off the sheet and looked at it, the image a newspaper clipping taped to a sheet of paper. Beside the clipping stood the word *Queller?* in perfect copperplate handwriting. Below the name in a smaller version of the same handwriting were the words *End Run.* Beneath these words in Mr. Lusker's jagged, barbed-wire script stood the word *Boat?*

The clipping itself came from the "Orange County" section of the *Los Angeles Times.* It described the headless body of an unidentified man washing ashore on an Orange County beach. Sharks had done substantial damage to the body, gnawing off the head, both arms and one leg. Only the torso, most of a pair of jeans and one cowboy boot remained.

"I'll make sure he looks at the file right away, sir," said Marv, kowtowed a few more times and got off the phone. He looked at me. "Anything?"

I passed him the facsimile. "You got me."

He read the page and shrugged, shaking his head. "Another wild hare."

"Probably."

He got up and started for Mr. Lusker's office. "I'll get you the file."

I heard the metallic sound of a file drawer rumbling open. Marv returned with a slim manila folder open in one hand, reading.

"So?" I asked.

"So nothing," said Marv, squeezing closed the folder with one hand and passing it to me. He smiled a particularly obnoxious smile. "It's *all* yours, Jerry. And Madeline Mundell, too."

"Thanks, Marv."

"Anything for an up-and-coming star."

Chapter Two

I took the folder back to my office and opened it. According to a scribbled note inside, Mr. Lusker started making entries the previous June, just after Horton Queller disappeared. The folder contained clippings from several magazines and newspapers, including a *Wall Street Journal* profile of Queller called "Good-bye to the Fast Lane?". I read the *Journal* piece first.

Good-Bye to the Fast Lane?

Horton Queller Only Made $3 Million Last Year; So What's His Problem?

Bollington Associates Super
Arbitrageur Complains About
Lack of Respect,
Resigns Amid Controversy

A Fair Wind to Tahiti

By Ellington W. Witherspoon
Staff Reporter of The Wall Street Journal

NEW YORK—At 33 years old, Horton Queller, III, comes close to breaking Wall Street's whiz-kid record, the youngest and brightest multimillion-dollar employee on the Street.

Trading options, futures and currency, Mr. Queller earned Bollington Associates over $300 million dollars last year, receiving just over $3 million in salary and bonus, an income twice the size of Ralph Bollington, his employer. Not bad for someone who only five years ago was putting the finishing touches on a Ph.D. in psychology and considering a teaching career.

But was the money enough for Mr. Queller? Last month, Mr. Queller abruptly resigned from Bollington Associates, leaving behind only a short note and no explanations. "I just came in one Tuesday morning," says Ralph Bollington, "and found the note on my desk—two words and Hortie's signature." Mr. Bollington declines to reveal the contents of the note but indicates the two words amounted to "I quit" in less polite language.

Mr. Queller's resignation forced Bollington Associates to answer more questions than simply the cause of an employee's resignation. The firm made $587 million last year both for its own account and for clients, most of it from currency and options arbitrage trading. Mr. Queller's single-handed $300 million contribution amounted to more than half the firm's revenues. Clients wanted to know how Bollington Associates hoped to match its past performance without Mr. Queller. Foreign exchange markets, following uncorroborated rumors of major losses at Bollington Associates, slowed to a trickle for several hours on news of Mr. Queller's resignation. The Securities and Exchange Commission—along with everyone in the financial industry—wanted to know what happened.

What happened, according to a close personal friend of Mr. Queller, was profound ideological disenchantment: "Hortie always believed you got rewarded for achievement. In our society, money is achievement. Money brings respect. Hortie made more money than anybody and it didn't matter."

From the outside, a $3 million bonus might appear

to be something that would go a long way toward salving wounded pride. Many at Bollington Associates consider the bonus obscenely high. Other industry observers, less involved in the immediate situation and perhaps less envious, consider the bonus obscenely low. "If he worked around here," says David N. Samuelson, First New Hampshire's V.P. for options trading in New York, "he would have taken away more like $15 million—minimum—for that kind of performance."

The story of Mr. Queller's journey to disenchantment and resignation is not just another tale of yuppie-dom. Nor is it, at least in the beginning, a story of genius. A Californian by birth, Mr. Queller's high school career was less than auspicious. "All he did was hang around and watch people," says John "Wolf" Wolverton, football coach for the Balboa High School Dolphins in Newport Beach, California and Mr. Queller's mathematics teacher in high school. "He did okay in math, but he always struck me as a little weird, you know, always on the sidelines and never willing to put it out there like the guys on the team. You never knew what was going on with Queller."

At the University of California's Berkeley campus in the late seventies, Mr. Queller again drifted. Described by former classmates as simultaneously introspective and gregarious, "a thoughtful guy who knew everyone," Mr. Queller frequently annoyed his friends with what he later called "Thought Probes," setting up apparently spontaneous events, then gauging people's response. "The guy was a jerk," remembers Arvin Denison, a Berkeley classmate of Mr. Queller. "He once filled up my dorm room with inflated balloons—floor to ceiling, the whole room—while I was asleep, then he popped one of the balloons to wake me up. I felt so disoriented, I just about lost it. I mean, waking up buried alive in balloons! My sense of direction was so confused I almost fell out the second-story [dormitory] window trying to get out of there. When I finally made it to the hall, there was Hortie. He clicked a stop watch and told me it took two minutes and twenty-three seconds for me to solve the problem. I mean, who cares?''

Mr. Queller, for one. Apparent pranks like forcing Mr. Denison to cope with a room full of balloons led to Mr. Queller's Ph.D. dissertation in psychometrics, the science of measuring human psychological response. ''All those experiments,'' says Mr. Queller, relaxing at his Basking Ridge, N.J., home in jeans and cowboy boots, the clothes a contradiction to the usually precise, professional cadences of his voice, speech habits left over from his years in academia, ''got me interested in measuring situational reaction time, trying to categorize and quantify it. What better place to study crisis psychology than financial markets. The whole thing's psychological to begin with. Take a concept like value, what something's worth—that's *totally* psychological.'' Mr. Queller combined psychology and catastrophe theory, a branch of mathematics developed by French mathematician Réne Thom, in his doctoral dissertation *Crisis Psychology and Catastrophe Theory in Free Market Economics,* an attempt to quantify market behavior. ''After that [developing the theory], there was only one thing left to do,'' says Mr. Queller. ''Try it.''

Mr. Queller took a job with First Boston's trading department and learned to trade options. He did well but became dissatisfied. Most banks set trading limits for individual traders at around $50 million, an amount sufficient to control about $15 billion in option positions. Mr. Queller found the limit confining. ''By then, I was hooked,'' says Mr. Queller. ''I traded at work, I traded at home, I had two phones in my car to trade on my way to and from work. A $50 million trading limit was peanuts.''

Two years ago in June, Mr. Queller moved to Bollington Associates on the promise of a substantially increased trade limit. As Mr. Queller's performance for his new employers improved, so too did his trading limit. At the time of his unexpected resignation, Mr. Queller's trading limit approached $1 billion dollars, letting him control approximately $300 billion in currency option positions. Mr. Queller typically made between 200 and 300 trades per day, a personal paper trail that kept two assistants working full time cleaning up details behind him. Mr. Queller's colleagues at Bollington Associates often complained about what they considered his poor manners. "He was like a greedy little kid," says a former associate who consented to discuss Mr. Queller's habits only on the condition he remain anonymous. "Sometimes he would move a billion dollars in a day and all by itself that would move the market. But did he tell us about it? No. And we were in the *same* office. In essence, he was making money off *us*."

When asked about such poor etiquette, Mr. Queller responds with a blunt obscenity and adds: "It was my job to make money. Situationally speaking, a trader in Hong Kong and a trader in the next office were the same thing, competition. I didn't make up the rules of the game, you know."

But Mr. Queller did, however, study the rules. Combining his academic work with his real world experience trading various markets, Mr. Queller developed a devastatingly effective programmed trading algorithm for currency and options arbitrage, a computer model of the marketplace that allowed Mr. Queller to squeeze pennies from situations others ignored. On advice of counsel, Mr. Queller declines to comment further on his trading techniques—the computer program embodying the market model is currently the subject of a lawsuit between Mr. Queller and Bollington Associates, who claim ownership of the program as something developed by an employee on company time—but Mr. Queller does note that the lawsuit itself seems to him typical of

"Ralph Bollington's perennial desire to get something for nothing."

The rest of the article described Queller's dissatisfaction with life on Wall Street, his feeling that superstar performance deserved superstar respect, i.e., superstar money, and ended with a tease kicker about Queller at a crossroads in his life. "I'll either come back to the Street and make them all kneel," it quoted Queller as saying, "or just go off to Tahiti and never be heard of again."

Just as I finished the *Journal* article, the phone rang.

"Well?" said Marv.

"Well, what?"

"Anything to it?"

"I haven't finished reading the file yet, Marv. All I know now is that Harold wants us to look into the disappearances of some Wall Street whiz-kid."

"Harold," said Marv, noting my use of Mr. Lusker's first name. "Don't push it, Jerry. You may be Mr. L's number-one boy this week, but if you fuck up, you'll be number one on his shit list. Rose is coming down there to get the file and dupe it. I'll read it. When you get done, come back here. We'll talk."

"Okay," This time, I hung up without a good-bye, taking advantage of my number-one boy status while it lasted.

Rose picked up the file, Xeroxed it and returned it. I leafed through the clippings and picked out one from—of all places— the *National Enquirer*—on Queller's disappearance.

Rocket Scientist Missing! ### *Secret Formula Vanishes!*

Horton Queller, III—very rich and very eligible—disappeared last week and apparently took with him a computer formula worth millions!

"Hortie," as his friends call him, was a rocket scientist, one of the new generation of Wall Street wizards who use computers and mathematics to make split-

second decisions and tons of money. Hortie was among
the best and the brightest, but unhappy. No respect,
Hortie complained. He threatened to go to Tahiti and
vanish into obscurity.

The article, using the same chummy, in-the-know style,
went on to give more or less the same background on
Queller as the *Journal* article, then suggested Queller ran
off with a lover.

. . . and Hortie, wherever you are, have fun! You too,
lucky girl, whoever you are.

I glanced through the rest of the clippings and walked
down to Marv's office.

He was still reading when I came in. He finished and
looked up at me, shaking his head. "There's nothing
here."

"Tell me about it."

"Some yuppie shithead is unhappy because they only
paid him three million dollars last year so he pulls up
stakes and goes off to Tahiti with his girlfriend," said
Marv, shaking his head again and shrugging. "B.F.D.
What are we supposed to *do* with it?"

"Good question."

Marv got up and started pacing. "There's not even room
to do a switch on Mr. L. About all we've got is this Hortie
jerk pouting about how he don't get no respect. What does
Mr. L *want?* Are we supposed to play it as small-minded
Wall Street that can't appreciate a good thing or a small-
minded shithead who didn't appreciate what capitalism did
for him?"

"You got me."

Marv stopped at his desk and picked up his copy of the
facsimile transmission. "And what about this piece of
crap? Sharks munch on some guy in cowboy boots and
there's supposed to be a connection." He tossed the fac-

simile on the desk in disgust. "The whole thing sounds more like *True Detective* than *Global Capitalism.*"

An idea occurred to me. "That's not bad, Marv. We could do a 'Murder on Wall Street' story."

"Murder?" said Marv. "Where do you get murder?"

"Guy disappears. Body appears. Big bucks motive."

Marv laughed. "They always say Wall Street's full of sharks."

"Right."

"Wrong," said Marv, shaking his head. "Even if we could trump up something like that—"

"It's controversy and Mr. Lusker wants controversy."

"It's not our beat. Money's our beat, Jeeter, not murder. Leave murder to that weasel buddy of yours."

"He pronounces it 'Wh-eye-sel,' " I said. "But I like your pronunciation better."

Marv meant Mark Weisel, a crime reporter for the Orange County section of the *Los Angles Times* and hardly a buddy. Weisel and I graduated in journalism together from Claremont. Weisel considered me someone with whom he competed or, more accurately, someone he attempted to lord it over, a journalist at a real newspaper doing hard news, not a staff writer at a trade magazine doing fluff. I usually avoided or ignored Weisel, probably the reason Marv liked reminding me of him.

"So what are we going to do with it, Marv?"

Marv stood at his desk and stared down at the folder, weary, depressed. "Forget it maybe. Sweep it under the rug and hope he doesn't remember."

"Okay," I said. "As long as it's your rug."

He shook his head. "We can't, can we?"

"I doubt it."

He looked up. "Fast shuffle?"

"Pardon me?"

"I do it sometimes with Mr. L. He gets on one of these hobby horses and wants me to mount up. You remember that hard-on he had for Senator Cranston?"

"Before my time."

"There was nothing to it, but Mr. L *wanted* us to find something. He wanted Cranston out and some John Birch Society jerk in. I made a few phone calls, came up dry on the leads Mr. L gave me, told him it was a dead end and immediately dumped a bunch of problems in his lap about the next issue, problems I already had solutions for but something to keep him busy. The fast shuffle."

My respect for Marv went up. Not much, but some. He was not, after all, a complete toady, which in no way meant he would back me if the idea bombed.

"And that's what you want?" I asked, trying to involve him. "A fast shuffle?"

Marv thought a second, weighing consequences and probably also locating escape hatches, then nodded. "Yes, dammit! I've got a magazine to put out here. I can't have writers running around the countryside writing sequels to *Jaws*. There is absolutely nothing to this, nothing! It's a waste of our time! Mr. L will thank us later."

I nodded, trying to reinforce his decision. "You're right, Marv."

"He *will*."

"You don't sound convinced."

His resolve crumbled. "You never know with Mr. L."

"That's true," I said, trying to regain momentum for the idea of dead-ending the story. "But then you never know with anyone, Marv. Life's like that."

Marv, not listening, nodded agreement. "Like that note. Where'd he get that damn note?"

"What note?"

Marv gave a dismissing wave toward the file folder. "In there."

I reached across the desk and got Marv's copy of the file. Halfway through the clippings I found the note, overlooked during my first pass through the papers. Another facsimile, this time of a few, hand-written words on a sheet of Bollington Associates stationery, it reproduced Queller's letter of resignation.

Dear Ralph,
   Fuck off.
                  Hortie

I laughed. "I'd say this Queller had an attitude."

"Had?" said Marv. "You're as bad as Mr. L. The guy's in Tahiti with a bimbo. The question is how Mr. L got that fuck-off letter."

"He probably knows Bollington," I suggested. "He knows everyone."

Marv grunted, acknowledging the suggestion as probably true. "Anyway, we'll try a dead end. It's the best I can think of." He gave a long sigh and looked at a sailboat picture on his wall. "Maybe someday I'll own one of those things and get to Tahiti myself." He looked at me. "And don't forget your lunch interview. Rose will give you the magazine's credit card."

"What's this Madeline Mundell do that I'm supposed to be interviewing her about?"

"Interior designer."

I saw it coming. Mr. Lusker frequently sent staff members to interview women he found interesting—models, actresses, interior designers—a form of flattery he hoped would work wonders later in the hot tub. The interviews never got printed. The models, actresses and interior designers stayed around a while and finally went away. Mr. Lusker's famous "eye for world-class talent" roved on. He considered the interviews rewards for staff members— a free lunch with an attractive woman—in this case a reward for my April Fool's joke.

"Off to fantasy land."

"You got it."

"I really do have a lot of work, Marv. Maybe if—"

"Jerry, Mr. L wants you to have this," said Marv as though he were a grandmother talking to a child, "so you're going to have it. That's all there is to it. It doesn't matter what you want. It doesn't matter what *I* want. It only matters what Mr. L wants and he wants you to have this.'' His voice returned to normal. ''In other words, you're it.''

I shrugged. ''I guess I've got to eat. What's her claim to fame?''

Marv looked at me as though I had just asked a dumb question.

Chapter Three

"**E**mptiness," said Madeline Mundell, a carrot stick from the garnish tray held in her hand like a lecturer's pointer. She gazed out the restaurant window at the marina and ocean beyond, her abstracted expression suggesting the vast emptiness of the Pacific Ocean somehow encapsulated her idea. "That's the key."

"Emptiness," I echoed and watched the carrot stick, the traces of lipstick on it provoking fantasies, the conversation, artsy, provoking boredom.

"It's not what you put *in* a space, Jerry," she continued, the well-practiced phrase timed to sound spontaneous, "but what you leave out."

"I suppose in your line of work, you have to do both."

"Both?"

"Put things in," I said, "and leave things out."

She nodded agreement, as though I had just contributed something significant to the conversation. "You have to take the exact measure of emptiness. That's what's important."

Marv, I decided, was right about Madeline Mundell's claim to fame. Elegant and expensive—definitely expensive—she suggested Alfredo's for lunch, an equally elegant and expensive Italian restaurant in Marina del Ray, picking a window table and beginning to expound on her philosophy of interior design even before the menus arrived. Everything she said sounded glib, rehearsed, quot-

23

able, the sort of patter she probably used to convince clients to pay too much for too little.

While she elaborated on the nuances of filling space with emptiness, I tried to look intelligent and watched the carrot stick. Occasionally, she nibbled at it, especially interesting moments. I kept wondering why so attractive and polished a woman annoyed me. The perfect coiffeur, the perfect makeup, the perfect composure—even the perfect backlighting from the bright day outside, giving her an aura—all of it annoyed me. I wanted to reach across the table and mess up her hair, smear her lipstick, push the carrot stick up her nose. I felt as though everything about her were superficial, designed like her philosophy of emptiness to produce the same knee-jerk response advertisers rely on when they show idealized women ducking into limousines in front of columned mansions. Nonetheless, I responded to the image. That bothered me most. I knew how the magician did the trick but fell for it anyway, cooperating to produce the illusion, enticed into fantasies by carrot sticks.

"Are you listening, Jerry?"

"Hm? Oh, sure." I smiled. "Got every word."

I watched her talk and nibble and appear to think. I sensed my own conflicting urges to both destroy the illusion and let myself be seduced by it. My mind wandered. I started thinking about conflicting urges in general and wondering why the older I got the more of them I had, an adult form of acne. Somehow Queller, the multimillionaire whiz-kid and super-yuppie, gave me the same kind of zits, mixed feelings of envy that anyone made $3 million a year doing anything and disdain for the values that let anyone believe he was worth more.

Before I left the office for lunch, I called the Newport Beach Police Department in Orange County—the body washed up on a stretch of beach in their jurisdiction—and asked about the headless torso wearing a cowboy boot. The officer I needed, a Sergeant Gahr, was out. I called a few marina offices in the area and asked about the "End

Run." No one knew the boat. I wrote a brief report for Mr. Lusker, pushed the facts to say the police considered the body unidentifiable, pushed them some more to say no marinas in the area recognized the "End Run," saved the report to Mr. Lusker's directory on the file server and went to lunch. On some level, I almost hoped the torso belonged to Horton Queller. His death, gnawed to pieces by sharks, might at long last make him an interesting human being.

I watched the carrot stick rest thoughtfully on Madeline Mundell's lower lip and thought about Mr. Lusker's hot air clique of important people, most of them important for the same reason Queller was important, money. All of them produced the same irritating attraction I felt looking at Madeline Mundell, more emotional zits. For that matter, all the people I praised once a month in *Global Capitalism* gave me emotional zits. My annual income amounted to pocket change for most of them. Nevertheless, they gave me large amounts of their expensive time just to see their names in print, a situation that often made me feel smug—the rich, the powerful, the famous on my doorstep—and at the same time irritated me for feeling smug. These people trusted me. They trusted *Global Capitalism*. Like parents with well-behaved children, they knew we would do the right thing; that is, make them look like worthwhile human beings. Once upon a time, when I picked journalism as a career in college, I thought a journalist's job was to make the Horton Quellers of the world— the rich, the powerful, the famous—uneasy. Instead, I spent my days making them look good, ensuring ongoing ad revenue for *Global Capitalism* and keeping my paycheck arriving on time, like Madeline Mundell, taking the exact measure of emptiness.

Lost in thought, I emerged to find Madeline Mundell waiting for an answer to some question or another, the carrot stick now held like a teacher's ruler, presumably about to rap me across the knuckles for inattention.

"Pardon me?" I said and smiled.

She gave a dismissing wave of the carrot. "Of course, it's none of my business."

"Ask anything you like," I said, hoping to catch the general drift of the conversation.

"Blondes? Brunettes? Redheads, perhaps?"

"That depends."

She smiled, amiable. "Anything will do?"

"Not exactly."

"You *do* like women, Jerry?"

"Definitely."

"Then what type?"

The missing question at last. "Usually unattainable women, the kind you see in ads getting into limos in front of mansions."

She laughed and gave me a cute, sidelong glance. "Really? Do you enjoy frustrating yourself? Or do you just like longing from afar?"

"I long from afar mostly," I said. "It's safer."

She laughed again. "I'd say you like women with a little style, a little class."

"Who doesn't?"

"Many men find them intimidating."

"They just give me zits."

"Too rich for you," she said, understanding what I meant.

"Exactly."

She used the carrot stick to toy with a piece of cauliflower on the garnish tray. I guessed she spent half her life in expensive restaurants toying with cauliflower on garnish trays. She stopped toying and looked at me. "Do you like me, Jerry? As a human being, I mean."

"As a human being?" I said and shrugged. "Sure. Why not?"

"As a woman?"

"As a woman," I said, uncomfortable, "you're just fine. As you were saying about emptiness . . ."

"Am I your type?"

The question made me even more uncomfortable, probably its purpose. At another time, in another place, under other circumstances—perhaps with another writer doing the make-believe interview—I might have read the question as a come-on. In an interview whose sole purpose was to flatter one of Mr. Lusker's diversions and give me a free lunch for writing a good editorial, I somehow failed to believe the question actually meant what it didn't say. I decided to play along for a while and see if the invisible ink emerged.

"As I said, who doesn't like classy women?"

"Do you have any money, Jerry?"

"Money?" I thought of my paltry bank account.

"On you."

"Oh, on me." I nodded. "Sure. Some. Why?"

"We can go somewhere," she said and thought, the carrot pensively against her lip. "Let's see. What would be nice on a pleasant winter afternoon? Somewhere with a view so we can leave the drapes open."

The invisible ink became readable. I glanced out the window to avoid eye contact, to avoid inappropriate fantasies. Instead of a soothing view of the ocean and marina, I saw a reflection in the glass, an image of reality, the maître d' escorting a short woman and even shorter child toward the table. I looked toward them. My daughter saw me first, let go of my wife's hand and ran across the dining room to the table, her usual miniature overalls and flowered sneakers replaced by a frilly white dress and shiny black shoes. She stood beside the table with her arms in the air, wanting up.

I avoided looking at Madeline Mundell and hoisted Joy with both hands, standing her on my lap in front of me.

"Hello," said Joy as though I were a genie who suddenly appeared in front of her.

"Hello," I answered and kissed her. Of the three women in my general vicinity, I found the one in front of me definitely my type and said so: "You look very pretty today, Sweetheart."

"I know."

"You do, huh?"

Joy nodded. "Mommy said so."

"Ah, then that makes it official."

Barbara arrived at the table, plain at best by comparison to Madeline Mundell, another juxtaposition of reality and fantasy, more zits. I introduced Barbara to Madeline, noticing polite distance on both sides, more on Barbara's side than Madeline's.

"I called the office," said Barbara while the maître d' found another chair. "Marv said you were here."

"I'll have to thank him."

Madeline, sans carrot stick, looked at her watch and stood up, offering Barbara her chair and both of us an excuse about a forgotten appointment. She edged out from behind the table and looked at me. "It's been very nice chatting with you, Jerry. Perhaps we can finish up some other afternoon. How does that sound?"

"Sounds good."

She got a business card out of a small purse and handed it to me. "Call my office."

I looked at the card, elegant and expensive, a name, a phone number, no address. According to Marv, she worked out of her home. "Maybe we can do the interview there."

"I'd like that."

Everyone got reshuffled, Joy into a child's chair, Barbara into Madeline's chair.

Barbara noticed me watching Madeline leave. "What does she do?"

"Keep Mr. Lusker relaxed, I suppose."

Barbara made a noise like a muffled grunt. She knew about Mr. Lusker's peccadilloes, including the fake but flattering interviews. That I participated in them only confirmed her poor opinion of me. Once, in the days when I still thought journalism could make a difference, our relationship was different. Neither of us felt inclined to discuss the change directly. I knew Barbara's attitude from the comments she leaked or, in this case, grunted. What irked her was not jealousy of Madeline Mundell or any threat to a marriage she only cared about to the extent it paid the bills but envy. If she had only been more realistic and picked someone else, she too could have spent her afternoons toying with cauliflower in expensive restaurants instead of working part-time in a department store selling naugahyde furniture, the adult price for her youthful idealism. As for me, Barbara no longer considered me a budding Woodward or Bernstein but a second-rate hack grinding out third-rate copy for a fourth-rate magazine, working under my ability to bring home a paycheck, not that she minded the paycheck. Though I felt uncomfortable with Barbara's opinion of me, I could live with it. I recognized it as substantially true. What bothered me most was Barbara airing her opinions, directly or indirectly, in front of Joy. At three, Joy understood none of it. Later, as an adult, I wanted Joy to understand. Adults make compromises. Many of them, I made for her.

Madeline, the fantasy, disappeared from the dining room. The waiter brought menus and a bib for Joy. I turned my attention to Barbara and reality. "Let's eat."

We did, silently. Barbara avoided looking at me, instead staring out the window. The expensive restaurant, the sunny marina, Madeline Mundell—all of it set her brooding. Halfway through lunch, Joy picked up Barbara's mood and got grumpy, flipping tomato sauce on my sport coat and the window. By the time the check arrived, I barely remembered what I ate.

On the way out of Alfredo's I held Joy's hand and calmed down. I thought about Barbara's unexpected arrival at the restaurant. She took time off from work. She dressed Joy to please me. She called the office to find out whether we could have lunch. In her way and in spite of her feelings, Barbara still wanted to try.

Crossing the parking lot, I put my arm around her. She let me. We walked in silence. At her Datsun, I strapped Joy in the baby seat and stopped Barbara from getting into the car.

"I've got an idea, Barbo," I said. "I'm kind of a fair-haired boy at the office this week. I can probably get away with taking the rest of the afternoon off."

Barbara looked up at me, started to say something, changed her mind and simply nodded.

She waited in the car while I walked to the pay phone at the edge of the parking lot and called Marv.

"No sale," said Marv.

"But—"

"No buts, either, Jeeter," he said, demoting me from Jerry back to Jeeter. "Mr. L reamed me over that piece of shit you wrote."

"I thought he liked it," I said, confused. "April Fool's joke and all that."

"Not that. The Queller thing. After expressing his—and I quote—'profound disappointment' at the 'shoddy job of investigation' you did, he made it extremely clear he wants the job done right—*extremely* clear, if you get my point."

"Not exactly."

"I'll spell it out," said Marv. "If you don't come up with something usable, you're gone. Clear enough?"

I looked past the phone at Barbara waiting in her car. "I understand."

Instead of spending the afternoon trying to keep my marriage together, I spent it trying to keep my job. My primary research tool, the telephone, faltered. I normally worked up stories for *Global Capitalism* by staying on the phone until my ear ached. I talked to everyone who knew anything about anything and put it all together later, total immersion. During three years at the magazine, I wrote stories on almost every aspect of the business and financial community. When new stories came up, I knew who to call to get answers. The Queller story—a missing whiz-kid, a chewed-up torso, maybe a boat—stumped me. What did any of it have to do with net earnings, mergers, currency fluctuations or corporate raiders, my usual beat?

Still, I tried. I got Yellow Pages out of the office library covering every county in Southern California and wore out several sets of fingers calling marinas. I asked about the "End Run." No one knew the name. One guy laughed and suggested I call a local tackle shop. I was halfway through punching out the number when I got the joke—football, end run, tackle. I shrugged and called the number anyway. No luck. I called the Newport Beach Police Department again. Sergeant Gahr had come and gone.

About two o'clock, surrounded by open phone books, each showing columns of marinas checked off in red to indicate I called, I sat back, ran my fingers through my hair, rubbed my sore neck muscles and tried to calculate how long Barbara, Joy and I could survive after my final paycheck. The answer depressed me.

I looked at Joy's picture on my desk. Hair perfectly brushed for the picture, wearing an immaculate polka-dot blouse with a white collar and enormous red bow tie, she looked angelic.

"Sorry, honey," I said. "Daddy's fucking up again. The mean Mr. Lusker bear is chasing Daddy through the woods and trying to eat him up. His big bear eyes are red and angry and his big bear teeth are sharp and pointy and he's howling and growling and snapping and biting and icky saliva's oozing out of his big bear mouth. And you know what? He scares the shit out of Daddy. Because if the mean old Mr. Lusker bear eats Daddy, Daddy won't be able to bring home porridge for Mommy and Joy, and Mommy and Joy will cry so loud something will come and eat them too, maybe a wild nauga from Mommy's store that's angry because Mommy's selling its hide for furniture or, worse yet, the lumbering, one-eyed idiot Marv. He'll come and hit Joy with his big club and steal her pretty sneakers."

"We wouldn't want that to happen," interrupted Rose from the doorway and handed me galleys for the March issue of *Global Capitalism*. "Hot off the presses."

I hefted the galleys in my hand. They contained at least one feature article I wrote and a half dozen of my shorter items, all needing a last-minute once-over for errors. "When am I supposed to do this, Rose?"

"Between two and three in the morning like everyone else." Rose studied me, her expression turning into an elongated frown. "You okay?"

"No."

"Poor baby. What has the mean Mr. Lusker bear done to you this time?"

"Fucked me over."

"Tell Rosie bear *all* about it."

I told her. Rose listened, thought, shifted the load of galleys from one arm to the other and finally shrugged, abruptly cheerful. "Why didn't you ask me something hard?"

"That's easy?"

"Don't call marinas. They don't know anything."

"Neither do I," I said. "That's the problem."

"Call the boat fueling stops. They keep accounts by boat name. It doesn't matter whether the boat belongs to a marina or not."

I thought about the suggestion, looked at the phone books on my desk and sighed. There had to be at least as many fuel stops as marinas. "You're right."

Rose smiled and nodded toward the galleys in my hand. "By tomorrow. And before lunch."

I went back to the phone. I called fuel depots in marinas. Once during the afternoon, Marv interrupted my efforts with a thoughtful reminder to hurry up. Near five o'clock, my ear aching, I found the Orange County directory under two other directories and started down the list of fuel stops. Eventually, I got to Lindy's Landing in Newport Bay.

"Landing," said a gruff voice.

"May I speak to . . ." My eyes tired and my memory dysfunctional, I checked the directory. "Lindy, please."

"You got him."

"You don't happen to sell fuel to a boat called the 'End Run,' do you?"

"Who wants to know?"

I told him.

"Jeeter," he said and mused on the sound. "Funny name."

"I won it in a lottery. Does a boat called the 'End Run' buy fuel from—"

"Yeah. And them two assholes owe me fifty bucks."

"Which," I said, trying to sound like someone sympathetic to his problem, "two assholes?"

"The two that own the boat. Who else?"

"Do these two assholes have names?"

"Most people do. Not like Jeeter, of course—that's a doozie!" I heard a boat engine in the background. "Time's up. That's the 'Dr. Doctor' with the doctor himself on board. Gotta pump some. Will you *look* at them two bimbos!" He hung up.

I called back. Busy, probably off the hook while he pumped some for the doctor and the doctor's two bimbos. The number stayed busy until I left the office.

Chapter Four

The next morning, I called Lindy's Landing from my apartment. Still busy or busy again. I left home and started for the office. The closer I got, the slower I drove, held back by bumper-to-bumper traffic and my own reluctance to enter the lion's dean without meat. I did have one morsel, a boat called the "End Run" near Lindy's Landing in Newport Beach. I finally decided the assignment, special, demanded special methods. Besides, the idea of spending the entire day trying to get through to one busy phone number left me cold, especially with Mr. Lusker and Marv looking over my shoulder. I bypassed the Wilshire Boulevard freeway exit and kept going toward Newport Beach.

An hour and a half later—the trip normally took forty-five minutes on a clear freeway—I merged into traffic on the Newport Freeway. The character of the traffic changed around me, dented Chevolets and dusty pickups giving way to BMWs, Mercedes and an occasional Porsche. At Pacific Coast Highway, I stopped for gas and directions. A surfer, wearing knee-length jams and a blue Exxon shirt, waited on me. When I asked about Lindy's Landing, he told me to find the ferry on Balboa Island and "look for an old fart in a straw hat. You get lost, dude, just ask anybody. Everybody knows Lindy. The guy's kind of a human monument."

I laughed at the phrase. "A human monument. I'll bet the engraving hurt."

"Not him," said the surfer and gave me my change. "You could engrave on that old bird all day and he'd never notice. He's tough."

I left the gas station, crossed a short bridge onto Balboa Island, parked on a side street and walked to a bay front sidewalk, following signs with arrows toward the ferry. I liked the idea of being out and around, wearing out shoe leather. Normal *Global Capitalism* stories kept me cooped up in a windowless office with a phone and a computer, wearing out the seat of my pants.

A winter wind, chilly, blew in off Newport Bay. A single sailboat, red and yellow spinnaker flying, tacked across the bay, perhaps the doctor himself and his two bimbos out for another day on the "Dr. Doctor." In any case, someone able to play with adult toys while everyone else worked, someone with too much time, too much money, someone who, face-to-face, would probably give me zits.

Ahead of me, the Balboa ferry, a barge for three cars and foot passengers, pulled away from its dock for the short trip across Newport Bay. Beyond the ferry, I saw a quay with two gas pumps and, near the pumps, an old man in a straw hat coiling rope, the human monument.

I walked past the ferry landing, stepped over boxes and tarps to work my way around the side of a corrugated metal building and started down the quay toward the man.

"Lindy?" I called.

"Who wants to know?" shouted the man without looking up from his rope coiling.

"Jeeter."

Bent over the pile of rope, he peered at me under his arm, scowled and grunted. "You don't look much like no Jeeter."

I ignored the comment. A gust of wind off the bay disarrayed my hair and flapped the brim of his straw hat. He stood up and looked at me. I guessed his age at about seventy, his skin as weathered as the corrugated metal shed.

"Can you tell me where I can find the 'End Run'?"

He used the limp end of the rope to point toward the middle of the bay.

"Sunk?" I asked, surprised.

He laughed, deep wrinkles surfacing around his eyes. "You ain't too nautical, are you, Jeeter? I was pointin' at them moorings."

I squinted against the glare off the water. A half dozen sailboats, grouped like cattle around a watering hole, stood moored in the middle of the bay. "How do I get there?"

"Can you swim, Jeeter?" he asked and snorted out a laugh. "Ain't that far. A Jeeter ought to be able to do it in no time."

"I could walk, too," I said, "but I forgot my halo."

He laughed again. "Walk! That's a good one! Jeeter, you ain't half bad. Let me tell you how you got to go about it. First, you get yourself a boat—" He frowned at me. "You know what that is, don't you?"

"I'll ask someone."

"Yeah, well, don't ask me. I got work to do." He went back to coiling rope. "Why you interested in that thing anyways? It's just an old Santana. Good boat. Wide beam. Good sleeper. But, like I said, nothin' special."

"I want to find out who owns it."

"Two faggots."

"Pardon me?"

"Faggots, flamers, swishes, mincers," he said, making a prissy expression with his weathered face. "Get the picture? You ain't one, too, are you?"

"Me?" I said. "No. I like women with limos and mansions."

"Yuppie, huh?" he said with equal contempt. "You yuppies is almost as bad as them faggots. Yuppies and faggots all over this place these days. Once we didn't have no faggots around here. We didn't have no yuppies neither. We had John Wayne. Now that was somethin'. Wayne used to keep his yacht here, you know, an old converted minesweeper. Big sucker."

"Wayne?"

"The boat. Armed, too. We had *men* in them days, Jeeter. Flynn kept a boat here and them Cagney boys, Jimmy and Billy."

"Billy?"

"Jimmy's brother. I remember one time old Pat O'Brian fell off the Cagney's boat"—he pointed somewhere out into the bay with the rope—"right there. Drunk as a skunk! That Irishman could drink! We had *men* in them days, real men, not a bunch of lily-livered faggot yuppies!"

"Those were the days," I said, at a loss.

"Damn right they was!"

"So I have to get a boat to go out there."

"Well, you see, Jeeter! You ain't half as dumb as you look. I only got to say a thing once and you pick it right up."

The human monument began to get on my nerves. "Are you always this—what? Pugnacious?"

"Only when a guy comes around here sticking his nose in other people's business. Then I figure the guy's an asshole and it don't matter what I say to him. Even faggots and yuppies got a right to be let alone."

"Do you think I could get their names?" I asked. "These faggot yuppies, or whatever they are."

"You still ain't told me why."

"I'd like to talk to them," I said, evading the question. "Do you have any records, something with a phone number maybe?"

"I got records," he said and coiled rope, "but I already told you I got things to do and them records"—he nodded toward the corrugated shed ten feet away—"is way over there in my office. You want me to walk all the way over there just to look. Don't see nothin' in that kind of a trip for me."

I started to get the point. Somewhere—maybe from John Wayne or James Cagney in the old days, perhaps even from Errol Flynn—he learned about checkbook journalism and liked the idea.

"I can't really afford—"

"Me neither," he said, beginning to uncoil the coiled rope. "I got work to do, payin' work."

I thought about Mr. Lusker, my job, Joy. I got out my wallet. Unfortunately for my negotiating position, when I took out one twenty, the bill tugged out the corners of two more bills.

The human monument noticed. "They owe me fifty."

I sighed and gave him three twenties.

He tossed aside the rope and started toward the metal shed. "I'll get your change."

The fuel card listed two names for the "End Run," John Wolverton and Leon Fairview, but only one phone number, Wolverton's. I remembered Wolverton's name from the *Wall Street Journal* profile of Queller, a high school football coach and Queller's mathematics teacher. Somehow, I felt as though I were making progress, connections, though what connections eluded me.

I found a pay phone on a pole near the ferry—the human monument refused to let me make even a local call from his phone—and called the number on the card.

"This is John Wolverton," said the answering machine, the voice strong, masculine, anything but gay, and went on to tell me Wolverton was out. It suggested I leave a message at the beep or call a second number.

I called the second number, Balboa High School. Coach Wolverton, I learned, was in the gym finishing up an off-season workout with his players. I got directions to the high school, more directions to the gym, called Rose at the office to tell her I would be late, retrieved my car and took the ferry across Newport Bay.

During the ten-minute trip, I got out of my car and stood at the rail of the ferry, watching the "End Run" at its mooring. I felt optimistic. Wolverton coached high school football. If the human monument's characterization of him was accurate, Wolverton liked all the butt-slapping football players did, probably encouraged it, perhaps even gave private lessons—potentially useful information.

* * *

"Wolf!" screamed an adolescent stacking towels inside the metal cage, then looked at me. *"That'll bring him!"*

I nodded thanks, the easiest form of communication in the noisy locker room. Around me, metal doors slammed, hulking teenage linebackers shouted obscene conversations, equipment clattered to the concrete floor, shoulder pads, helmets. At the far end of one aisle, a naked man emerged from clouds of steam and looked toward the cage.

"Guy here!" shouted the kid in the cage and pointed at me.

The man snatched a towel off a bench, wrapped it around his waist and started toward me. In his late forties and well built, Wolverton looked like an older version of the team around him.

He reached me and held out one hand, using the other to hold the towel at the waist. *"Wolf Wolverton!"*

"Is there somewhere quiet we can talk?" I yelled.

"About what?"

"Horton Queller!"

Wolverton nodded, got a second towel from the boy in the cage and started toward the glass-paneled office, holding one towel at his waist and drying his hair with the second towel.

I followed.

In the office, a cubicle with wide windows in all four walls to let him keep an eye on the chaos, Wolverton sat in one of two student chairs to avoid dripping water on the leather chair behind his desk. A trophy case beside him displayed plaques and statuettes. Among the small gold quarterbacks cocked to throw small gold footballs stood a small gold hunter in a game vest, a tiny shotgun aimed at the sky as though ready to shoot down the footballs. Football, skeet shooting—I began to doubt the human monument's characterization of Wolverton.

Wolverton hiked one ankle on the opposite knee and smeared the towel around his head. "Queller, huh? Weird duck."

"You told the *Wall Street Journal* Queller was standoff-ish."

Wolverton nodded, his wet hair going in several directions over a prominent bald spot. "How about that article, huh? Was that something, me in the *Wall Street Journal!* The sports page, maybe—but in there with all those pin-striped suits. And the guy they sent to talk to me was real pleasant, too." He glanced at me briefly from under the towel. "No offense, but I always thought reporters were dicks."

"Some are," I said. "Can you tell me anything else about Queller?"

"I told it all to the *Wall Street Journal* guy," said Wolverton and stopped rubbing his head. "I taught Queller math. I guess I can take some credit there, right?"

"Did he play football?"

"That runt?" he said. "You're kidding."

I decided to fish for information. "What's Leon Fairview got to do with Queller?"

Wolverton looked at me a second, then started rubbing his head again. "Leon? You talked to him?"

"Not yet," I said, improvising. "But he's on my list."

"Where is the little peckerhead, anyway?"

"You don't know?"

Wolverton smiled at me, the towel hesitating on his head. "And you don't know either, do you, Mr. Jeeter?"

"A better question might be *who* is Leon Fairview?"

Wolverton shrugged and went back to rubbing, most of his expression obscured by the towel. "Just an old student of mine. Nobody important."

"You own a boat with him."

Wolverton stopped rubbing his head and put the towel in his lap. He thought about saying something, held it back and stood up. "I think we're pretty well done with this interview, Jeeter."

"Are we?" I asked and decided to goad Wolverton for a reaction. After all, real journalists twisted arms to get information. "What happened? Did Fairview cheat on you with Queller?"

I wanted a reaction. I got one. Wolverton glared at me, his freshly scrubbed face abruptly beet red. He raised a thick index finger and pointed it at me. "If *one* word of this kind of crap, just *one* word, gets into print, Jeeter, I'll find you wherever you are, drag you into the street and kick your teeth down to your asshole!" He glared at me. "You got that?"

"I—"

Before I could finish answering—not that I had much of an answer—Wolverton reached over, jerked open the office door and shouted to three large adolescents in street clothes. *"Roberts, Garcia and Williams—in here!"* He indicated me with a flick of his towel. *"This asshole's leaving!"*

I sat in the car a long time after Wolverton's bouncers escorted me off campus, at first angry, finally depressed. I kept asking myself what I thought I was doing. Playing at street reporter? Sabotaging myself? Both? Instead of exploiting Wolverton and using him to open doors for me, I managed to antagonize him and get the only door worth opening slammed in my face.

"Dumbshit," I concluded, annoyed with myself.

I started the car and drove up the Balboa Peninsula toward Pacific Coast Highway, both the weather and my mood degenerating. The sky, overcast, darkened, threatening rain. One or two oncoming cars showed headlights, anticipating the storm. Near the head of the peninsula, I found the surfer's gas station and pulled in, parking near the phones. I still had one or two doors to knock on, Sergeant Gahr's at the Newport Beach Police Department and Leon Fairview's. Neither sounded promising. I imagined Sergeant Gahr reciting the number of shark bites on a John Doe torso and Leon Fairview—whoever he was—saying he never heard of Horton Queller and just owned a boat with a former high school teacher. End of story. End of job. Considering Mr. Lusker's connections in the publishing community, end of career. Maybe the surfer needed help pumping gas.

I called the Newport Beach Police Department. The operator put me through to Sergeant Gahr.

"Gahr," she said, making the name sound like a noise.

I introduced myself and explained what I wanted.

"You mean old John Doe Four," she said with a slight laugh.

"The one with the cowboy boot."

"That's him. Or what's left of him. We don't have a name yet."

"Do you have anything?" I asked, expecting at least a lecture on the difficulties of identifying half-eaten corpses. The details might help me justify coming up with nothing when I talked to Mr. Lusker.

"What was the name of that magazine again, Mr. Jeeter?"

"Global Capitalism."

"Never heard or it and"—papers shuffled—"it's not on the list."

"I can understand that," I said. "We don't normally cover this kind of story. But if you could just tell me—"

"Can't," she said. "Not without clearance, press credentials. We do have procedures, Mr. Jeeter. Assuming this magazine of yours is real—"

"It's real."

"We need proof," she said. "We get nut calls, you know."

"This isn't one of them."

"I'm sure it's not. Nevertheless—"

"What kind of proof?"

"A letter on the magazine's stationery will do. We have an officer who clears press people. He'll check you out. Then I can talk. It'll only take a couple of weeks."

"A couple of weeks!"

"Sorry," said Sergeant Gahr, her voice genuinely apologetic. "Procedure."

"Ma'am," I said, "I really do need this information. If you could at least tell me whether you have anything more than appeared in the papers—torso, jeans, cowboy boots. Is that it?"

"We have several other details."

"Like what?"

"Mr. Jeeter—"

"Listen, Sergeant, if I have to beg, I'll beg. My ass is on the line here. If I don't come up with something—not in two weeks but yesterday—I'll have a new career pumping gas at Exxon. My publisher wants this story a lot and what I've got for him right now is zilch. I either have to get the story or the world's best excuse why it's ungettable."

"I understand, Mr. Jeeter, but procedure—"

"Believe me, I'm not a weirdo. I'm not a nut."

"There is a way to speed things up."

"Tell me and I'll love you forever."

She laughed. "I've heard that one before from men."

"No one ever meant it as much as I do."

She laughed again. "I've heard that one, too. Okay, Mr. Jeeter, assuming you *are* a real journalist . . ."

"I am."

". . . then you probably know someone in the local press corps, someone who already has acceptance credentials."

I disliked even saying the name. "Mark Weisel?"

"The *Times* guy," she said, a studied neutrality in her voice. "He'll do. Have him call me and get the information for you. That way, everything's kosher."

"Weisel and I aren't exactly friends."

The neutrality left her voice. "You're sounding more like my kind of man all the time, Mr. Jeeter."

"Cheater Jeeter!" said Weisel, recognizing my voice and using his old nickname for me. Weisel originally thought up the nickname to both irritate and demean me, one of his extracurricular hobbies at Claremont. He came up with it after I got what he considered too much attention for a story in the school paper, a sports piece about our notoriously poor football team. My story claimed the team played an entire quarter with two balls on the field and still failed to score. Inevitably, half the student body believed the story. I became *persona non grata* in the locker room and celebrity of the week in the newsroom. Everyone liked the story so much, the paper ran a correction in the next issue saying the team in fact played the quarter with no ball on the field and failed to notice. Weisel scoffed, called the story fake journalism and came up with the Cheater Jeeter nickname. His own nickname, Weasel Weisel, had more substance, suggesting Weisel's ability to ingratiate himself to people—weasel his way in—gain their confidence and later stomp all over them in print, the perfect personality for a street reporter but less than attractive in a friend. Or associate. Or rival.

"Can we skip the crap this time, Mark?" I asked. "I'm really not up to it today."

"Sure. What do you need, old buddy?"

"Information."

"You came to exactly the right place," he said. "That's what we do around here, sell information, two bits at your local newstand."

"I'm doing a story for *Global Capitalism* . . ."

"You still work there, do you?"

". . . and I need some information from the Newport Beach Police Department on a John Doe—John Doe Four to be exact."

"And you want to know who to call," he said, incorrectly anticipating my question, his voice patronizing. Real journalists, after all, people who worked for real newspapers, knew who to call. "Try Kathy Gahr. She does that kind of thing. She can at least get you on the right doorstep. That it?"

"I talked to her," I said. "There's a problem."

Feeling as though I were confessing to not being a real journalist, I explained about press credentials and having no time to get them.

Weisel acted as though he believed the confession. "And you want me to use my credentials to get the poop for you."

"I'd appreciate it."

"Anything to this, Jeeter?"

"What do you mean?"

"Whatever you're working on," he said. "If I get something useful for you, does it mean there's a story here?"

I saw his next move coming and played dumb. "For you? I doubt it."

"Newspaper, Jeeter," he reminded me. "I work for a newspaper. We print news. If there's a story here—"

"Even if there is a story," I said, "I can't do that, Mark."

"Sure you can," he said. "It's like elementary school, sharing."

"I can't give away a story we're going to print."

"So there *is* a story here!"

"I didn't say that," I said, dodging. *"If* it turns out there's a story here, I can't just give it to a newspaper. It would mean my head. You know that. It would be like you giving a story to the *Herald Examiner.*"

"I've done that before," said Weisel. "Besides, we're local. You're—I don't know what your stuff is but whatever it is, it doesn't compete with us. If there's a story here, the *Times* wants a piece of it."

Weisel's attitude annoyed me. "Stop being an asshole, Mark, and just do me a favor for once—*please!*"

"Interesting," said Weisel, gauging my reaction. "You really want this, don't you? Either it's hot or they've got you by the short hairs, do or die."

"The latter."

"I doubt that, Jeeter," he said, smug, evidently thinking my situation gave him some advantage. "It's hot, isn't it? I want it."

I tried to convince Weisel to do me the favor and forget twisting my arm. He refused and twisted. I thought, looking for a way to get what I wanted without spilling Mr. Lusker's beans. If the information about John Doe Four came to nothing, no story existed and I could only use the information to convince Mr. Lusker I looked under every rock. On the other hand, if John Doe Four turned out to mean something, Weisel, grinding out copy for a daily newspaper on a daily deadline, would get a beat on me with my own story, a fate almost as bad as pumping gas for a living. I remembered Marv's tactic of diverting Mr. Lusker onto different stories.

"Mark—"

"I want it, Jeeter," he repeated. "And that's that."

"You're not giving me much of a choice."

"No choice at all."

"Okay," I said and lied to him, picking the first credible story that came to mind, improvising. I told him about a coach at a local high school with a preference for hands-on instruction. I promised to give him the coach's name if he got me the information about John Doe Four from Sergeant Gahr.

Weisel thought a few seconds and agreed, promising to get back to me at the office with the information. At the time, I had no intention of actually giving him Wolverton's name.

I stood at the pay phone behind the gas station and checked out my final lead, the wind picking up around me. The Orange County phone book listed twenty-seven Fairviews spread out from Alhambra in the north to San Clemente in the south, none of them named Leon, or even L. I bought some quarters from the surfer and remembered Wolverton saying Fairview was a former student, meaning he once lived in the area and probably had relatives nearby. I called the only Fairview near Balboa High School.

A woman answered.

I asked for Leon Fairview.

"Leon doesn't—" she began, then broke off, distracted

by someone in the room. I heard a gagging noise, as though the person in the background were choking on food.

"Mrs. Fairview?"

The phone went dead.

I called back. The phone rang but no one answered.

I copied the address out of the phone book and checked it against a map in the car, locating it about a half mile from the gas station. I decided a personal visit might be worth a try, a final rock turned over.

I drove back down the peninsula, the sky even darker around me. Just as I found the Fairviews' street, the rain started, a sprinkle too light for the windshield wipers. I drove slowly down the street checking house numbers, occasionally flicking on the wipers for a single, smeared pass.

I found the address toward the end of the block, a boxy, wooden beach house, the veranda decorated with fish net and cork floats. The house looked left over from the fifties, out of place among the glass-and-wood creations from the seventies and eighties, as though its owners bought the house and froze time, ignoring any changes in the neighborhood around them.

I parked in front of the house and got out. A gust of wet wind blew my hair and slammed the car door. I started through the drizzle to the front door. Everything—porch, windows, fish net and floats—looked dusty, uncared for. I walked up on the porch and knocked on the screen door.

I heard footsteps from inside and the sound of a woman's voice, followed by the same gagging noise I heard on the phone. The door finally opened. A small woman in her sixties, one hand on the door and the other holding her house coat closed at the throat, smiled at me through the screen.

"Yes?"

I introduced myself, got out one of my business cards and, when the woman made no move to unlatch the screen door, pushed the card through a rip in the screen.

She took the card and studied it. I glanced past her at the living room. A man about her age sat in an easy chair facing the door, staring at me. He looked vaguely like Wolf Wolverton—not a relative but a similar type, big, bald and rugged but ill. His complexion showed the pasty remains of a once deep tan. Beside him on the floor stood an oxygen bottle, a plastic hose running up over the arm of the easy chair and forking into his nose. I smelled cigarette smoke from inside the house and noticed an ashtray on a table beside him.

Mrs. Fairview finished examining my card and looked at me. "We don't read that kind of magazine, young man. You might try directly across the street. I believe the Webbers subscribe to several magazines."

"I'm not selling magazine subscriptions, Mrs. Fairview," I said. "I'm a writer for the magazine. I'm looking for Leon."

The man in the easy chair came more or less alive, making angry, gagging noises. Mrs. Fairview excused herself and waddled across the room to the man, soothing him and checking his hoses. "Yes, dear," she said to him. "I understand but—"

The man made more angry, gagging noises.

"All right, dear," she said and waddled back to the door, talking to me through the screen. "I'm sorry, young man, Mr. Fairview says you have to leave now. We don't know anyone named Leon."

"But—"

"Please go," she said, closing the door, upset. "We don't have a son."

I sat in my car in front of the Fairviews' house and debated whether to knock on their door again. The storm arrived, heavy winds, heavy rain, in the distance, heavy thunder. I watched the distorted image of their house through the windshield and wondered why the Fairviews disowned their son. The reason seemed obvious. Mr. Fairview, macho outdoorsman, refused to accept the idea of a gay son, values that matched the boxy house from the fifties. I wondered whether Fairview turned to Wolverton in high school as a more sympathetic father figure. Perhaps. I also wondered how I would react if Joy one day swaggered out of the closet and told me she was a lesbian. I hoped I would love her anyway.

I turned the car around and started back toward Los Angeles. Rain slowed traffic, giving me too much time to think. I had followed every lead the story offered, knocked on every door, and still found no one home. The prospect of actually losing my job started to seem real to me for the first time.

I drove and brooded, working my way through a long series of gloomy thoughts, dredging up ancient mistakes to justify my mood. Once upon a time, I remembered, everything seemed different. Once upon a time, I saw myself getting Pulitzer prizes, writing books about whatever got me the Pulitzer prizes, enjoying the admiration of my peers, the esteem of my banker, even winding up in a job like Marv's, editor-in-chief but editor-in-chief of a magazine that made a difference. Pure fantasy, all of it. People who worked for the *Washington Post* or the *New York Times* got Pulitzer prizes—even people who worked for the *Los Angeles Times*—not people who worked for *Global Capitalism,* a rinky-dink business magazine whose only reason for existence was ad revenue, money to keep Mr. Lusker's balloon filled with hot air. Whatever I wound up doing rather than working at *Global Capitalism,* I told myself, would probably be an improvement. That's what I told myself.

Chapter Five

Marv, after a silent query with raised eyebrows, sighed, shook his head and disappeared into his office, closing the door.

"I don't think Marv loves me anymore," I said to Rose.

"Worse," said Rose and glanced at the matching closed door to Mr. Lusker's office. "Harold feels the same way."

I studied Mr. Lusker's closed door. "Maybe if I talked to him—"

"I wouldn't," said Rose.

"But—"

"There's more."

"Do I want to hear it?"

"Probably not."

"Tell me anyway."

"Marv assigned that venture capital piece to Sharon Kahn."

I understood immediately what Rose meant. The article, venture capitalists with international connections, fell into my usual area of expertise. Kahn, a free-lancer, wrote about business startups. *Global Capitalism* only used free-lancers when no one around the office could write the story. Marv was already planning for the day when no one around the office would be able to write about venture capitalists.

"That asshole."

"And don't forget the March galleys," said Rose. *"Please!"*

On the way to my office, I walked past Mr. Lusker's door, sensing his looming presence behind it. I sat at my desk and tried to correct the March galleys for Rose. My mind wandered. I fantasized about Madeline Mundell, imagining her ducking into a long white Mercedes in front of a tall white mansion. Unfortunately for my fantasy, both the mansion and the Mercedes I visualized belonged to Mr. Lusker. Still, the fantasy appealed to me. Though it smacked of self-destructive behavior, the idea of cheating on my wife with my employer's mistress promised a quick end to two depressing situations.

I spent the rest of the afternoon finishing up my regular work. I checked the March galleys and returned them to Rose. I translated dreary statistics on Japanese business acquisitions in the United States into English. I spent an hour explaining data for a pie chart to Willie Lien, the magazine's nonverbal art director. Finally, I settled down with phone tapes from an interview with a self-important New York investment banker—a V.P. for mergers and acquisitions, no less—who said four or five times he considered "Europe the next battleground of M and A," as though he considered the remark clever and quotable. I kept imagining him standing in the back of a jeep—power tie flapping over the shoulder of his pin-striped suit, telescoping pointer raised in the air above his head like a battle baton—shouting, "To Berlin! To Berlin!"

Even working gave me mixed feelings, more emotional acne. I wanted to finish as much work as possible to give Mr. Lusker as few reasons as possible to fire me. At the same time, the more work I left unfinished, the more the magazine still needed me. The longer I worked, the more annoyed I got with everyone and everything, especially myself. I remembered Marv's face when I came in the office, his sigh, the disappointed shake of his head. I felt as though I were simply marking time until the axe fell, waiting out the last few seconds until my head fell into the basket.

I reached the investment banker's graduate school years and was in the middle of trying to make his revelation to go into banking sound something like the Roman emperor Constantine's vision of a cross against the sun, when Mark Weisel called.

"I got the poop, Jeeter."

"That's something we should all have," I said, "poop."

Weisel laughed. "That's what we do in the news biz, Jeeter, get poop."

"I've always said that. Tell me about it."

"Aside from Gahr making it *very* clear she was doing *you* a favor, not me . . ."

"That was nice of her."

". . . she says a reconstructed I.D. from the wallet in the stiff's jeans says 'Horton Queller.' Is that important?"

"In the ultimate scheme of things, is anything important? Zen teaches us—"

"Fuck Zen," said Weisel. "Is it important?"

"To whom?" I asked. "Probably to this Queller. To me? I'm into existential doubt today."

"You're into being a pain in the ass today."

"That too."

"I had our research people do a search on this Queller—"

"*Real* reporters for *real* newspapers call it the morgue, Mark," I said. "Appropriate in this case."

"Do you want this stuff, Jeeter," asked Weisel, exasperated. "Or do you just want to go fuck yourself and forget about it?"

"Sorry," I said. "Rough day."

"The guy's a New York stock trader type, which is probably your angle on it, right?"

"You got me."

"Gahr says she tried to contact relatives but can't catch up with anyone."

"But she's sure it's this Queller person?" I asked, trying to keep the questions as off-hand as possible.

"You're not listening. *Real* reporters listen."

"I'm listening."

"The reconstructed I.D. *said* Queller. That's all she
knows."

I shuffled possible responses to the information, searching for one consistent with the facts I already gave Weisel
but simultaneously pointing him in the opposite direction,
away from Queller. "Damn, wrong guy!"

"What's this Queller got to do with anything?"

"Nothing," I said. "It's the wrong guy."

"What guy did you expect?"

"Another guy," I said. "This one's the wrong guy."

"Wrong for what?"

"The story."

"What story?"

"Mark, there isn't any story. Not now. I was just elim-
inating possibilities. Now they're eliminated. This
Queller—you say he's a Wall Street type?"

"Right. Hotshot trader of some kind. Dow Jones News
Retrieval showed an old story on him."

"No," I said, trying to sound convincing. "That doesn't
fit at all."

"Fit what?"

"My idea."

"What idea?"

"Mark, don't start that again. There's nothing to this. I
appreciate your help. You saved me a lot of wheel spin-
ning. Now I can go do something more productive with
my time."

"What, for example?"

"A different story."

"Jeeter, I don't believe a fucking word you're saying."

I tried to put weary resolution in my voice. "Believe
what you like, Mark. If you want to waste a lot of time
chasing wild geese, be my guest. By the way, do they need

any business writers around the *Times?* I know someone who may need a job."

Weisel ignored the question and thought, evaluating my response. "We'll see about this Queller."

"Mark—"

"What's the coach's name?"

"What coach?"

"The gay coach," said Weisel. "We had a deal: I got the poop from Gahr, you gave me the name."

I hesitated. Originally, I intended to get the information from Weisel about John Doe Four and give him a phony name for the coach with the roving hands, a diversion to keep him from thinking about Queller. With Weisel close to my story, I needed something real to keep him busy. Besides, after my forced exit from Balboa High School, I considered Wolverton a jerk who deserved what he got, a delicate piece of self-justification since I provoked Wolverton into throwing me out in the first place.

"Wolverton," I said.

"Wolf Wolverton!" shouted Weisel and gave a lupine howl of pleasure. *"The Wolf's a flamer! I always knew that guy was weird! All that macho shit of his on the sports page about building hard, young bodies!"*

I already regretted giving Weisel the name. "My information may not be any good, Mark. In fact—"

"This is hot, Jeeter! Maybe I'll call it 'Bugger-gate: Scandal in our Schools.' How's that sound?"

"A little strong for the *Times,"* I said, trying to temper his enthusiasm. "Besides, it may not be true. It's just a rumor. Not even a rumor, actually. It's more like a vague hint of a rumor, one that probably has no substance to it at all, so—"

Weisel, off and running, ignored me. "This is *great,* Jeeter! I'll have one *hell* of a good time with this one! What's this Queller got to do with it?"

I hesitated, almost ready to tell Weisel the truth to calm him down. I thought better of it. "Not a thing."

"Okay, dude," said Weisel. "I owe you one."

* * *

The rest of the afternoon, I worked on the heroic profile of the investment banker. The job took only part of my attention. In the back of my mind, I mulled over the implications of Weisel's information. Implications were few and far between. I put everything I read about Queller together with the few bits of information I dug out myself, added the reconstructed I.D. on the chewed-up torso, and still came up with nothing. So what if sharks ate Queller? So what if sharks ate all of Wall Street's finest? It probably served them right.

I thought about the one-legged corpse in the cowboy boot. If I wrote down everything I knew about Queller and gave it to Marv, I would still be on the street for failing to deliver. The guillotine blade inched closer. I decided to make my last moments pleasant and went back to fantasizing about Madeline Mundell.

Perversely, fanatisizing about Madeline Mundell, sleek and elegant, reminded me of Barbara, short and dumpy. More emotional acne, more mixed feelings. I remembered Barbara in the parking lot of Alfredo's restaurant on the verge of almost talking. I wondered whether my Madeline Mundell fantasy amounted to more sabotage, a way to short-circuit any real effort to talk to Barbara about our real problems. If I tried to talk to her again, openly and honestly, would she listen? In my heart, I doubted it. How could I expect someone to listen who blamed me for all life's disappointments? Almost talking, after all, wasn't actually talking. Almost talking was all we had left of once talking all the time about everything, a happier time, a less realistic time.

Typing my way to Berlin with the investment banker, I even wondered whether all my ramblings about Barbara were just another form of self-justification, the misunderstood husband trying to give himself permission to avoid dealing with his problems by cheating on his wife. The thought passed through my mind with utter clarity just before I found Madeline Mundell's business card, sniffed it—cardboard with no traces of perfume—punched up an outside line and called her number.

"Jerry," she said, sounding pleased to hear from me. "You're calling about finishing up our little chat."

"Something like that," I said. "When would be a good time?"

"This evening? We can do it here. Do you know the address?"

"No."

She gave me the address, an expensive section of Westwood. "I talked to Harold today. He seems peeved with you."

"Peeved is probably an understatement," I said. "Try totally pissed off."

"What did you do?"

"It's more what I didn't do. Or what I can't do, an impossible story he wants me to write anyway."

"Harold's like that. He wants impossible things. That's part of his charm."

"That and his bank account." My second line rang. "Could you hold on a second? I've got another call."

"Why don't we just make it eightish?"

I hesitated, my emotional complexion breaking out. "I—"

"What?"

"Madeline," I said. "I don't think I can do this."

"Surely you've done it before."

"Not really."

She laughed, a charming and pleasant laugh. "I can hardly believe that. I thought people in the magazine business did this sort of thing all the time."

"Some do," I said, thinking of Mr. Lusker. "I guess I'm weird."

"Not at all," she said. "I can understand how difficult it must be. I can barely do it myself."

"Really?" I said, surprised.

"It makes me nervous."

"Me too."

"And you'll have Harold looking over your shoulder."

"I hope not."

"But you will," she insisted.

I had a brief image of video tape and one-way mirrors. "I didn't know he was into that sort of thing."

"Doesn't he read the interviews you write up?"

"Oh," I said, finally tracking on the conversation. "Interviews. Yes, he reads every word in the magazine several times." The second line rang again, insistent. "Listen, Madeline, I think maybe we ought to postpone the rest of the interview again. It's probably still raining outside . . ."

"It is," she said. "It's quite lovely from here."

". . . and I'm tired and generally contrary. I'd probably be terrible company. I'll call you."

I heard something tentative in her voice, as though she thought she recognized a brush-off. "You *will* call."

"Of course."

"I'll be expecting you."

I hung up and answered the second line.

"In here, Jeeter," said Marv and hung up, reality again intruding on fantasy.

On the way to Marv's office, I put on my coat and cinched up my tie, the condemned man trying to retain as much dignity as possible before the execution. Somewhere during the long walk down the corridor, my generally contrary attitude reasserted itself. I decided both Marv and Mr. Lusker were jerks. For all I cared, both of them could take a flying leap. Someone else could go brain dead writing about conquering investment bankers. I also decided to take as little shit as possible from Marv. If he intended to fire me, he could suffer for the privilege.

I reached Marv's door, took a deep breath and went in.

Marv glanced up from a mess on his desk, talking even before I closed the door. "*Five* times I've talked to him today, Jeeter—*five!*"

"So?" I said, walked over to Marv's leather couch and flopped on it, my feet on one armrest and my head on the

other. I put my arms behind my head and looked at the
ceiling between my elbows. "Isn't that what you do around
here, talk to Mr. Lusker?"

"Get off there."

"No."

"I don't have anything to *say* to him," said Marv.

"That must make all those conversations difficult."

"Impossible is what it makes them." He noticed me on
the couch again. "Get off there."

"No. Why am I here, Marv?" I asked, staring at the
ceiling. I noticed a stain on a soundproofing tile and wondered whether Marv kept a bottle behind the removable
tile. "I mean in general, on the planet."

"To cause me grief, probably."

"At last, my true calling revealed."

"Will you get *off* that couch?"

"No."

"This situation's *impossible*, Jeeter," continued Marv.
"I've never seen him like this. He's got this giant hard-on
about Queller being the story that will put *Global Capitalism* on the map. I'm afraid we're *both* going out the
door on this one."

"As opposed to just me," I said to the ceiling.

"He's got Willie doing a new cover for the March issue,
a composite cover of dead bodies from those pics of
Queller in the *National Enquirer.*"

"A cover story," I said, any hope I had of surviving at
Global Capitalism rapidly vanishing. Botched cover stories amounted to instant suicide.

"He keeps sending Willie's sketches back and telling
him to make the images more decomposed or more
bloated. We've *never* run a cover like that and we've already got a perfectly good cover for March. We've already
got the whole damn issue and he starts redesigning the
entire fucking magazine!"

"Now there's an idea, Marv," I said between my elbows. "A whole new look for *Global Capitalism.*"

"He's tying up this entire place with this . . . this—"

"Drivel?" I suggested, remembering Marv's comments about my April editorial. "That's a word we could all use more often around here."

"*Drivel!*" said Marv, taking the suggestion. "That's *exactly* what it is! Or lunatic obsession!"

"How about lunatic drivel?" I said. "That has a ring to it. When we redesign the magazine, we'll put that right on the cover: 'Lunatic Drivel Inside,' along with the Surgeon General's warning about brain cancer. Truth in packaging—that's what we need around here, Marv. We'll run two pictures inside to help explain the new format, one of a normal human brain and the other of a prune. The cut line will explain that the prune was taken from what was left of an old subscriber, someone who fell off a boat and was eaten by sharks like Queller. We'll give all the scientific evidence in a nice chart. We'll show conclusively that just three issues of *Global Capitalism,* whether eaten directly or taken intravenously, will cause measurable brain shrinkage and the beginnings of the dreaded prune brain. On the editorial page, instead of words, which no one cares about anymore anyway, we'll put one of those little perfume inserts like we had in last year's December issue, but instead of perfume we'll fill it with barf smell. That should do it. Everyone will know exactly what the magazine's about. When we close the first issue of the *New Global Capitalism,* we'll all go out and cheat on our wives to celebrate." I glanced at Marv. "Oh, sorry. I forgot. You already do that, don't you?"

Marv stared at me across the litter on his desk, his expression peculiar. I expected anger. Instead, he looked as though I had just suggested the perfect format for the magazine. "What did you say?"

"I never repeat myself."

"You said Queller was eaten by sharks."

I nodded. "So what?"

"Are you sure?"

"Who can say what's certain in life?" I said. "Zen teaches us—"

"Are you *sure?*"

"Reasonably."

"Why didn't you tell me this in the first place?"

"Is it important?"

"You still don't get it, do you?"

"I guess not," I said. "Explain the joke."

"It's no joke. *Global Capitalism* is currently dedicated to the memory of this shit Queller. Don't ask me why."

I nodded. " 'Why' is often an impermissible question."

"Anything about Queller's important. Is that all you've got?"

I nodded.

"Then get *more, dammit!"*

"You're saying I still work here."

"Of course you still work here," said Marv, getting up from behind his desk, walking over to me, taking my arm and tugging me off the couch. He pushed me toward the door. "We *both* still work here, for now. Get *more,* Jeeter, *more!"*

"Like what?" I asked, resisting the push toward the door.

"That's up to you," he said, reached the door, opened it and pushed me out into the lobby. "And *call* the instant you've got it!"

His door closed.

Glancing over my shoulder at Marv's closed door, I walked over to Rose's desk. "Rose, this entire place has gone nuts."

"Is this new information?" she asked.

I kept looking at Marv's door. "He's over the edge."

"That's not new."

I looked at Mr. Lusker's closed door. "And him—God knows what's going on with him."

"That's not new either."

"They want me to make something out of nothing, a silk purse out of a sow's ear, a mountain out of a mole hill, a—I don't know what."

"We're still looking for something new here," said Rose. "You make mountains out of mole hills all the time."

"This one's different."

"How?"

Before I could answer, Rose's console beeped. She answered the call, listened and held out the phone to me, shrugging and mouthing, "A woman."

I expected Barbara with a honey-do or perhaps Madeline Mundell.

"Mr. Jeeter?"

I failed to recognize the woman's voice. "Yes."

"This is Leona Fairview, Leon's mother. I need to talk to you."

Chapter Six

The trip back to Orange County took two hours—rain, accidents and clogged freeways turning me into a sullen hunk of meat behind the wheel. I set the appointment with Mrs. Fairview for eight o'clock to allow for the weather. I was close to on time but, given a choice, would have preferred to skip the appointment altogether. If I had successfully provoked Marv into firing me, I would have at least been home—unemployed, true, but warm, dry and comfortable.

By the time I started down the Balboa Peninsula, squinting through the rainy night to find the donut shop Mrs. Fairview suggested for our meeting, I wondered why I bothered at all. One more non-fact for the Queller story would do nothing to save my job. That Marv and I would look for work simultaneously only marginally improved my disposition. What, after all, could Mrs. Fairview tell me? I tried to get her to talk on the phone. She refused. Presumably her husband, listening between snorts of oxygen, might overhear.

When I got off the phone, I told Marv about the call. His face took on the look of a child's at Christmas. Mrs. Fairview, he assured me, would turn out to be a wonderful present, just what we needed, a breakthrough. I used his enthusiasm as an opportunity to get reimbursed for the fifty dollars I spent buying information from the human monument and tried to calm him down. I failed, told Rose

to find him an Alka-Seltzer—or, alternatively, a bourbon—
and left the office.

I finally found the donut shop and parked in a small lot
beside it, looking through the rain at the bright windows
for any sign of Mrs. Fairview. The place looked deserted.
I got out and trotted through the drizzle to the glass door,
pushed it open and stepped inside.

I managed to eat half a stale donut before Mrs. Fairview
arrived. She stopped outside the shop and, looking in
through the window, an umbrella held over her head, saw
me, collapsed the umbrella and came in. She stood just
inside the door long enough to shake off the umbrella. The
attendant, a teenager with a bad case of inflamed acne,
waited on her, putting a single donut in a paper bag and
waiting while she counted coins from a change purse. She
brought the purchase to my table.

"Thank you for coming, Mr. Jeeter," she said, resting
her umbrella against the wall. "It's a terrible night out."

"No trouble," I said, remembering the long wet drive
from Los Angeles.

Mrs. Fairview sat across from me, holding the donut
bag with both hands as though she thought I might make
a grab for it.

"You're not going to eat your donut, Mrs. Fairview?"

"I seldom eat them. Fattening."

"Stale too, if the one I had was a sample."

"Not this one," she said, indicating the bag. "That
nice young man always saves me a fresh one. He likes
them fresh."

I tried to imagine Mr. Fairview eating donuts with a
plastic hose up his nose. The image spoiled what was left
of my appetite. "Why, if I can ask, *did* I come, Mrs.
Fairview?"

She let go of the donut bag, evidently trusting me, and
unbuttoned the top of her raincoat. She reached in and
took out a slip of paper. She studied the paper a moment,
then looked at me, her expression faintly official, as though

she were conducting a survey. "What is your magazine's circulation, Mr. Jeeter?"

The question, from left field, threw me. "Pardon me?"

"The circulation of this"—she consulted the paper again—"*Global Capitalism,* what is it?"

"About seventy thousand."

"Paid or newstand?"

"Mostly subscription. It's a controlled circulation book. Why?"

She ignored the question. "And the readership?"

I felt tempted to say people looking for their name in print but restrained myself. I had no idea where the conversation was headed. "Middle and upper management in larger corporations and financial institutions, maybe a few investors looking for ideas."

"Brokerage houses?"

"Yes. In fact, almost all of them. Mr. Lusker, our publisher, prides himself on that. He thinks of brokerage houses as 'influence subscribers,' people who read something in the magazine and because of their jobs spread the word about our good work to their customers."

"Almost *all* of the brokerage houses."

"That's right. Mrs. Fairview—"

"And you, Mr. Jeeter, what sort of thing do you usually write?"

I skipped the honest version of an answer. "A little of everything, profiles, industry pieces, anything of special interest to the world's business and financial community."

"If you did write something now," she asks after another glance at the paper, "when would it appear?"

I remembered Marv's complaints about Mr. Lusker forcing the art director to work up covers of decomposed bodies. "Probably in the next issue, the March issue. Our publisher considers this a special case so our normal lead time is cut way down."

She studied the slip of paper and shook her head. "It was supposed to be at least one hundred thousand."

"What?" I asked. "Our circulation? That's our target

by the end of the year. You sound like you're going to place an ad.''

"Oh, no," she said. "It was just supposed to be one hundred thousand or more, but seventy thousand will simply have to do, won't it?" Her face lost its official look. "This is very painful for me, Mr. Jeeter. Edward wants nothing to do with Leon. Edward blames me.''

"Your husband blames you for your son's homosexuality.''

She nodded, looking distracted. "It's not something I like, the way Leon is, but he is our own flesh and blood. How can I simply abandon him?''

"I have a daughter," I said. "I feel the same way.''

"Is she . . ." Rather than use the word, Mrs. Fairview let the sentence trail off.

"I don't think so," I answered. "She's three.''

"Oh," she said, disconcerted. "I'm sorry.''

"I'm not," I said. "She's the best thing in my life right now.''

Mrs. Fairview's expression took on a distant look. "I remember when Leon was a baby. He was a very pretty baby.''

"I'm sure.''

"He cried too much, but he was very pretty. And he wasn't always—that way. In high school, he even played football. He wasn't very good—too skinny, they said—but he managed to stay on the team.''

"He probably cooperated with the coach.''

"Yes," continued Mrs. Fairview, nodding. "Leon was always very cooperative. He likes pleasing people. And then one day he just—" She shook her head. "I don't know. He just changed. He just stopped liking girls, I guess. He told us about it and Edward simply would not believe it. 'No son of mine,' he used to say. Leon even brought one of his . . . friends home, a short young man in a suit. That was when Edward told him never to come to the house again and refused ever to speak to him.''

"It must have been difficult for you," I said, feeling

genuinely sympathetic and using my sympathy to make
her trust me.

"It was." She studied me a moment, then made up her
mind. "You will do, Mr. Jeeter."

"For what?"

She stood up, tucked the donut bag under her raincoat
and picked up her umbrella. "Please follow me."

I expected us to go wherever we were going by car.
Instead, Mrs. Fairview led the way down the street, waddling ahead of me, the umbrella open above her. I caught
up with her and walked beside her, the umbrella threatening to poke me in the eye. Rain, pattering on the umbrella fabric, ran off and soaked my sleeve. I suggested I
hold the umbrella.

"A gentleman," said Mrs. Fairview and smiled.
"That's very nice."

"Where are we going, Mrs. Fairview?"

"To see Leon, of course."

We walked two more blocks and turned on a street lead-
ing toward Newport Bay. Ahead of us, I saw the landing
facilities for the peninsula side of the car ferry. We reached
the landing and walked out on a pier used by foot passengers on the ferry.

Mrs. Fairview stopped at the end of the pier and pointed
out into the bay. "Leon's out there."

I squinted across the rainy bay. A ferry, halfway across
the bay, came toward us carrying a single car. Nothing
else showed signs of life. "On the ferry?"

"No," she said. "On the 'End Run.' "

I could barely make out the "End Run," a dot bobbing
in the choppy water. "How do we get there?"

"Mr. Pemberton."

"Who?"

"He owns the boat fueling place," she said. "He's a
very nice man."

"Lindy?" I asked, confused by her description of him
as a nice man.

She nodded. "He takes me out to see Leon. I give Leon his donut and talk to him." She unbuttoned the top of her raincoat, took out the donut bag and handed it to me. "Please give this to Leon. That way, he'll know you came from me."

I returned Mrs. Fairview's umbrella and put the donut bag inside my coat. I looked toward the "End Run." Heavy rain, slanting through the windy air to the surface of the bay, obscured any lights on the boat. It looked forsaken, a sailboat moored and abandoned, waiting for summer.

"You're sure Leon's out there, Mrs. Fairview?"

No one answered. I looked around. Mrs. Fairview, the umbrella pulled down close to her head, disappeared around a corner in the direction of her house, a waddling, toadstool silhouette under a corner lamppost.

The car ferry arrived, bumping to a stop against the dock. A hydraulic valve hissed. Metal plates clanged. A barrier vaguely like an enlarged version of the nose guard on a football helmet swung up in front of the single car on the ferry. The car bounced up the ramp and onto the street. I boarded the ferry.

Crossing the bay, rain soaked me, plastering my hair to my forehead. The sole passenger on the ferry and probably an object of ridicule for the boy in the yellow slicker who took my fare, I watched the "End Run" and remembered why I became a business writer instead of a street reporter—warm offices, regular hours, more or less pleasant people. It seemed like a good idea at the time.

I pulled my attention from the "End Run" and picked out Lindy's Landing on the far side of the bay. Light showed in the window of the corrugated office shed. I anticipated at least one more problem before I got to the "End Run."

"You fucking nuts, Jeeter?" said the human monument, seated on a hard wooden chair and rubbing his hands together in front of a glowing electric heater. He squinted at me. "You ain't on drugs, are you?"

"No," I said. "I just need to get to the 'End Run.' "

"And I need somebody to do all that damn"—he gestured in the general direction of a rolltop desk, its pigeonholes feathered with slips of paper—"paperwork. We *all* need somethin' in life and that's what I need right now, Jeeter. How am I supposed to make a living if I don't bill the reg'lars?"

I understood the point of the conversation immediately. "I'll pay you to take me out there."

He paused with his hands in front of the heater. "How much?"

I got out my wallet. "Fifty bucks."

He went back to rubbing his hands. "Piss on that, Jeeter. It's colder than your mama's ass out there. I go out there tonight, I catch my death." He glanced at me. "And *who's* gonna pay for *that?*"

"Okay, sixty."

"Ain't enough by half."

"It's all I've got."

"You got a checkbook?"

"No." I lied.

"Then you got a problem." He rubbed his hands.

The human monument's attitude, petty and small-minded, angered me. I decided to skip tact. "Listen, you old pirate, sixty bucks is all I've got. Take it or leave it. I'm *sick* of you trying to gouge every dime out of me you can. And believe me, when I write this story, you're going to be in it, you and Lindy's Landing. By the time I'm finished, you'll have city inspectors and harbor authorities and God-knows-who all over you. And it'll serve you right for being a money-grubbing asshole."

I doubted whether anything I wrote in a magazine like *Global Capitalism* would cause anyone problems with local authorities.

Pemberton, on the other hand, looked at me, rubbed his hands and considered the idea. "Sixty bucks, huh?"

"And not a penny more."

"For sixty bucks," he said, shaking his head. "I ain't taking you."

"Then fuck you," I said, starting for the door.

"But for sixty bucks . . ."

I hesitated, hand on the doorknob.

". . . I'll rent you a boat."

Walking down the concrete quay in the rain, unlashing the tarp from Pemberton's dinghy, straddling the dinghy to jerk the starter rope on the ancient outboard, I finally calmed down. For sixty dollars, I got a boat and a single-sentence lesson in seamanship: "Don't sink her."

I settled into the boat and I started out across the water, my hand on the outboard throttle and the seat of my pants soaked. By the time I reached the "End Run," the rest of me was soaked, including the donut bag. A ladder hung over the side of the sailboat. I tied off the dinghy on the ladder and climbed aboard, wondering about the best way to announce myself. Steadying myself on the rigging, I walked toward the rear of the boat, wind and rain off the bay chilling me. I found the main cabin hatch, started to rap on it with my knuckles and, instead, sneezed.

Chapter Seven

The stubby cabin doors opened. The hatch cover slid back and thumped. A man in his early thirties with a narrow face and neat brown mustache looked up at me from the stairs inside the cabin. The man's hair—curly, brown, meticulously cut—showed blond streaks on both sides, as though the hairstylist had an unfortunate accident with a bleach bottle in the middle of an otherwise perfect haircut.

"Leon Fairview?"

The man nodded and backed down the stairs into the cabin. "Come in, Mr. Jeeter. It's terrible out there."

"You're telling me."

I started down the cabin stairs, turning sideways to get through the narrow hatch. When I reached the bottom, Fairview squeezed past me, went back up the stairs and slid closed the hatch cover, locking the double doors from the inside. He came down the stairs and edged by me toward the boat's galley. "Would you like some cocoa?"

I smelled it in the air. "Definitely."

Fairview tossed me a towel to dry off and fixed cocoa in the galley. I wiped my face with the towel and sat down at a fold-out table jutting from the bulkhead. Eventually, Fairview placed two steaming mugs of cocoa on the table and sat across from me.

I warmed my hands on the mug and sipped the cocoa, glancing at him. "Good."

"It's very hot, too," said Fairview.

"That's the good part."

"This is going to be difficult for me, Mr. Jeeter."

"Take your time."

Fairview sat back on the cushions opposite me and sipped his own cocoa. "I don't know how to start."

"Just start," I said. "You can come back later and pick up details. Start with Queller."

"Hortie," said Fairview—even saying the name caused a twinge in his expression. "Hortie was my best friend, really my only friend. I loved Hortie."

Uncomfortable with whatever he meant by the word *love*, I put down my cocoa, reached inside my coat and took out the soaked donut bag. "Before I forget, your mother sent this."

He looked at the soggy bag and smiled. "I don't even like donuts, you know. She thinks I like them and it makes her happy to bring me a donut but I really just like seeing her."

"She told me about your father's attitude."

Something flitted across Fairview's tan face. "It's difficult, but I love him too."

I thought of Wolverton, Fairview's original substitute father. "I'm sure you do. Tell me about Horton Queller."

Fairview disposed of the donut in the galley trash, sat down again with his cocoa and collected his thoughts. I watched him, trying to gauge what I saw. In a crowd, I might or might not have pegged him as gay. He wore jeans and a sport shirt, both as meticulously neat as his hair and mustache, a persnickety style I had noticed once or twice among gays. The peroxide streaks argued trendy, though not necessarily gay, an adult echo of a punk style. Even his movements around the boat making cocoa or disposing of the soggy donut seemed to me at worst simply neutral, not feminine. As a teenager and one of Wolf Wolverton's students, he probably looked cuter.

"I met Hortie in high school," began Fairview. "He was always very good at math, and I needed help in math."

"Wolverton's class."

Fairview nodded. "Hortie never studied math. He just kind of read it, if you know what I mean. He sat down the night before an assignment was due and worked through all the problems on first sight."

"Bright."

"Very bright," he said. "I think Hortie was a genius of some kind."

"They thought so on Wall Street."

"They didn't," said Fairview, shaking his head. "Those people didn't appreciate Hortie."

"They gave him three million dollars last year," I said. "I wish someone would appreciate me that much."

Fairview continued shaking his head. "They didn't appreciate Hortie at all."

Queller and Fairview became friends over a math book.

"Good friends?" I asked, stressing it.

"Not then," said Fairview, understanding what I meant. "That was later."

After high school and during college, they stayed in touch, phone calls, occasional visits or letters, still only friends. When Queller started working on the East Coast, they saw each other when Queller made business trips to California.

"Hortie always liked visiting me. He said it was peaceful. In New York, people were always after him to make money for them. The pressure—" Fairview shook his head. "Hortie looked like he aged ten years during the five years he spent in New York. I don't think the people he worked with were very nice to him."

"Three million dollars is nice," I said. "Take my word for it."

The comment angered Fairview. "He deserved more, Mr. Jeeter! They took and they took and they took from him. They used him and he made millions and millions of dollars for them and they paid him *nothing* for it! Without Hortie, *they* would have nothing. It was Hortie's brains and Hortie's system and Hortie's algorithm that turned that Ralph Bollington into a big name on Wall Street and he *owed* Hortie. Three million dollars is nothing compared to what he was worth!''

Fairview's whining tone during the outburst reminded me of a wife complaining about the lack of respect shown her husband at the office. ''When did you become lovers?''

''Last year,'' said Fairview. ''Hortie started coming out here a lot and staying with me.''

Queller occasionally flew out to California for short weekends, arriving Saturday morning and leaving Sunday night. Fairview and Queller seldom went anywhere. They stayed at Fairview's apartment.

''We cooked and made love,'' said Fairview. ''It was very nice.''

''How did Wolverton take it?'' I said, fishing.

Fairview frowned. ''That part was difficult.''

I remembered the girl I dated in college just before I met Barbara. ''A little overlap, huh?''

''Wolf was always very nice to me. He helped me when my modeling wasn't going well.''

''Helped you financially?''

Fairview nodded. ''At first he was upset about Hortie. He said horrible things about Hortie and what he was going to do to him. At the time, I thought he might kill him. John has a terrible temper.''

''I noticed,'' I said, remembering my unceremonious exit from the gym. I also remembered the corpse with the cowboy boot. ''Do you think he would actually do something like that?''

''Like what?''

''Kill Queller.''

Fairview shook his head vigorously. ''No. John finally saw how Hortie and I felt about each other. You can't really argue with how someone feels, can you?''

I thought about Barbara. ''I suppose not.''

''He finally accepted things. He's been very supportive.''

''Go on.''

Over successive visits, Fairview noticed Queller's attitude toward Wall Street begin to change. When Queller first started flying to California for weekends, he talked constantly about the challenge of his work, how it made demands on every aspect of his skills and personality, his understanding of crisis psychology, his ability to model that psychology mathematically with computers, his insights into international financial markets.

"He used to say, 'They don't understand that it's all so simple. Markets are just ordered catastrophes.' I don't know what he meant by that but he always laughed when he said it like he thought everyone on Wall Street was stupid for not knowing something he thought was simple."

I remembered the *Journal* profile of Queller, his Ph.D. dissertation in psychometrics, *Crisis Psychology and Catastrophe Theory in Free Market Economics*. "Simple to him, maybe."

Fairview nodded. "And he was very kind, too, at least to me."

As time passed, Queller became more and more frustrated with his work, as though he cracked the Japanese code before World War II and no one either appreciated or cared about his accomplishment. He set out to show them, to earn more money single-handedly than any option and currency trader in the history of Wall Street. He worked days, nights and, except for his vacation trips to California, weekends. He traded from the office, the car, the bathtub in his Basking Ridge home.

"The bathtub?" I said and laughed.

"He had a phone in the bathroom."

I imagined Queller splashing around his tub, phone in one hand, rubber duck in the other, making currency trades in Hong Kong. Fairview noticed my repressed smile. "Is something funny, Mr. Jeeter?"

"Not at all," I said, controlling myself. "It's been a long day and I'm a little giddy. Sorry. Go on."

"He even had a computer terminal in the bedroom in case he woke up in the middle of the night with an idea."

"He sounds driven."

"Very driven," said Fairview and made an odd expression, a determined frown I took as an echo of Queller's face when he talked to Fairview about Wall Street. "He wanted to show them. He wanted them to notice."

"I'd say they noticed," I said. "Anyone who can generate three hundred million a year in revenues gets noticed."

"But not in the way Hortie wanted to get noticed," said Fairview. "All they talked about was the money. Money, money, money. Not Hortie."

"Money's what Wall Street's about."

"But it's not what Hortie was about. They never saw how beautiful the thing was he created. They just saw all that money. It was greed, that's all, just greed."

"That's what Wall Street's about, too."

I remembered Queller's comments in the *Journal* article about feeling underpaid for his efforts. "And you're telling me all Queller really wanted was love, right?"

"He wanted *respect*, Mr. Jeeter. He wanted them to acknowledge his achievement. Is that so much to ask?"

I tried to respond sympathetically to keep the conversation going. "Maybe. For them."

"They only respected one thing."

"Money."

Fairview nodded. Queller, he said, decided to get their respect in the only way they understood. If they refused to respect him for getting them what they wanted, they would respect him for taking it away. At the height of his career, freight cars full of money rolling up to his employer's doorstep from his efforts, Queller quit, taking away the one thing they respected.

I decided I almost liked Queller—not quite, but almost. "He had balls. I'll say that."

Confused by my statement, Fairview peered at me,

frowned, realized what I meant and nodded. "He was very courageous. And they killed him because of that."

"For quitting?" I said. "Are you saying Ralph Bollington—"

Fairview made canceling motions in the air with his hands. "Not Bollington. Or maybe Bollington. I don't know. Someone. Someone greedy."

"That narrows it down to just about everyone," I said, finally starting to believe I might have something to justify Mr. Lusker's enthusiasm as well as a decomposed body on the cover of *Global Capitalism*. "Could you be a little more specific?"

Fairview shook his head. "So many of them wanted what Hortie could give them."

"Let's back up a little," I suggested. "So Queller quit Bollington Associates. Then what?"

Queller moped. He sat around his Basking Ridge home for weeks, calling Fairview ten times a day to complain about "those assholes," meaning everyone in general who failed to appreciate him and Bollington Associates in particular. To go back to work, Queller wanted a fifteen-million-dollar bonus for past services and a half interest in Bollington Associates. Ralph Bollington refused. Queller fumed. Finally, convinced no one would pay what he considered himself worth, Queller vanished, walking away from his Basking Ridge home and flying to California to live permanently. He stayed with Fairview, intending to buy a house somewhere in Newport Beach.

"They found him," said Fairview.

"Who?"

"Men."

Queller lived with Fairview six months. One night, after both men went to sleep, Fairview found himself awakened in the middle of the night by unfamiliar noises. He got out of bed and looked through the apartment without turning on the lights but found nothing. When he started back toward the bedroom, he heard more noises, a scuffle, a muffled cry. He saw vague shapes in the bedroom, two men standing over Queller in the bed.

"Didn't you do anything?" I asked.

Any composure Fairview retained telling the story vanished completely. He began sobbing. "I *couldn't*, Mr. Jeeter! I just *couldn't!* They were killing Hortie and I was so afraid I just . . . I just—"

"You just what?"

"I *hid!* I went into the bathroom. I got in the shower. I heard them outside doing things to Hortie and I . . . I pee-ed all over myself I was so afraid."

While Fairview stood in the shower peeing on himself, the men searched the apartment. He heard drawers pulled out and their contents dumped on the floor. He heard fabric rip as they cut into furniture. He heard china shatter as they went through the kitchen. Once, one of the men came into the bathroom. Fairview held his breath as long as possible, felt himself about to gag and slowly, carefully, silently, breathed.

"The man was *two inches* from me. I could see his shadow on the shower door. He was going through the medicine cabinet and the dirty clothes. He found some condoms and Vaseline in the cabinet and I heard him say, 'Fucking faggots,' and he threw the Vaseline so it hit the shower door. The door doesn't catch right so when the jar hit it, the door sort of came open a crack."

"Did you see him?"

"I was too scared to even look. Once I got beat up by some . . . people and—"

"Because you're gay?"

He nodded. "And I knew his type. If he found me in the shower, he would have killed me. He'd have said, 'Fucking faggot,' and hurt me. All I saw was his dark clothes. He even took the toilet apart and looked in the tank."

"For what?"

Fairview stood up, steadied himself on the bulkhead and opened a head-level cabinet. He reached deep into the cabinet and came out with a three-inch square of plastic, a hard-shell floppy disk. He tossed it on the table in front of me.

"A computer disk," I said. "So what?"

"It has Hortie's algorithm on it."

I looked at the plastic square. We used them occasionally at the office. Capable of storing several hundred pages of text or an equivalent amount of programming, the disk in essence contained Queller's brain, the total of his mathematical and psychological insights into international currency and options trading markets, $300 million a year worth of insights.

"Where was it?" I asked.

Fairview sat down opposite me and smiled for the first time during the interview. "On the coffee table."

I laughed. "You're kidding."

"Do you use a computer, Mr. Jeeter?"

"Yes, unfortunately."

"The kind of people who do this, who hurt other people and kill them, don't know much about computers."

"That's probably true," I said. "Leg-breakers don't have much use for computers. So what?"

"Whoever hired these men probably told them to look for a floppy disk. These"—he picked up the disk and tapped the plastic case on the table—"aren't very floppy like the other kind."

"Five-and-a-quarter-inch disks?"

Fairview nodded. "The older ones. Maybe someone showed them one of those and said to look for one like it."

I laughed again, thinking of Fairview's demolished apartment and the disk on the coffee table in plain view. "You're saying they didn't know what they were looking at."

"It doesn't even look like a disk," said Fairview and ran his finger around the square shape. "It looks like—I don't know what."

"A coaster, maybe," I suggested, imagining it on a coffee table.

"Anyway, they searched everything and didn't find anything and they took Hortie away."

"Took his body away, you mean."

Fairview shook his head. "He was still alive. They probably wanted to torture him to find this." He indicated the disk on the table. "They made him get dressed. I heard the front door close and I waited a long time in the shower and finally I came out."

At first, Fairview wanted to call the police. The three phones in the apartment were disabled, two with cut cords and one ripped from the wall. Fairview calmed down enough to get dressed and was about to leave the apartment to find a pay phone when he remembered Queller telling him that under no circumstances was anyone to know his whereabouts.

"I don't think he meant *these* circumstances," I said.

"I didn't *know* what he meant, Mr. Jeeter," said Fairview, distraught. "Maybe he even knew people like that would come."

"I doubt it."

"Hortie knew everything. He could always predict everything anyone did ahead of time."

I had difficulty swallowing the idea of Queller as a complete clairvoyant but let the point pass. To Fairview, someone like Queller, a psychologist used to predicting human behavior in complicated market situations, probably seemed like a clairvoyant.

"I thought maybe Hortie didn't want me to call the police. I mean, he knew I was in the apartment and he didn't yell for help or anything."

"Maybe he couldn't," I suggested.

"You mean they hurt him so bad."

"That's right."

"Or maybe he wanted to save me," said Fairview. "Hortie was very brave."

"Or save that disk."

"I thought of that, too, after I found it." Fairview tapped the disk with a meticulously manicured fingernail. "This is all there is left of Hortie. It's Hortie's achievement. It meant more to him than anything."

"You could still have called the police."

"I was confused, Mr. Jeeter," said Fairview, pain in his expression at the memory. "I loved Hortie and I wanted to do what he thought was best but they took him and I didn't *know* what was best."

"The police—"

Fairview, upset, interrupted. "If those men knew I had it . . ."

"The disk."

". . . they would come after *me!* I don't understand computers but Hortie showed the program to me because he wanted me to admire it and he told me about it and I knew if I called the police, someone would find out I had it! And besides, I thought maybe they were just going to talk to Hortie and let him go."

"Not likely."

"But it was *possible!*"

I let the point go and remained silent.

"I was scared, Mr. Jeeter. I had that disk"—he nodded toward it—"and it was what they wanted and if they didn't get it from Hortie and Hortie was already dead, they would come back and hurt me! They'd wait until the police were gone and they would come back and hurt me!"

"Not if the police caught them."

"Someone else would come."

"Okay. So what did you do then?"

"I took the disk and I came here," he said. "I've been living here ever since."

I looked around the cabin. Even living aboard the "End Run" for six months, Fairview, as neat about his housekeeping as about his clothes and hairstyle, kept everything shipshape.

"Wolverton knows?"

Fairview nodded. "He doesn't know why. I told him not to tell anyone. Wolf is a good friend."

The answer explained Wolverton's strong reaction to my questions in his office and my escort off campus. He probably believed any contact I had with Fairview, any explanations in print of their relationship, threatened both his job and Fairview.

I thought about Fairview's story. I still had a few questions. Someone wanted Queller's algorithm and its precise description of market behavior bad enough to kill him for it, then dump his body in the ocean. They either had a boat of their own or threw him off a cliff somewhere along the coast. Either way, little evidence remained to link them to the body.

As for my own story, I only needed to explain the "whys" in *Global Capitalism,* not the "whos." Greed stood out as an obvious why. Reluctantly, I decided Mr. Lusker was right. The story might push the magazine's circulation toward a hundred thousand. After all, everyone likes reading about greedy people who go to extremes, a form of smug self-defense, letting them prove to themselves they are merely acquisitive.

I also realized I still had a job.

"One other point, Leon."

He nodded, waiting for the question.

"Why tell me?"

"I don't want to hide anymore, Mr. Jeeter. Hortie's dead and I feel bad about it but I have a life, too. I can't live"—he gestured around at the boat—"like *this* the rest of my life. I want the story to come out and then the police can do whatever they do and these people will all go away and leave me alone because as soon as you leave"—he picked up the floppy disk and held it by its corner like a dead thing—"I'm going to destroy this. Then no one will have any reason to find me and hurt me."

By the time I left the "End Run" an hour later, I felt convinced Fairview only wanted to be left alone. He saw me as the means to that end. As I putted back toward Lindy's Landing, the rain faded to a light mist. I tied the dinghy at the end of the quay and walked to the pay phone near the ferry. I got out some change and glanced at my watch, five after ten. The office would be empty but I could at least leave a voice-mail message for Marv to show him I followed orders.

I pumped change into the phone and called. The equipment at the *Global Capitalism* office answered immediately. Rose's recorded voice informed me I had reached the offices of *Global Capitalism* and told me the next issue would be available February 20th.

"I know," I said, impatient.

Instead of telling me to punch out the extension I wanted on any Touch Tone phone, the equipment started through a hunt group, ringing a phone three times then moving on to a new phone, searching the empty office for someone at a desk. I was about to hang up when it found someone.

"Yeah."

"Mr. Lusker?"

"No, Adam Smith," said Mr. Lusker, evidently impersonating his favorite economist. "Who is this?"

"Jeeter."

A long pause ensued.

"Sir?"

"I'm waiting, Jeeter," he said. "Everyone in this office is waiting."

Since Mr. Lusker was evidently alone in the building—even Marv escaped the vigil—his statement was literally true. "I think I've got something on the Queller story, sir."

"Let's hear it."

I told him. He listened, occasionally saying, "Hmm," a noncommittal reaction to let me know he was still awake. As I got further into the story, Mr. Lusker's "hmm" got more cheerful. Once, he even said, "Interesting, Jeeter," high praise. When I finished, he thought a long time before he gave his final opinion.

"Jeeter."

"Sir?"

"I knew my faith in you was justified. You're one *hell* of a reporter! Write it up, my boy! And put the best writing you've got into it! Give me the *feel* of it—heroes, villains, this poor jerk Fairview in the middle of it all and out of his depth! That," he concluded, more exhilarated than I had ever heard him, "should get their goddamn attention!"

"It's not exactly a *Global Capitalism* story, sir."

"Jeeter," he said, irritated, "just write the damn thing." He hung up.

I took the ferry back across the bay, shivering in the cold night air and watching the "End Run." A single light showed in the cabin, Fairview, alone, trapped on board. The story still needed work, details nailed down, corroboration. Nevertheless, in spite of my wet clothes and the bone-chilling wind off the water, I felt good, tired but relaxed. I felt as though I had done a solid job, produced solid results and gotten solid praise for my efforts.

I also found myself agreeing with Mr. Lusker, a rare enough event to mark on a calendar. Poor Leon Fairview, out of his depth. Queller wanted the world's respect for his ability to make money, yuppie values that got him eaten by sharks. Mr. Lusker wanted the attention of subscribers and, more important, advertisers. Marv wanted to keep meeting his alimony payments. I wanted a job that let me eat regularly. Economics moved all of us. More than civilization, sex or religion—in Queller's case, holding out against leg-breakers, more even than survival—economics manipulated us all, everyone but Fairview. I watched the "End Run" bob at its mooring like a forgotten buoy and thought about what Fairview wanted—love, first his father's, later Wolverton's, finally Queller's. Failing that, Fairview wanted to be left alone.

Chapter Eight

"*Ahhhh—*" I said and tried to hold it in, "*—CHOO!*"

"You're sick," said Marv and took a step back.

"No shit." My head ached. My nose dripped.

"Should you be here?"

"As a career move, it sucks."

"Well, you're here," concluded Marv, stating the obvious, "so tell me how you got it."

"Standing out in the rain all night," I said, sneezed and blew my nose into Kleenex, prolonging it to convince Marv I was in fact sick.

"I mean the story," said Marv. "How'd you get that?"

The question annoyed me. Being in the office instead of at home in bed annoyed me. Marv, pacing the reception area in front of Rose's desk and giving me a cheerful greeting the instant I came through the door, annoyed me. Marv got almost no practice being cheerful and did it poorly.

"Piece of cake," I said, hoping a short answer would make him go away.

"That's great, Jerry! Just great! I want to hear *all* about it."

"I want to go to bed."

Marv waved aside concerns about mere life-and-death illness. "Forget that. Tell me about—"

"I'm sick, Marv."

"I understand, but—"

"I already told Mr. Lusker everything. Ask him. All I want to do right now is go to my office and write up this crap before my brain turns to silly putty." I sneezed again, this time intentionally. "Assuming I live."

"You'll live," Marv assured me and tried another tack. "You've got the March cover."

"The decomposed body," I said, my general condition letting me empathize with it.

Marv nodded. "Willie did a good job. The body looks like a decomposed dollar sign floating in the ocean. The leg is sort of crooked so—"

"I don't think I want to hear this in my condition," I said. "I might barf on you."

"Okay. I still need the details for the inside illustrations. I had to move that crap about the Nips buying California farther back in the book. I need—"

"I need rest, Marv, sleep, maybe a doctor."

"Aspirin," said Marv, as though he had discovered a miracle cure that would take care of everything and let me give him the details. "I need details to get the illustrations done."

"I'm too sick to argue," I said. "Talk to Mr. Lusker. Tell him you need help."

Rose, listening, heard the last sentence and smiled.

"Jerry—" began Marv.

"I'll show you copy as soon as I get copy," I said, starting toward my office. "You can *read* all the details while I sleep."

I went to my office, stacked Kleenex beside the computer keyboard and started on a first draft of the Queller story.

Or tried to start on it. I stared at the blank screen and mulled over a lead, my soggy brain debating between Queller's resignation from Bollington Associates and the break-in at Leon Fairview's apartment. I decided on the break-in, a little drama at the beginning to catch people's interest.

I put my fingers on the keyboard.

They refused to move.

I checked my notes from the interview with Fairview and tried again, fingers poised above the keys.

Still no movement.

I decided to write up my notes verbatim to prime the pump and get a flow started. The notes came out disjointed sentences.

I kept trying. The more I tried, the worse it got. I tangled up sentences, split infinitives, dangled participles. Two or three times I derailed myself into dependent clauses with no logical way out. When I reread the copy, it sounded like a fourth grader's first composition.

Sniffing, blowing my nose over the keyboard, I forced myself to keep at it, an exercise in pushing string. Finally, after a pause for an especially long and juicy workout with my nose, I recognized the symptom: ignorance. I had no idea what I wanted to say, always an obstacle to writing anything. My unconscious mind grappled with the jumbled pieces of the story but wanted more time to organize them. My conscious mind collaborated with my obstinate unconscious, refusing to care that Marv, Mr. Lusker and the entire staff of *Global Capitalism* hung on our every word. All either of them wanted was sleep, antibiotics.

Just before lunch, my nose sore and red, I saved a few garbled paragraphs to the file server, locked the document under the password BIGDEAL to keep out inquisitive Marvs and went home, looking forward to losing consciousness for the afternoon in bed.

I pulled the Toyota out of the ground-floor parking garage and settled into traffic on Wilshire Boulevard. My head ached. My joints ached. I felt full of phlegm. Distracted, probably running a temperature, I failed to notice the black BMW behind me until I got to Verdugo.

At first, I just noted the car in the sideview mirror, a potential traffic obstacle. I drove, blew my nose and thought about phlegm, one of journalism's unacknowledged occupational hazards. Even when the BMW started following me through holes in traffic, I paid little attention, assuming the driver simply liked my driving style and mimicked it. I mulled over the Queller story and tried to make the pieces fit. Some did, some didn't. After about ten minutes of mulling, I finally became aware of the BMW as a distinct entity. I changed lanes to get around a slowing city bus. The BMW changed lanes. I shifted back into the lane ahead of the bus. I expected the BMW to follow. It hung back, slowing traffic instead of passing. During the rest of the trip home, it hung back, changing lanes when I changed lanes, turning when I turned, pacing me.

"Weird," I said to its image in the mirror.

I parked in the garage under my apartment building and took the elevator up to the apartment. The elevator climbed a shaft with windows overlooking the street. Groggy, feeling as though the elevator were intentionally taking an especially long time just to get on my nerves, I glanced out the windows at the street. A black BMW drove along the street below me, slowed near the entrance to the apartment garage and proceeded down the street.

"Paranoia, Jeeter," I concluded, watching the black car vanish around the corner. "Must be the fever."

The fever, along with a collection of plugged orifices, kept me vegetating in bed for the next three days. Barbara, once she looked at a thermometer, insisted I stay home, claiming my health was more important than any "silly story." The phrase simultaneously showed Barbara's spousal concern for my physical well-being and demeaned my work, suggesting I was either a fool for considering work in my condition or a fool for considering the kind of work I did in any condition.

At the height of the fever, Joy came into the bedroom and asked whether I was dead yet. I told her no. Marv called the second day. I told him the same thing. On the afternoon of the third day, alone in the apartment while Barbara sold naugahyde and Joy did whatever people do at daycare centers, I tried to work on the Queller piece.

Too weak to sit at the computer in the living room, I propped up a TV tray on my knees and scribbled on a yellow legal pad.

Even writing longhand, a slow process with time to think between words, I had trouble getting the story to gel. I surrounded the bed with crumpled balls of yellow paper, false starts. I tried outlining chronologically, hoping a time line would clarify events. The time line joined the rest of the paper on the floor.

Something other than the flu, I decided, was wrong.

But what? Me? The story? Both? I had no idea. I stared at the bedroom ceiling, pen in hand, wondering why the story stumped me. I still had questions, true, but I wrote stories for *Global Capitalism* every day without knowing all the answers or even half of them. *Global Capitalism*, in fact, made its living simply ignoring most of life's important questions. I put aside the yellow pad and turned on the bedroom TV, hoping an hour with a mindless soap would clear my head. Just as I settled into "Another World," the apartment doorbell buzzed, bringing me back to this one.

"Go away."

The doorbell buzzed again, more sustained, more insistent.

I threw back the covers, got up, struggled into a pair of jeans and lumbered toward the noise. I stopped at the hall mirror and checked my pallid face, deciding anyone rude enough to drag me out of a sick bed could take me like he found me, splotchy face, bloodshot eyes and fright wig hair included.

A sustained buzz started from the direction of the living room, someone leaning on the button.

"I'm coming, dammit!"

I crossed the living room and opened the front door.

A large man in a cheap suit showed me a badge. I guessed his age at mid-fifties, his hobby as alcohol. Large veins showed on his cheeks and nose.

"Garvey," he said.

"Jeeter," I responded.

"I know. May I come in, Mr. Jeeter?"

I pushed aside the door and walked back to the couch. "As long as you don't mind being exposed to bubonic plague, be my guest."

Garvey came in and closed the door, taking up a position just inside, legs apart, as though preparing to block any escape attempt.

I sat down on the couch and looked at him. "I thought you guys came in pairs."

"Sometimes we do," he said and glanced toward the hall, the noise from the bedroom attracting his attention.

"TV."

He returned his attention to me. "Your office informed me you were here."

"I guess they were right."

Something, probably irritation at my sarcasm, passed across his face. "You don't seem too cooperative, Mr. Jeeter."

"If I knew what I was supposed to be cooperative about," I said, "it might help."

"Horton Queller," he said, watching me carefully for a reaction.

"Okay," I said, finding his alert manner tedious. "Now we know the subject. What about Horton Queller?"

"You're writing an article about him. Is that correct?"

"Trying to write one," I said, nodding. "At the moment, I'm not getting much useful out of my sick brain."

"Writer's block?" he asked and scrutinized me more closely, as though he knew the name of the tragic disease but had never actually met someone afflicted with it.

"Flu," I explained. "What about Queller?"

"As you no doubt know, we're investigating his disappearance."

"I didn't, but so what?"

"We thought you might be able to help."

"How?"

"We would like to find him."

"You work in L.A. ?"

"Yes."

"Try the Newport Beach police," I suggested. "Talk to a Sergeant Gahr. She'll give you the only lead you'll ever need."

He took out a spiral notebook and wrote down the name, asking me to spell it, then looked at me. "And what would that lead be?"

"Queller," I said. "Or what's left of him."

"He's dead?"

"I'd say so. I'm no doctor but they tell me it's difficult to survive a shark attack when the shark bites off your head."

He frowned, puzzled. "Dead is no good."

"I'm sure Queller feels the same way."

"You're positive he's dead?"

"Sergeant Gahr will tell you *all* about it," I said and stood up, a hint he should leave and let me go back to bed.

Garvey showed no sign of leaving. "Dead doesn't fit our facts."

"Dead fits my facts."

He moved his pen to his notebook. "Which are?"

"Privileged."

"Mr. Jeeter—"

"I know it's an obscure law and one most policemen ignore, but the First Amendment—"

"Won't fly in this situation."

"The First Amendment won't fly?" I said. "The First Amendment *always* flies. That's why it's the First Amendment."

"If you were dealing with the police—"

"I'm not?"

Garvey gave me a look of feigned puzzlement, as though he, for one, never led me to believe otherwise. "I showed you my I.D."

"Show me again."

"Mr. Jeeter—"

"You're not a police officer?"

"Private."

I looked at the cheap suit, the veined nose. I decided it was time Garvey left. I walked across the living room to the breakfast counter and picked up the cordless phone, holding it so he could watch me punch the numbers. I tapped out the first two digits of 911. "I think it's time to leave, Garvey."

He studied me a moment, perhaps gauging whether he could take the phone away from me before I hit the last number. He relaxed, shrugged and smiled. "At least I got something from you, didn't I?"

"If you're not gone in thirty seconds," I said, "what you'll get from me is a ride in a police car."

Reluctantly, after a final glance at the phone and a final shrug, he left.

When the front door closed, I walked over to the window and waited for him to appear on the sidewalk below me. He came out from under the entrance awning and walked down the sidewalk to a four-door Chevrolet, a cheap model with a radio antenna on the trunk. Like the badge and the I.D., the car looked semi-official, a resemblance he probably cultivated. I went back to bed and tried to work on the Queller story. I thought about Garvey once or twice and finally dismissed him as lucky, someone hired to find Queller who stumbled on my trail. The trail, thanks to Mr. Lusker and Marv, turned out to be well marked and Garvey only the lead hiker in an expedition of people looking for Queller.

Friday, when I got back to the office, the rest of the expedition started appearing on the trail, a tall stack of pink message slips from people looking for information about Queller. I told Rose to give everyone the same answer, read all about it in the next issue of *Global Capitalism.*

Ensconced in my office, the computer booted and waiting, I stared at the blank screen and wondered whether they would have anything to read. After ten minutes, I typed a single character.

The phone rang.

I answered, irritated at this interruption to the creative process. "What?"

"You don't have to take my head off," said Rose.

"Sorry," I said. "Long day."

"You've only been here fifteen minutes."

"Still a long day. What do you need?"

"I have a Jim Langford for you."

"What's a Jim Langford?"

"A reporter."

"What's a Jim Langford, reporter, want?"

"You, he says."

I looked at the single character on the screen and considered telling Rose to take a message, then changed my mind. Professional courtesy never hurt. Whatever Langford wanted from me, someday I might want something from him, whoever he was. "Okay."

My second line rang.

I punched the button and identified myself.

"Jim Langford," said a man's hoarse voice. *"Basking Ridge Star-Dispatch.* I won't take much of your time, Jerry."

"I'd appreciate it," I said.

"I hear you. We're as busy as one-legged figure skaters ourselves," he said, evidently thinking a tired joke would get us off to a good start. "We're doing a piece on the disappearance of Horton Queller, the Bollington Associates options trader. Are you familiar with the affair?"

I hesitated. Occasionally I got calls from writers tilling some field I already plowed, someone who turned up my by-line on a *Global Capitalism* article. I never got calls from writers while I was still staring at a blank page in the computer. "How did you wind up on my doorstep, Jim?"

"Legwork," he answered, "pure and simple. That's how it's done, isn't it? Hard work, long hours—"

"Low pay."

"You got it. There's probably nothing to this Queller thing but they've got me out here beating the bushes anyway."

"And you found my name under one of the bushes."

"In a manner of speaking."

His answer sounded more like fancy footwork than diligent legwork. "What can I do for you?"

"I thought we could trade info, make both of our lives easier."

"Okay," I said. "You first."

He laughed. "Right. You'll pick my brains and that'll be that. Listen, Jerry, I figure since you're on the West Coast, you're further along on this thing than I am. What I've got is background material. It'll fill out anything you write."

I looked at the single character on the screen. "It needs filling out."

"Good. We'll trade, tit for tat. Try this. Did you know Queller was gay?"

"Is that important?"

"You tell me," he said. "Does it fit with anything you've got?"

"It fits."

"How?"

"I don't know," I said honestly. "Unless I wind up writing a story about AIDS on Wall Street, I don't think it fits at all. You said you had more background material."

"His parents," said Langford. "You got that stuff? Father died in a car wreck in eighty-four and his mother's as good as dead from the same wreck."

"I've got most of that," I lied. "What do you mean as good as dead?"

"Vegetable. The same accident did it. She sits around all day in a nursing home staring at the air."

"Nursing homes are expensive."

"You got that right," said Langford. "A trust account pays the bills. I'm *way* ahead of you on that one, Jerry.

Queller set it up with his first million. The guy has beau-coup bucks.''

"I know.''

"The account takes care of everything automatically through an offshore bank.''

"Where?'' I asked.

"Your turn.''

For the same reason I sent Mark Weisel off on a wild-goose chase, I decided to tell Langford less than the whole truth, but enough to get more information. "There's a rumor Queller's dead.''

"A rumor,'' he said, surprised. "From where?''

"That I can't give you.''

"Okay, but—''

"Where's the bank with the trust account?''

"Grand Cayman. Why does this source of yours think Queller's dead?''

Grand Cayman—somewhere in inventory *Global Capitalism* had a story detailing banking practices on Grand Cayman Island. I made a note on a pad to read it. "You don't remember the name of the bank, by any chance.''

He answered with a question of his own. "Have you talked to any of Queller's friends on the coast? He grew up out there. Witherspoon at the *Journal* gave me a few names. Someone named Fairview seemed to be important.''

"Do you always do your stories off other reporter's notes?''

"Only when I can,'' he joked. "It saves time.''

I decided to end the conversation and summoned my most sincere voice. "Jim, I'm turning up zip around here. The whole thing's driving me nuts. I'm sitting here right now with a single character on screen, not even a word. That's as much of the story as I've got right now.''

"Maybe we can sort it out together,'' he said, fishing for more information with a wide cast of his net.

"It's good of you to offer, but I've got to do this myself.''

"I mean just the story line," he said, persevering. "Of course you have to write it yourself."

"I don't even know enough to do that," I said. "I tried making a chronology of events . . ."

"What events?"

". . . but that bombed, too. Maybe if you gave me the rest of your background stuff—"

"Jeeter."

"Hmm?"

"You're not going to give me anything, are you?" he said, changing strategies, substituting aggressive for co-operative. "You're just going to be an asshole about the whole thing."

"I'd say so, Jim, yes."

I expected him to hang up. Instead, he continued, prob-ably deciding the longer he stayed on the line the greater his chance of getting information. "But you say Queller's dead."

"A rumor."

"It's something."

"Not much, I'm afraid," I said. "Listen, Jim, I've got to go. If you need any more help on this, feel free to use anything you like from my piece in next month's issue of the magazine or call me after it's out. Maybe I can let you use my notes."

I went back to the story, deleting the single character on screen and starting over. To my surprise, I found my-self spewing out copy, describing the break-in at Fair-view's apartment and setting up a succinct billboard paragraph that let me jump back to Queller on Wall Street and give the reader a history lesson. The material, orga-nized by my unconscious during three days in bed and triggered by the idea of another reporter dogging my foot-steps, tumbled out, the logjam broken.

Marv called once to find out how the draft was going. I heard relief in his voice when I mentioned the page num-ber, five. He got off the phone immediately, claiming he wanted me to have as much time as possible but probably calling Mr. Lusker in his balloon to report what a fine job he did motivating me.

Later—I was too involved in the story to notice when— the phone rang again. Reluctantly, I answered, my attention on the screen, typing.

"What?" I asked.

"A Ms. Fairview," said Rose.

I stopped typing. "Ms. or Mrs.?"

"She said Ms."

"Okay."

The second line rang. I answered.

An unfamiliar woman's voice responded. "Mr. Jeeter, this is Cynthia Fairview. I'm Leon's sister. I understand you're writing an article about my brother and Horton Queller."

I remembered Mr. Fairview's reaction to even the mention of his son's name, much less his son's name in print, and tried to anticipate her problem. "Ms. Fairview, there's absolutely nothing defamatory in the article. I do mention Leon's homosexuality. I can't avoid it. I understand how your father feels and I've tried to keep that part as straightforward as possible but, beyond that, I don't think I can help you."

"I need to find Leon, Mr. Jeeter."

The statement brought me up short. "You don't know where he is?"

"No," she said. "Can you help me with that?"

"I'm not sure," I said, trying to change gears from writing to thinking, two distinct and often unrelated activities. Somehow, the conversation seemed wrong. Talking to Leon and his mother, I never got any impression of a sister. I remembered Mrs. Fairview bringing Leon a donut in the rain, an act more characteristic of a doting mother with an only child than someone with a house full of children or even two. More important, I remembered the sound of Leon's voice and the sound of his mother's voice.

Though both spoke standard American English with no obvious regional accent, both sounded similar, a family resemblance missing in the woman's voice. "Could you hold on a second, Ms. Fairview? I have to check a file in another room for a possible address."

"Thank you very much, Mr. Jeeter," she said. "I appreciate the inconvenience I'm causing you."

"No trouble," I said and put her on hold.

I got Rose on the other line. "Rosie dear, do me a favor."

"Why not," said Rose. "I do everything else around here."

"Call this number." I flipped through my notes, found the Fairviews' phone number and read it off. "A woman will probably answer. Her name is Leona Fairview. Tell her you're calling for me and ask her whether she's got a daughter."

"That's it?" said Rose. "Just whether she's got a daughter?"

"If the answer's yes, get details. Otherwise, that's it. If I'm still on the other line, interrupt me."

I took the woman off hold, intending to stall her. "Ms. Fairview?"

"Yes."

"I'm sorry about that. The person I need to get the information for me is in the john. It'll be a few minutes before I can get it. If you could give me a number—"

"Actually," she said, "I'm calling from my hotel. I live in New York."

"Which hotel? I'll call you back."

"It's the hotel lobby I'm afraid," she said. "I've checked out. I'm on my way to the airport right now. I thought if I could get the address from you, I could see Leon before I left."

My phone chirped. "Hang on another second, Ms. Fairview. I've got another call."

I put her on hold again and brought up Rose.

"No daughter," said Rose.

"Interesting. I wonder who I'm talking to. Do me another favor, Rosie."

"Only if it's within arm's reach."

"It's not. Go into the library. Check *Standard Rate and Data.* Tell me about a New Jersey newspaper called the *Basking Ridge Star-Dispatch.* "

I went back to Leon's fake sister. "How did you say I could contact you, Ms. Fairview?"

She sensed something going wrong and abruptly hung up.

Rose called back. "You did say the *Basking Ridge Star-Dispatch?* "

"Right. A local paper."

"A nonexistent paper," she said. "At least according to that book."

Standard Rate and Data listed advertising rates for almost every publication in the country, along with a general description of each publication. If a publication the size of a daily newspaper existed, it showed up in the book. Rose checked under *Star-Dispatch, Basking Ridge Star-Dispatch* and *Basking Ridge Star.*

I thanked her, called Directory Assistance for New Jersey and asked for the paper's number. The operator checked and apologized. No listing. Fake policemen, fake reporters, fake sisters, plus an inch of message slips from brokers and bankers—the trail was starting to look like a rush-hour freeway.

I told Rose to hold my calls and worked through lunch, arranging, rearranging, re-rearranging, finally polishing. At first, I made Queller sound sympathetic, a misunderstood and unappreciated financial genius; in short, the usual sort of *Global Capitalism* hero, a jerk with money. The characterization rang false. I remembered the shark-eaten piece of meat in the Newport Beach morgue and changed the characterization. I turned Queller into more a victim of his values than their personification, a naturalistic touch I doubted Mr. Lusker would approve.

When I got to the question of who dumped the body in the Pacific, I equivocated. Without facts, I had little choice. I remembered the phony cop, the phony reporter and the phony sister, the brokers and bankers, some of them probably phony. I generalized them all into "the system" and made them the cause of Queller's death, a system that valued money even above life. The explanation sounded more like it came from a sixties radical than an eighties writer for *Global Capitalism*. I shrugged. The explanation fit the facts. Besides, Queller stood about as far as anyone could get from a counterculture victim of establishment repression, more like the victim of some beast that ate its young.

Late in the afternoon, I finished a draft of the article, saved it to the file server and walked down the corridor to Rose's desk, planning to leave early and get a start on sleeping my way through the weekend, a final recuperation from the flu. Rose handed me a new stack of messages, more brokerage firms, more banks.

I leafed through them. "You know what I'd like to know, Rosie?"

"I couldn't possibly guess."

"I want to know *how* they know I know something," I said. "Or think I know something."

"Who?"

I fluttered the message slips. "These people. I just finished the piece two minutes ago and these guys have been lining up for days. How do they know I know anything they want to know? Telepathy?"

Rose dug under some papers on her desk and came up with the February issue of *Global Capitalism*. She opened it from the back, thumbed past several pages of ads and turned the magazine so I could read it, tapping a box at the bottom of the page labeled, "In The March Issue."

I read it.

In the March Issue

SCANDAL—

"Horton Queller—A Whiz Kid's Last Gasp!"

IN JUNE OF LAST YEAR HORTON QUELLER VANISHED, ENDING A CAREER AS THE MOST SUCCESSFUL ARBITRAGEUR IN THE HISTORY OF WALL STREET! WHAT DO RALPH BOLLINGTON, LEON FAIRVIEW AND THE STREET HAVE TO DO WITH IT! IN NEXT ISSUE OF *GLOBAL CAPITALISM* AWARD-WINNING JOURNALIST GERALD JEETER TELLS US ALL!

ALSO IN THE MARCH ISSUE

TRENDS—

"First Hawaii, Now California!"

JAPAN BUYS AMERICA—CHEAP!

PROFILES—

"Carlo De Bennedetti—A New Roman Emperor?"

LIRA-TOTING LEGIONS MARCH INTO BELGIUM!

TRAVEL—

"Grand Cayman Island"

A GREAT HIDEAWAY—FOR YOUR MONEY!

Aside from the usual *Global Capitalism* style (heavy on the exclamation points), I noticed Marv's dig at me. "Award-winning journalist" meant an award I won in college as the most valuable staff member on the school newspaper for one semester. I posted it in my office at *Global Capitalism* as a joke. Marv noticed it one day and for the next month went around calling it "Jeeter's Pulitzer" and me "Jeeter, the award-winning journalist." I also noticed the ambiguity of the last line. The award-winning journalist "tells us all" meant either tells us everything or tells all of us, a waffle phrase in case I screwed up.

"The shit is getting pretty deep around here, Rose."

"I've been wearing waders for years," said Rose, leaned forward and glanced at the upside-down box. "What's the problem?"

"When Marv wrote this," I said, poking the box on the page, "the story didn't even *exist*. He stuck my dick out on the chopping block and hung the sword of Damocles over it."

"There's an image you might want to save and use in an article."

"Is the shithead in?"

"Which shithead?" asked Marv, hearing my voice and coming out of his office.

"Speak of the devil," I said and held up the magazine, boxed promotional blurb toward him. "You wrote all this crap blind, Marv. At the absolute latest, it was done . . ." I thought about the magazine's printing schedule. "Three days ago."

"Last-minute stuff," he said, nodding. "So what?"

"So you really put me out on a limb," I said, angry. "It pisses me off."

"I can see that, but—"

"What was it, an insurance policy?"

"Insurance?" said Marv, mystified. "I don't see—"

"That makes it even worse," I said, working myself up. "You don't even see it. You play your little office politics game so much you don't even see when you're playing it!"

"Jerry—"

"If I flamed out on the story, you could use"—I poked the box with my finger—"this to blame it all on Gerald Jeeter, award-winning fuck-up!"

"It wasn't that way, Jerry."

"I can see your fingerprints all over it."

"Calm down."

"I'm just *tired* to death of the shit around here, Marv," I said. "I'm going to talk to him about this."

Marv shrugged and gave up. "It's your funeral."

I walked across the reception area to Mr. Lusker's door, put my hand on the doorknob, took a deep breath and walked in.

Behind me, I heard Marv say, "He wrote it."

Chapter Nine

Mr. Lusker looked up from a file on his desk, morning sunlight from the window behind him catching the fringe of gray hair around his bald head, illuminating it, a halo effect that had little to do with his character. He sat back. The halo vanished. The sunlight on his skull gave it a convoluted look, a more characteristic appearance.

"Jeeter," he said. "Feeling better?"

Committed the instant I opened the door, I walked across the office and dropped the magazine on his desk, the page with the boxed promotional blurb open in front of him. "What's this shit?"

He looked at me a moment, his attention caught by my tone of voice, then inspected the magazine. "It appears to be a copy of my magazine. This month's issue, I'd say."

"The box."

He looked at the box, read it and looked up at me, bewildered. "Is there some problem here I don't see?"

"That was written before we even had a story."

He shrugged. "So?"

"So?" I said, frustration letting me regain some of the emotional momentum I felt talking to Marv. "You don't see the problem, do you?"

"Frankly, no," he said. "We've got a story now, thanks to you, and one hell of a story it is. When can I read it?"

"When you wrote that blurb," I said, refusing to let him change the subject, "we didn't *have* a story. What if it never happened? What if it all turned out to be nothing, zip, zilch? You stuck my . . . eh . . . neck out on the chopping block.''

He smiled at me. ''Worked, too, didn't it?''

''It *worked!*'' I shouted. ''Is that all you think about?''

Mr. Lusker nodded. ''Pretty much, Jeeter. I'm running a magazine here. If I have to stick some pusillanimous writer's neck out there once in a while to make this magazine happen . . .''

''Pusillanimous!'' I said, insulted.

''. . . I'll do it. Now where's the story?''

''But—''

''Jeeter, when was the last time you looked back at the previous month's issue of any magazine to compare the promo-ed material to this month's table of contents? The answer is never, right? People don't do that. If your story came to nothing, no one would have noticed, except me, of course.''

I hesitated. He had a point. ''Ethically—''

''This is a magazine, Jeeter, not a nunnery.''

''You mean this is no place for ethics.''

He ignored me, swiveling his chair to face the computer beside his desk. ''What directory's the story in?''

I debated continuing the conversation. My steam, already diminished, evaporated. ''Mine.''

Mr. Lusker accessed my directory on the file server and tried to pull up the story. He glanced at me. ''Locked?''

''I wanted to keep Marv out until it was finished.''

''Password?''

''Bigdeal.''

He laughed at the password and typed it in. My article appeared on screen.

While Mr. Lusker read, I stood in front of his desk and stared at balloon pictures on the wall. Gradually, I calmed down. Even more gradually, I began to feel like an idiot. My paranoia, sparked by people bombarding me with inquiries about Queller, was out of hand. After all, I did get the story Mr. Lusker wanted. Running the promotional box even worked to my benefit, a published claim to be first with the story if that turned out to be important. I looked at the gun collection on the wall, Lugers, Mausers, Berettas. Even without the guns, I managed to shoot myself in the foot.

Mr. Lusker finished reading, sat back and smiled. "Not bad, Jeeter."

"It's not finished yet," I said, considering the piece more or less finished but wanting to deflect criticism. I needed more rest, not criticism.

"It's still not bad, but I can see it's not finished."

"Hm?"

"That crap about the system killing Queller, his yuppie values eating him up."

I sensed a blue pencil at work. Aware I had deviated from the party line, I avoided looking at Mr. Lusker and nodded. "Do you want me to change that?"

"Leave it," he said and shrugged. "It may be true. The other stuff you can fix."

"What other stuff?"

He waved one hand at the computer screen. "That sentimental crap."

I peered across his desk at the screen. "What sentimental crap?"

"Fairview," he said. "He sounds like a high school girl who just wants to be loved."

I nodded. "He is."

"Bullshit."

"I was there, sir."

"But evidently not awake," said Mr. Lusker, looking directly at me. "He sold you that bill of goods and you bought it lock, stock and barrel."

"He didn't sell me—"

"*Everyone's* selling something, Jeeter. Even you."

"Me?"

He patted the computer monitor as though it were a pet dog. "Your ability to get a damn good story like this. You'll get a raise for it. And that, Jeeter, is capitalism.

This prick Queller understood it. It got him killed, but he understood it. The trick is to sell what you've got and not wind up like he did."

" 'In the long run—' " I began.

" 'We're all dead,' " said Mr. Lusker, completing the quotation. "I've read Keynes. It's the short run that counts. In the short run, making a buck is what everyone's about—*every*one, Jeeter. If they get you"—he indicated the balloon pictures on the wall—"your balloon busts. You get eaten by sharks. If that blurb you object to so much because it offends your delicate journalistic ethics sells magazines, that's what I've got to sell. It keeps the sharks from eating me. And you too, for that matter. Is all this obvious?"

It was. "No, sir."

"It should be. *Everyone* sells something, even you, even this Fairview."

"I don't see—"

"I know," interrupted Mr. Lusker, his tone sounding like a college professor lecturing a class of dull students. "How old is this Fairview?"

"The same age I am, thirty-three—no, he met Queller in high school. That makes him thirty-four."

"How many thirty-four-year-olds do you know who are *that* stunted emotionally? Especially gays?"

"Why especially gays?"

"Most of the gays I know," said Mr. Lusker, surprising me that he knew any, "bounce around from relationship to relationship. Whether you do that with someone of the opposite sex or someone of your own sex, you learn a lot doing it. You grow up. You get realistic. You stop acting like some gushing little dipshit."

I thought about Fairview, remembering him on the boat, still unconvinced. "Some people don't grow up."

"Jeeter," said Mr. Lusker, losing patience with me, "did the man strike you as an idiot?"

"No, sir," I said. "Normal, I suppose."

Mr. Lusker smiled briefly. "I won't touch that one."

"Maybe he was in love," I said. "That makes idiots out of people."

"Maybe," said Mr. Lusker, as though love were generally irrelevant to adult life. "So what? The point is how *anyone*—gay or straight, in love or not—could sit around under these circumstances moaning about his poor dead lover and just wanting to be left alone with his delicate feelings."

"According to Freud," I said, "mourning causes—"

"Fuck Freud, Jeeter," said Mr. Lusker, angry at my obtuse reaction. "There was still *three hundred million dollars* on the table!"

I frowned. Mr. Lusker had another point, a rather large one.

"Money, Jeeter," he continued, his expression exaggerated, as though demonstrating the word's pronunciation to someone hearing it for the first time. "This magazine is about money, capitalism, not love. Think about it. Why did we get that newspaper clipping about the body on the beach with Queller's name scrawled on it and the name of the boat? It came in faxed from one of those private mailbox places with no way to trace it back. I'll bet your man Fairview sent it."

I finally got Mr. Lusker's point. "Shit."

Mr. Lusker sat back and smiled, the corona from the window reappearing around his head. "You even said it in your story. 'Economics manipulates us all.' Trite but true."

"The disk."

Mr. Lusker nodded.

I felt even more like an idiot than at the beginning of our conversation. "You're right, sir."

He smiled. "I'll bet that was difficult to say."

"It helps explain quite a few things."

"Such as?"

I told him about the phony policeman, the phony reporter, the phony sister and the stack of messages from brokerage houses.

He thought, slowly doing a 360-degree swivel in his chair and stopping with his attention on me. "Brokerage houses are taking a big interest, you say?"

I nodded. "Evidently so."

"They're still after Queller."

"Who?"

"Or his brains anyway," said Mr. Lusker.

"Who's still after him?"

"Anyone interested in making three hundred million dollars a year, I suppose." He swiveled another complete circle. "This is good, Jeeter, very good."

"What, sir?"

"We're giving Fairview all this free advertising on the cover of *Global Capitalism*. We're helping him find his customers and they're coming out of the woodwork in droves." He looked at me. "How many calls have you gotten so far just on"—he indicated the In-The-March-Issue box—"this?"

"Thirty, maybe."

Mr. Lusker laughed. I disliked the sound of the laugh. "Jeeter, I want us there."

"Where, sir?"

"When Fairview sells that disk, I want to know *all* about it." He beamed at me. "Part Two of your series on Horton Queller."

"Series?"

I left Mr. Lusker's office and walked back down the corridor to my own, dazed. I sat a long time in front of the computer, scolding myself for missing the obvious so utterly. I listened to Fairview and watched him toss the plastic disk on the table in the "End Run," a computer program embodying Queller or at least Queller's ability to earn $300 million a year. Even dead, Queller lived. If a mediocre options trader used Queller's algorithm and updated it with data that matched current market conditions, he could come close to duplicating Queller's performance.

I asked myself how much that kind of performance was worth.

The answer startled me. A business capable of earning $300 million a year would be worth—minimum—four times earning, $1.2 billion dollars. I had difficulty comprehending an amount that size and got out my calculator. If I spent a thousand dollars a day from the day Christ died to the end of the twentieth century, I would still have over $250 million in my wallet for my old age, not counting interest. Under the circumstances, the only reasonable estimate of the algorithm's value was a lot; that is, what someone was willing to pay for it or how many people someone was willing to kill for it.

I retrieved my article and reread it. In the light of Mr. Lusker's comments, my naiveté showed. Love bulked large, not economics. Love might have played a part, I decided, but economics manipulated everyone, even Fairview, who in turn manipulated me. I remembered his mother's list of questions in the donut shop, the magazine's circulation and readership, my own background and qualifications, the sort of questions advertisers ask. I even asked her at the time whether she intended to place an ad. Fairview knew exactly the sort of magazine he needed for his ad and exactly the sort of writer he needed to work up the ad copy.

The more I thought about it, the angrier I got. Fairview got one by me. And what could I do about it? Nothing. Even knowing Fairview used me to drum up customers for Queller's computer program meant nothing. The story served *Global Capitalism*'s economic interests as much as it served Fairview's, gaining us readers and advertisers, keeping me from pumping gas for a living. I thought about the meticulous man with the neat mustache and the bleach streaks in his hair. Evidently he learned a thing or two about high-roll financial markets as Horton Queller's lover.

I read through the story yet again, adding notes to myself in brackets on points I wanted to change. When I got to the end, I made a note to omit any suggestion Fairview destroyed the floppy disk. I intended to stay with the facts I actually knew, emphasizing the floppy disk by leaving it where I saw it last, on the table in the "End Run."

I thought about the new ending. Something—some way to express my anger at Fairview—was missing. My original ending, the floppy disk destroyed and Fairview alone on the boat mourning his dead lover, left the reader feeling the story was finished, a neat wrap-up of all the loose ends. With the disk still on the table—as Mr. Lusker put it, $300 million still on the table—the reader wanted more. The question it raised—and then what?—remained unanswered, a setup for Part Two.

Which brought up another question, namely, did I really want to write Part Two? Even thinking about writing it made me feel like a fool. Actually writing it, I would have to show Fairview sailing off into the sunset with a pile of money after making me look like a fool. Did I really want to look like a fool in my own article?

I picked up the phone and tapped out the number of Mr. Lusker's extension.

"Sir," I said, trying to think of some neutral way to start the conversation, "it's about Part Two."

"It'll be a knock out, Jeeter!"

"*If* we do it."

"If?" he said, irritated, probably anticipating more qualms for Jeeter The Ethical. "Why would we *not* do it?"

"It will make us look like fools, sir," I said. "Fairview used us."

"So what?" said Mr. Lusker. "It'll sell magazines."

"Okay, but don't you think—"

"When someone begins a sentence that way, Jeeter," he said, his mind set on having Part Two and resisting any objection to doing it, "they're usually talking about something I *don't* think."

"Don't you think we should call the police?"

"About what?" asked Mr. Lusker, as though the idea never occurred to him.

"Fairview."

Mr. Lusker laughed. "We'll have them arrest him for living on a boat without a permit, right?"

"No, we'll have him arrested for this crap he's trying to pull with Queller's computer program."

"Crap's a pretty serious charge, Jeeter," he said. "What, exactly, do you mean by it?"

"For selling the program."

I heard a long, exasperated sigh. "First of all, Jeeter, this magazine is not a policeman. Second, neither are you. You write what happens. You don't make the rules and you don't enforce them."

"I understand all that, sir, but this is different."

"How?"

"We're not talking about what happened," I said. "We're talking about what's *going* to happen, the future, not the past. If I were a crime reporter . . ."

"Which you're not."

". . . and knew about a murder that happened yesterday and wrote it up, okay. That's history. But if I know about a murder someone plans to commit tomorrow, wouldn't I have some ethical obligation to do something about it?"

"Ethics, again," said Mr. Lusker, disgusted.

"Honestly, sir, yes."

"This wouldn't have anything whatsoever to do with the fact that the next article is going to make you look like a monkey for letting Fairview work you into a position to write a story that made him several tons of money?"

I hesitated. "No, sir."

"Jeeter, the story here is *economics,* not ethics. Get that through your head. Unless, of course, you *do* know about someone who's going to be murdered tomorrow—do you?"

"No, sir, but the principle's the same."

"Is it? Do you know of *any* illegal act that is going to take place at any time in the future?"

I thought. "Fairview—"

"Is selling something he has a legal right to possess. I know that because *you* told me."

"I did?"

"In your story. You said Queller hid the computer disk at Fairview's apartment, right?"

"Yes, sir, but—"

"And when the bad guys dragged Queller out of the place and Fairview was wimping out in the shower too chicken-shit to try to help when someone was beating the daylights out of the most important person in his life—at that point, Queller knew Fairview had the disk, right?"

"Okay, but—"

"And Queller didn't say a word, Jeeter. They beat him, they probably tortured him and they finally killed him—and he didn't say a word. That tells me something."

"What?" I asked, feeling especially dense. "That Queller wanted Fairview to have the disk because he didn't say anything?"

"Exactly."

"Maybe he hoped Fairview would call a cop and save him?"

"Jeeter, what did Fairview say when you asked him why he didn't call the police?"

"That Queller didn't want him to tell anyone where he was. He said he was just following Queller's orders."

Mr. Lusker laughed. "And you bought that one, too! Queller may have thought Fairview would call the police at first, but when it came down to it, Horton Queller had to know he was a dead man, no cavalry coming to the rescue. I think we've already established as a fact that the man wasn't stupid, right?"

"Yes, sir,"

"And when people are beating on you and doing God-knows-what to you and you figure out the people are serious enough to kill you and even then you keep quiet, you just made a very clear choice. Gay or straight, the man had stones. I'll give him that. He took whatever they dished out and kept quiet. Otherwise, we'd have *two* corpses instead of one—Queller *and* Fairview.''

I resisted Mr. Lusker's interpretation of the facts, probably resisting any argument that led back to me writing Part Two. "Maybe.''

"There's no maybe about it, Jeeter. Think about it. What does Fairview do for a living?''

"He said he was a model.''

Mr. Lusker laughed. "Now there's a lucrative profession. What else?''

"What do you mean, what else?''

"Only a handful of models make a living at it. The others—gay, straight or neuter—call themselves models so they'll have something to tell people they do. Believe me, I'm an authority on models. What else did he do?''

"I . . .'' I rifled through my notes, at the same time trying to remember whether I even asked the question. At the time, I accepted Fairview's occupation as a model uncritically. It seemed irrelevant. "I can probably find out from his mother.''

"Oops,'' said Mr. Lusker and laughed, enjoying my discomfort. "Don't bother, Jeeter. The guy's a social parasite. He lived off Queller. That's easy. Queller had more money than he knew what to do with. Of course he supported his main squeeze.'' He hesitated. "Do people still say that? Squeeze?''

"I haven't the vaguest idea, sir, but—''

"We have to keep *au courant,* as Madeline would say. Anyway, I'll bet that little shit Fairview had it all figured out while he was still peeing in his pants in the shower. Someone was dragging his meal ticket out the front door, maybe never to return. What would you do under the circumstances?''

"Try to stop them.''

"If you were this sniveling wimp?''

"Snivel, I suppose.''

"*Think,* Jeeter! I pay you to use your head. Your first act would be to save the only thing of real value in the apartment. You knew all about how Queller made his money and what that floppy disk might be worth. You would grab it and figure out some way to hold a garage sale that would keep you in condoms for life. The last thing you would do is call the police.''

I thought about Mr. Lusker's explanation. Again, he made sense, more egg on my face. "You're pretty good at this, sir.''

"That's why I own this magazine and you just work here. So—to get back to your precious ethical dilemma— if Fairview inherited the disk from Queller, he's got a perfect right to sell it, doesn't he?''

"Yes, sir.''

"And that, Jeeter—''

"Is capitalism,'' I said. "I know.''

I rewrote the story. I stayed at the office until past seven getting every detail right. I told the story from Fairview's perspective but downplayed his broken heart, instead portraying his romance with Queller as more economically motivated. Aside from the gay aspect, their relationship read like a typical yuppie romance: Queller, a good catch with a heavy checkbook, Fairview, a man in love because he was getting what he wanted, a life of leisure. I followed most of Mr. Lusker's suggestions, especially Fairview's first act when he crept out of the shower. I showed him looking for the floppy disk before he even considered calling the police.

Rewriting the ending, I paused with the floppy disk on the table in the "End Run.'' I thought about all the people trying to find Fairview, the people knocking on my apartment door and calling me at the office. Eventually, one of them would find him and either give him a large amount of money or kill him. To write Part Two, I would have to recontact Fairview and arrange to be in the vicinity when it happened. If they killed him, I might find getting the story difficult. In addition, if I were Fairview, my ad copy already written and published in *Global Capitalism*, I would not want me within a thousand miles of the transaction. Whoever got the disk from Fairview would feel the same way, reluctant to tell the world in print. I needed a reason for Fairview even to talk to me. Short of holding his mother hostage, nothing occurred to me.

Economics, I mused, trying to find any reason why Fairview still needed me—or anyone. Everyone needed Leon, but Leon needed no one.

"Maybe no one needs Leon," I said, an idea occurring to me, a way to simultaneously end the article and sabotage Fairview, something that would help vent my annoyance at him for using me.

Smiling, pleased with myself, I rewrote the end of the article. I liked the new ending, the floppy disk still on the table in the "End Run," Fairview looking at it and believing he had a million dollars in front of him when in fact the algorithm was worthless.

Economic logic argued Fairview had no intention of selling the floppy to only one customer. If he wanted only one customer, he could simply pick up the phone and call brokerage houses until he found one. Any firm on Wall Street would bend over backwards to have Queller's disk. Economics assumes everyone always wants more. Fairview, as greedy as anyone, wanted more, as many customers as possible. Otherwise, why place his—in my opinion, extremely well written—ad in *Global Capitalism?*

Economic logic also argued that Fairview shot himself in the foot. If *everyone* had Queller's algorithm and *everyone* used it in financial markets, *no one* had a competitive advantage. Everyone's actions balanced everyone else's actions, a zero-sum game—in short, no winners. The situation was precisely the same as if *no one* used Queller's program.

I read over the ending and felt smug. I envisioned brokers, traders, investors—Fairview's potential customers—reading the article. All of them were financially sophisticated. All of them would get the point. Fairview could never guarantee any of them exclusive use of Queller's program, the competitive advantage they needed to use it effectively. Consequently, the best—and cheapest—solution for all of them was simply to ignore Fairview and let him sit on his boat and dream, another zero-sum game.

I saved the article to the file server without a password. Almost immediately, someone accessed my directory and pulled up the article. Ten minutes later, just as I was about to leave the office and at long last go home, my phone tweeted.

"Not bad, Jeeter," said Mr. Lusker. "Not bad at all."

"Are you still in the office, sir?"

"I'm at the estate," he said, probably sitting at the computer in his home office with a tall drink. "I used the modem. You got just about everything right."

"You were a big help, sir."

"I can see that," he said. "I particularly liked your ending. That zero-sum argument fits nicely. You're finally using your head. We may make a capitalist out of you yet, Jeeter, instead of a Democrat."

In my tired condition, I almost said thank you. "An economist, maybe."

"Run it," said Mr. Lusker, sounding thoroughly pleased. "Run it as is. If Marv gives you any shit, tell him to see me."

He hung up. I stared at the phone a few seconds, thinking. Mr. Lusker liked the story, including the zero-sum ending. That worried me.

Chapter Ten

For the next week and a half, I procrastinated, finding reasons to avoid recontacting Fairview and reasons to avoid thinking about Part Two. Fundamentally, I wanted nothing to do with either one of them. Instead, I tried to catch up on other work. I sat at my computer and digested mounds of statistics, writing short paragraphs describing them. I expounded at length on brief footnotes in government reports to show "trends" consistent with *Global Capitalism's* skewed view of the world. Normally, I felt oppressed doing that sort of work, Sisyphus pushing his computer uphill. This time, I almost enjoyed it, a justification for letting Part Two slide. I did call Fairview's mother twice. Each time the phone simply rang. I assumed she was out filling her husband's oxygen bottle or buying Leon a donut.

When the March issue of *Global Capitalism* left the printer and started hitting mailboxes—a decomposed and half-eaten something, man or dollar sign, on a sea-green cover—my volume of mail and phone calls went up. One letter, from a Tokyo arbitrageur, was typical. The only Latin alphabet word among the laser-printed pictograms told the story: "Fairview." Brokerage houses, banks with options trading departments and individual investors called me at work and at home. They all had the same idea, getting their hands on Queller's computer program. As one of them put it when he got me out of bed at 6:00 A.M., "You could make a lot of money with a thing like that."

"No shit," I said, hung up and went back to sleep.

With the March issue out the door, Marv's attention turned to the April issue and Part Two. Frequently but politely, he pressed me for "the story." I assured him everything was under control and ended the conversations with excuses about my work backlog. Finally, he stopped me on my way out of the building to the public library.

"What's that?" he asked, looking over my armload of books.

"Stuff."

"What kind of stuff?"

"Charts, graphs, tables—that kind of stuff," I said. "Grist for the mill."

Marv eyed the books. "Which mill?"

" 'Next Time Fifty Percent Inflation,' " I answered, quoting the article's title.

"The Fairview piece—"

"You'll get it."

He looked directly at me. "Let me be blunt, Jerry."

"Do I have to?"

"When?" he said. "When will I get it?"

"Soon."

"How soon?"

"Marv—"

"Do we have a title for this masterpiece? A title would help."

I shook my head. The missing title had already kept Marv from listing Part Two as "Coming in The April Issue," though he did manage to end "A Whiz-Kid's Last Gasp" with the tag line "First of a Series."

Marv started to say something, glanced at Mr. Lusker's closed door and abruptly turned away, walking back toward his office and muttering, "He ties my hands, he ties my hands."

Rose watched Marv disappear into his office and close the door. "He worries."

"*I* worry, Rose," I said. "This story's screwing me up. It's giving me zits."

Rose, sorting mail, glanced at me. "You look okay."

"Emotional zits," I said. "I just don't want to do it."

"I suppose you could always quit."

I nodded agreement. "That's the option, isn't it?"

Rose stopped sorting mail and looked at me. "You're serious."

"I don't know what I am these days."

I left the office and took the books back to the library, any pleasure I felt in menial work obscured by my growing preoccupation with Part Two, more a carbuncle than a zit. When I got back to the office, I called Mrs. Fairview four times. Four times, no one answered.

Mail and phone calls increased. The phone calls, especially, irritated me. Everyone started by blowing smoke, telling me what an excellent job I did on the article, then getting to the point, Fairview. Even when they blew smoke, they got it wrong, particularly the zero-sum ending. When I started writing in college, I learned quickly that most people are poor readers, tune-whistlers who get the melody but miss the orchestration, the details I slaved over. At first, I thought everyone's reaction to "A Whiz-Kid's Last Gasp" came from slipshod reading. Finally, taking a call from an options trader in order to avoid thinking about Part Two, I understood my mistake.

"You got that all wrong, buddy," said the options trader when I finished explaining the story's zero-sum ending.

"Maybe you can explain what I meant."

"Sure."

He explained his own zero-sum theory. At first, it matched mine. If everyone had Queller's computer program, no one benefited. The game had new rules but everyone knew the new rules and no one got an edge. Similarly, if no one had the program, no one benefited. The old rules applied. "But if just *one* guy gets his hands on that program—*that* guy's got something worth having!"

"Ahh . . ." I said, hesitating, reevaluating, resisting

the man's characterization of the situation and at the same time knowing he was right, knowing my zero-sum ending did absolutely nothing to dampen people's enthusiasm; if anything, it highlighted opportunity, whetted appetites, motivated people to find Fairview and become, one way or another, the exclusive owner of Queller's program. Mr. Lusker, this time letting me put myself out on a limb instead of doing it for me, understood the situation the instant he read my ending. He wanted people motivated. He wanted Part Two.

"You still there, buddy?"

"I have to go."

I drove south. A Santa Ana wind, hot and dry off the desert, blew dust and pushed the temperature toward ninety, a record level for late February. My shirt stuck to my back. My mouth tasted gritty. I parked on Balboa Island and started toward Lindy's Landing, my coat over my shoulder and my tie undone, sweating. Sailboats, more plutocrats at play, dotted the bay, sails luffing in the fluky wind. Ahead of me I saw the car ferry, one of three daytime ferries grinding back and forth across the bay. Beyond the ferry dock, I could see the human monument coiling rope on the quay, evidently his hobby.

I walked past the automobile ramp for the ferry, worked my way around the corrugated metal office shed and started across the quay toward the mooring for the "End Run."

I stopped halfway across the quay. Something—I squinted against the glare of the sun off the water and held my hand over my eyes—was wrong.

Pemberton noticed me and tossed a last coil of rope on the pile. "Well, if it ain't that old son of the sea, Jeeter."

I pointed out across the water. "It's gone."

He peered at the bay, wisps of gray hair sprouting through the straw in his hat. "Heavens to Betsy, Jeeter, you're right."

"Where?"

"Sunk. Like the Titanic. Terrible tragedy."

"Leon Fairview—"

Pemberton shook his head. "Nobody aboard her when she went down."

"You said tragedy."

"She went down owin' me seventy-two dollars," he said. "That's a tragedy."

"What happened?"

"Yes, sir-ree, Jeeter, I hated to see that sucker sink. I rented that mooring to 'em and seventy-two bucks ain't chicken feed."

I got out my wallet and gave Pemberton a twenty-dollar bill.

He dangled the bill by one corner as though it were a dead fish. "Kind-a puny."

"The Harbor Patrol can tell me about boats that sink."

He reconsidered and put the twenty in his pocket. "But a keeper, Jeeter. Sunk a week ago. By the bye, you made this a real pop'lar attraction, sort of a Disneyland of the sea. One of them guys—"

"What guys?"

Pemberton eyed me. "Harbor Patrol don't know nothin' about them guys."

I gave him another twenty.

"Five, maybe six guys come around here. Suits, all of 'em. They wanted to know about the old 'End Run' just like you. And I told 'em the same as I told you."

"Pay up or leave."

He smiled, unoffended. "I'm here to make a livin', Jeeter. Anyways, one of them boys showed me that article you wrote in the magazine. Pretty slick. The first time you come around here, I figured you was a bill collector and just usin' that reporter crap to get information. I guess I was wrong there."

"I guess you were."

"You even spelled my name right. Pemberton. Don't too many people even know it. Most people think Lindy's the only name I got. Anyways, one of them boys showed me the magazine and I told him and I'm tellin' you, I don't know nothin' about Leon Fairview. I don't know where the sucker is and I don't give a holy rat's ass. After that night you come out here and almost sunk my dinghy in the storm . . ."

"I didn't almost sink anything."

". . . Leon up and moved out. That's all I know. His mama didn't even know he was gone. She come out here the next night as usual and I took her out there and no Leon. She was pretty upset."

"I can imagine."

"Nice woman, Leona. I hated to see her all upset like that just because somethin' terrible might of happened to that faggot kid of hers."

"But you charged her for the ride out anyway."

"I never charged Leona."

"What do you mean by something terrible might have happened to Leon?"

Pemberton shrugged. "That's what she thought. I think he just up and moved. I walked that old Santana stem to stern and everything was battened down and shipshape."

I looked out across the water. "How did he get off the boat?"

"You got me, Jeeter. Either he swum off or somebody picked him up. I didn't have nothin' to do with it."

"What made it sink?"

"Harbor Patrol diver says she was scuttled."

"Scuttled," I said, puzzled. "Why?"

Pemberton gave me a disgusted look. "Now just how the hell am I supposed to know a thing like that, Jeeter? For a guy smart enough to write them articles, you sure ask some dumb ones."

I nodded agreement. "Sometimes the dumb ones are the important ones. Have you seen Mrs. Fairview recently?"

"Nope. If you see her, say hello from me." He smiled. "Handsome woman."

I remembered the little old lady waddling down the

street in the rain with an umbrella, her silhouette like a toadstool. Tastes, I decided, differed. "You're talking about a married woman, Lindy. Mr. Fairview's a macho guy. He's liable to come after you with a big stick."

"He ain't gonna last, Jeeter," said Pemberton, starting back toward his office. "Me—I'm gonna last forever."

I let the human monument go back to coiling rope and boarded the ferry as a foot passenger, leaning on the rail and looking at the place in the bay where I once saw the "End Run." The mooring bobbed in the water, the missing boat a serviceable symbol for the missing Fairview, a possible lead paragraph for Part Two. I watched the mooring and wondered why anyone would scuttle the "End Run," especially without Fairview aboard. Did someone search the boat and accidentally turn the wrong petcock? Or search it and decide to wash away any incriminating signs of the search? Whatever the reason, I momentarily felt as though the act were aimed at me personally, the fates making my life difficult, probably trying to scuttle my career.

I got off the ferry on the peninsula side of the bay and walked the few short blocks to the Fairviews' street, starting down it. Even before I reached the Fairviews' house, I saw the yellow tape stretched between the wooden posts on the veranda, the fates at work again. I went up the concrete walk and stopped at the tape, its large black letters repeating the same message along its length: POLICE BARRIER—DO NOT CROSS.

I stood on the veranda steps. *"Hello?"*

The tape rustled in the warm breeze.

I tried again. *"Hello? Mrs. Fairview?"*

No answer. I looked around the neighborhood. Across the street, a tan woman in a white tennis skirt and matching white visor watered a flower bed. She watched me, the hose in her hand on automatic sweep.

I crossed the street and introduced myself, asking whether she knew anything about the Fairviews.

She smiled, displaying teeth as white as the visor. "Do you mind if I ask why you want to talk to Leona?"

"I work for a magazine," I explained. "I'm looking into—"

"The murder."

The word brought me up short. I managed an uncertain nod.

"Terrible, wasn't it?" she said, her voice as casual as her clothes, its tone suggesting something interesting had at last happened in her neighborhood rather than something terrible. "The police were all over the street, lights flashing, sirens, ambulance—everything."

"Interesting," I said, trying to coax more information out of her.

"Interesting?" she said and frowned at me from under the visor. "It was terrible."

"That's what I meant," I said. "Terrible."

"At first I thought it was Ed Fairview. Ed was doing poorly, you know."

"Emphysema," I said to show I knew the Fairviews. "It must have been difficult for Leona."

The woman nodded. "Very. I thought maybe he ran out of oxygen. Actually, both of them ran out of oxygen."

The comment, less than sympathetic, confused me. I decided what the woman wanted was to be considered interesting herself for knowing such interesting information and probably cared little for the Fairviews, members of the previous and less affluent generation on her street. "Hm."

"They brought them both out in plastic bags."

"Do you know what happened?"

She looked annoyed by the question. Without an answer to my question, she probably thought I would find her less interesting. She shrugged, inadvertently moving the hose. Water spattered my shoes. "I never found out."

"Do you think anyone else in the neighborhood would know?"

"I doubt it," she said, moving the hose again. Water soaked the cuffs of my pants.

"What about Leon?"

"You mean Leona."

"No, their son, Leon."

"I didn't know they had a son."

I thanked her and started back toward the ferry, walking slowly and thinking, distracted by the idea of the Fairviews dead, evidently murdered. Even without knowing whether their death was in any way related to their son or, more important, my story in *Global Capitalism,* I felt guilty, as though I had something to do with it whether or not I had something to do with it, another emotional zit and one probably caused by having to cope with the idea of death at all. I visualized men carrying black body bags down the steps of the Fairviews' house and placing them in an ambulance. I decided I needed to talk to Sergeant Gahr.

Walking past the donut shop where I talked to Leona Fairview and approaching the street that led to the ferry landing, preoccupied with thoughts of death and the Fairviews, I almost failed to notice the black BMW in the traffic on the street. It moved past me, slowed, sped up and turned at the next corner.

I took the ferry back across the bay and used the phone on the post near the landing to call Sergeant Gahr. Waiting for the police operator to find her, I looked out across the water, my attention stopping at the ferry loading cars on the opposite side of the bay. A black BMW, the last of three cars, rolled down the ramp and bounced onto the deck of the ferry.

The phone clicked. "Gahr."

"This is Jerry Jeeter, Sergeant Gahr. I was wondering if—"

"Just the man I want to talk to," she said. "I read your article."

"And like everybody else in the western world, you

want to find Leon Fairview," I said, anticipating her question. "The answer is I don't know. I'm trying to find him myself right now. I'm supposed to be doing a follow-up piece for the magazine."

"No offense, Mr. Jeeter, but that sounds like bullshit."

"It isn't."

"You're supposed to do a follow-up article and you don't know how to contact your key source," said Sergeant Gahr, pushing me. "No journalist worth his salt would agree to do an article under such circumstances."

I considered explaining about Mr. Lusker. Halfway across the bay, I noticed the ferry plowing toward me with the BMW on board. I doubted I had enough time to explain how assignments happened at *Global Capitalism.* "Frankly, ma'am, there are people at the magazine who are beginning to believe I'm not worth my salt or much else. Besides, I didn't have much choice. If I didn't do the story, I wouldn't work there anymore. But I think I can help you, assuming we can make a deal."

"We don't usually make deals, Mr. Jeeter," she said. "If you have evidence—"

"Information," I corrected, deciding to push back. "I've got information. I've also got the First Amendment."

Sergeant Gahr sighed. "There are times when I wish Thomas Jefferson died young. All right. What's the deal?"

"Tell me what you know about the Fairviews' deaths and I'll tell you anything I know that seems relevant."

She thought a moment. "Credentials."

"You've got a copy of the magazine," I said. "You know I'm real."

Sergeant Gahr sighed. "All right, Mr. Jeeter."

Sergeant Gahr outlined the police reconstruction of the homicides, the apparent motive, robbery. Someone unknown—possibly two someones unknown—entered the Fairviews' house sometime during the preceding week, probably Tuesday.

"Tuesday," I said, uncomfortable.

"Is that important, Mr. Jeeter?"

The March issue of *Global Capitalism* with my story on Queller and Fairview appeared the previous Tuesday. "I don't think so. Actually, I don't know. I just wanted to get the day right."

The Fairviews' neighbors heard nothing. Neighbors, allowed Sergeant Gahr, seldom heard anything. Neighbors disliked missing work to testify in court about other people's problems. The Fairviews' house showed no signs of forced entry, indicating whoever did it probably came in the front door. They ransacked the house, jerking out drawers and dumping the contents on the floor, pulling apart beds and slashing mattresses, emptying the kitchen cabinets. "We found flour, coffee and sugar containers upended on the kitchen floor. They even took the housing off the microwave."

"Thorough."

"Very."

Every object in the living room was either broken, ripped apart or otherwise searched. Even the Fairviews' bodies were strip-searched.

"How were they"—I felt a twinge saying the word— "killed?"

"Suffocation," answered Sergeant Gahr. "Someone put a pillow over the old woman's face until she quit breathing and just unplugged the old man."

"Unplugged him?"

"Shut off his oxygen."

"Fingerprints?"

"You're kidding, Mr. Jeeter," she said. "This was very professional. We didn't even find Leon Fairview's fingerprints."

"He was *persona non grata* around there," I said. "Mr. Fairview had a problem dealing with his son's homosexuality."

"Figures," said Sergeant Gahr. "My parents had the same problem for a while. Your turn, Mr. Jeeter. How does any of this fit with what you know?"

I glanced toward the bay. The ferry with the black BMW sat twenty yards out, waiting in the water for the second ferry to finish loading and clear the dock.

"Mr. Jeeter?"

"I'm here."

I told her about the "End Run," a name I never mentioned in my article, and its location in Newport Bay. "With a little legwork, anyone could find it the same way I found it. It sank about the same time Mr. and Mrs. Fairview were killed. The Harbor Patrol says it was scuttled. I don't know what it means but it sounds related."

"Interesting," said Sergeant Gahr.

"Maybe someone searched the house and the boat, then scuttled it," I said. "They tell me salt water and fingerprints don't mix."

"Or salt water and blood," she suggested. "Maybe someone found what they wanted on the boat."

"I doubt it. Fairview wasn't on the boat, at least according to the man who owns Lindy's Landing." I told her about Pemberton taking Mrs. Fairview out to visit Leon on the boat and finding nothing. "Fairview was already gone."

"The real question, Mr. Jeeter, is why. They killed two people, perhaps three. They searched a house and a boat with a fine-toothed comb. Why?"

"You said you read my article."

"Yes, one of the officers here showed me— Oh," she said. "The computer disk."

"It sounds to me like something someone might kill someone else's parents for."

Hydraulics hissed from the direction of the ferry dock. Metal clanged. The barrier in front of the cars went up. Cars—a Chevrolet, a Mazda, a black BMW—bounced off the ferry and started up a slight grade toward the street. I moved behind the post for the pay phone and tried to glimpse the driver of the BMW. Just as the car reached the top of the incline and leveled out for the street, my best opportunity to see inside, sunlight glared across the windows, momentarily blinding me.

"Mr. Jeeter?"

The BMW continued down the street. I glanced at the trunk lid. The car, new, still showed a paper insert in the license plate frame and no paper plate in the rear window. It continued down the street and disappeared around the corner.

"Are you there, Mr. Jeeter?"

"I'm here."

"You've been extremely helpful," she said. "Frankly, I'm surprised. Your friend Weisel . . ."

"I just know him," I said. "We went to school together. We're not friends."

". . . called here a while back asking about arrest records on a local school teacher. I talked to the teacher. He seemed quite upset by Weisel's innuendoes. Weisel said you put him onto the story."

"Me?" I said, trying to sound incredulous. "About the only thing I would put Weisel onto is a wild-goose chase."

She laughed. "Very good, Mr. Jeeter. It sounds like something I should try. I can't tell you how that man gets on my nerves."

"He gets on everyone's nerves," I said, the mention of Wolverton giving me another idea. If anyone knew how to contact Fairview, assuming Fairview was still contactable, it was Wolverton. "Listen, Sergeant, I've got to go. If I come up with anything else that will help you find Fairview, I'll let you know."

I used my last quarter and called Wolverton at Balboa High School. The school operator put me through to the locker room.

"Cage!" shouted a teenage voice.

I asked for Wolverton.

"You a newspaper reporter?"

"Newspaper?" I said. "No."

"Okay," he said and shouted, *"Wolf! Guy on the phone!"*

I heard a metal locker slam and a metallic echo, a hollow sound as though Wolverton and the student were alone in the locker room.

"Who?" shouted Wolverton.

"Says he's not a reporter!"

I heard hollow footsteps on concrete. Wolverton came on the line.

"Mr. Wolverton," I said, hoping to get out my question before he recognized my voice and hung up, "I need to contact Leon Fairview—"

"Jeeter!" he shouted.

"Sir—"

"Don't 'sir' me, you prick! You're the cause of all this!"

"All what?"

"First the boat!" he yelled. *"Now this!"*

"Sir, I just want to find Leon Fairview—"

"Well, come right over here, Jeeter. I'll give you anything you want! First, I'll kick your wimpy ass from here to Arizona, but after that we'll talk."

"Sir—"

Wolverton hung up.

I considered driving over to the high school. It sounded like a bad idea. Instead, I got my car and started back toward the office.

I took Pacific Coast Highway, the slow, scenic route, hoping stoplights and traffic would give me time to think. The ocean view helped, though it kept reminding me of sharks and torsos. I thought about the Fairviews' murders. I remembered Mrs. Fairview with her umbrella and soggy donut. She cared about Leon, she cared about her husband—a small personal dilemma she resolved by loving them both. She deserved better than to be suffocated and strip-searched.

When my thoughts turned to Leon Fairview, my feelings got more complicated. I considered Fairview's murdered parents, the scuttled "End Run" and Fairview's own disappearance a good start on Part Two, but only a start. To finish it, I needed Fairview himself. If he floated ashore somewhere, with or without shark bites, the story died with him. If he simply vanished, the story vanished. Either way, I had no chance of finding out what happened.

Near Seal Beach, pulled from my thoughts by a lane change, I glanced in the sideview mirror. Four cars back, a black BMW sat in traffic, the license frame on the front bumper filled with paper. I considered stepping on the gas. A high-speed chase seemed more dangerous than simply letting the BMW follow me back to the office. I settled into traffic and turned my attention to the next problem, placating Mr. Lusker, convincing him both Fairview and the story were probably dead.

Chapter Eleven

"**B**ullshit, Jeeter."

"Sir, it's a dead end," I said. "Very dead."

Mr. Lusker, standing at the window of his office with his back to me and his hands in his pants pockets, a silhouette looking out at the world, shook his head. "Wrong, Jeeter. *Think* about what you're telling me."

"I *am* thinking, sir," I protested. "Fairview's probably dead by now. You just don't want to hear it."

Mr. Lusker turned from the window and walked around to the front of his desk, his expression exasperated. "Jeeter, the man is *not* dead. He is *not* tied to a chair somewhere being tortured. And it has absolutely nothing to do with what I *want* to hear. It's simple logic, something in short supply around here. The man knew your story on him was coming out and he didn't want any unexpected midnight visitors, so he vanished."

"And he didn't tell his own mother where he was going," I said. "She showed up at the 'End Run' after he was gone and, according to Pemberton, was very upset not to find Fairview."

"Would you tell *your* mother?" asked Mr. Lusker. "The less she knew, the safer she would be."

"It didn't turn out that way, did it?"

"A little black humor," said Mr. Lusker, annoyed by my comment. "How quaint. Use it in your damn article, Jeeter, not around here."

"Sorry."

"He's out there. He probably sank the damn boat himself. Find him."

"I don't think he can be found."

Mr. Lusker leaned back against the edge of his desk and folded his arms across his chest, unexpectedly tolerant of my protests. "Convince me."

"Someone sank the boat. They probably did it to get rid of any evidence of Fairview's abduction. Fairview wouldn't sneak off the boat, then come back later and sink it. That would just call attention to the boat and to him."

"Okay. I'll buy that so far," said Mr. Lusker, nodding. "Someone else sank the boat and someone else searched it but *not* someone who already had Fairview. No one who already had Fairview would need to kill his parents, search their house, then search the boat. If they had the little wimp tied to a chair, he'd talk."

Mr. Lusker had a point. "Maybe."

"There's no maybe about it," said Mr. Lusker, pushing himself off the desk and walking to the glass gun case on the wall. He took his keys out of his pocket, unlocked the case and removed a pistol from its display pegs, a 9mm Beretta. He brought the gun back to the desk.

"What are you going to do with that?"

"Shoot you for being an idiot," he said, expertly jerking the action. He handed me the gun, grip first. "Take it."

I looked at the gun. "And do what with it?"

"Bear with me, Jeeter."

I took the Beretta, holding the grip between two fingers and letting the gun dangle.

"Careful, dammit," said Mr. Lusker, frowning. "It's loaded."

I laid the gun carefully on his desk and released it.

Mr. Lusker smiled, enjoying my squeamishness. "How did you feel holding that weapon, Jeeter?"

"Anxious," I said, moving away from it. "Do you always keep loaded guns around the office?"

"Of what earthly use is an unloaded gun?" he asked, as though I had just justified his intention to shoot me as an idiot. "The point is professionalism. That gun is not a tool of your trade. Do you remember the first time you used a computer?"

"Yes."

"How did you react to it?"

I looked at the gun. "Pretty much the same way. I didn't want to touch it."

"These men handle guns with the same confidence you handle a computer," said Mr. Lusker. "They're professionals. That's the key concept. Though I have my doubts about you, *these* professionals at least don't make very many mistakes. If you make a mistake, I chew you out. If they make a mistake, they either go directly to jail or die. That Beretta, for example. To my knowledge, that Beretta has been fired exactly eight times since it left the factory in Italy."

"I'm sure it's killed a lot of good men, sir."

"Four," said Mr. Lusker. "I have no idea whether or not they were good. Dead, definitely. Eight rounds fired, four men dead."

"It sounds like the guy missed four times," I said. "That's not very professional."

Mr. Lusker gave me a disgusted look. "Two rounds in the head each, Jeeter. It's standard killing procedure with a nine-millimeter weapon."

I looked at the Beretta again, at a loss how to go about admiring a piece of metal that killed four people. "Very interesting, sir."

"Carlos owned it."

"*The* Carlos?" I said, surprised. "The terrorist? How did you—"

"I acquired it," interrupted Mr. Lusker, leaving the gun's route from a terrorist's hand to Mr. Lusker's office obscure. "That's not the point. The point is he fired it eight times and killed four people. All very deliberate. No mistakes. The man was a professional—professional scum, perhaps, but professional nonetheless." Mr. Lusker walked back to the glass case and took out a second gun, a World War II vintage Mauser. He jacked a shell into the chamber, brought it back to his desk and placed it beside the Beretta. "This weapon was carried by one of the officers involved in the June 1944 attempt on the life of Adolf Hitler. If the bomb failed to kill Hitler, the man who owned this"—he tapped the grip of the Mauser—"was supposed to walk into the bunker where the attempt took place and do the world a favor. He bungled it. Hitler escaped both the bomb and the Mauser. The officer died for his treason and I—" Mr. Lusker hesitated, "acquired the weapon. Do you get my point?"

"Not exactly, sir," I said, wishing he would unload the guns before he got an urge to do the world a favor by ridding it of journalists. "Unless you mean the terrorist was more professional about his work than a professional army officer."

"And you, Jeeter, are a professional journalist."

"I try, sir."

"You work here and I'm sure you find yourself writing stories with which you personally disagree."

"Occasionally."

He looked at me a moment, probably considered disputing how frequently I found myself writing something I detested, shrugged and continued. "In any case, the officer who carried the Mauser bungled it because of slipshod professionalism. Carlos, professional scum, thought out every detail and succeeded. You don't kill people without thinking out the details. The people who killed the Fairviews and searched their house were professionals, Jeeter, just like the people who dragged Queller out of Fairview's apartment—in fact, they might be the same people. If they left no fingerprints when they tore the house apart, they would certainly leave no fingerprints on the boat. If they did kidnap Fairview off the boat and wanted to destroy evidence of the kidnapping, they would scuttle the boat at the time, not later. As you pointed out, no one would come back two days later and scuttle it."

"Maybe."

"Bank on it."

Unconvinced, I decided to stand my ground. "Maybe."

"Jeeter—"

"You've got another point, sir?"

Mr. Lusker took a deep breath, making it sound as much as possible like a tolerant sigh. "An obvious point. Fairview left the boat voluntarily. That coach probably helped him. The men searched the boat several days *after* he left. We know that because your boat fueling man told us Fairview was gone before the boat sank. They searched the boat, found nothing of use and scuttled it to make it *look* like Fairview was abducted."

Mr. Lusker's logic baffled me. "Why would they want—"

"Just because a few people are dead, Jeeter, don't start thinking this is any less a business story. Think like a businessman. Think capitalism, competition. These men are professionals. They know if they are looking for Fairview, they have competition. They know other people are looking for Fairview."

"Half the world."

"By making it seem like Fairview was abducted, they cut the trail. They give anyone looking for him—*you*, for example—a message. The message says, 'Too late, someone else won, time to give up.' That way, when they do find Fairview, they have him all to themselves. At the same time, they eliminate one more place for Fairview to hide."

I thought about Mr. Lusker's speculations and found them persuasive. "It's possible."

"Probable," he corrected. "Almost certain."

"I suppose Fairview's dead parents sent the same kind of message."

"Absolutely," said Mr. Lusker. "And you're the person who told them how to send it."

"*Me?*"

" 'A Whiz-Kid's Last Gasp,' " said Mr. Lusker. "They read it."

"Leg-breakers read financial magazines?"

"Professional leg-breakers do background research. Whoever hired them probably gave them a copy." He smiled. "I would. They read it and decided Fairview was a wimp. The best way to get a wimp's attention is to scare the shit out of him. Killing someone's parents often does that. I think you have a certain responsibility to this Fairview to find him and get him to sell that computer program to someone and write it all up. *Then* they'll leave him alone."

"Don't go in there," I said, passing Marv on my way out of Mr. Lusker's office. "He's armed."

"Hm?"

I went back to my office and sat staring at air a long time. No matter how obvious the logic of the situation seemed to Mr. Lusker, the logic of how to act on his conclusions seemed to me less than obvious, more like completely obscure. Rose interrupted my paralysis several times with phone calls from brokers looking for Fairview. I told her to take messages.

Mr. Lusker was manipulating me. That much, at least, I understood. He evidently assumed guilt motivated liberal Democrats. He decided to use my role in the death of the Fairviews to generate as much guilt as possible and get me to write the story he wanted for the magazine. Whether or not he was right in general about Democrats and guilt, in my case, he succeeded. I did feel some responsibility for the Fairviews' deaths. And guilt. Without my story, no one would have known Leon Fairview existed. No one would have tried to find him through his parents.

At the same time, Mr. Lusker pushed my guilt buttons, he juggled carrots and sticks in front of me, probably insurance in case I were fundamentally unfeeling or obtuse, a nonguilty Democrat. He commented on the difficulty of finding another job in journalism when someone lost a job due to incompetence (the stick), and promised to let me pick my next assignment after I wrapped up Part Two (the carrot). He even suggested a story idea, profiles of international options traders from Europe to Japan, on-the-spot interviews with all expenses paid by *Global Capitalism;* in short, a trip around the world. Normally, only Mr. Lusker traveled on the magazine's money.

All of which brought up another question.

I called Marv.

"Tell me something, Marv."

"Your wish these days," said Marv, "is my command."

"Why does Mr. Lusker want this story so much?"

"In a word?"

"If you can put it in a word."

I heard papers rustle. "Here's the word. Got a pencil?"

"Go ahead."

"Forty-two thousand seven hundred and twenty-three."

"That's several words."

"It depends whether you spell it out or use the number."

"Either way," I asked, "what does it mean?"

"Newsstand sales."

"Newsstand?" The idea threw me. *Global Capitalism,* most of its readers subscribers, seldom sold well on newsstands. The number, minuscule by the standards of *Playboy* or *Cosmopolitan,* was impressive for a fundamentally dull magazine. "Is that in addition to our normal numbers?"

"You want the grand total?"

"If you've got it."

"Mr. L and I just went over them in detail this morning," said Marv, sounding as though he had something to do with the magazine's improved sales. "Here it is. One hundred and fifteen thousand four hundred and fifty-six. Sanchez says the new subscription rate is already up twenty percent in the first week over our best issue last year. You don't get all the credit. Willie's cover helped."

"People thought they were buying the *Police Gazette.*"

"Who cares what people thought they were buying?" said Marv. "It worked. Mr. L has wanted to do something like this for a long time. He decided 'Gasp' was the story to launch it with. That's why he had Willie do the cover over until he got it right and that's also why he's given you more of his time recently than he's given anyone, me included.''

"And that's why he wants Part Two so bad.''

"He wants to keep the ball rolling. Instead of reaching a hundred thousand by the end of the year, we'll be closer to two hundred thousand. And that, O Holy Scribbler, is worth big ad bucks.''

"And a raise.''

"That's already happened,'' said Marv, his sarcastic attitude giving way to annoyance. "Your next check, contrary to sane fiscal policy . . .''

"And your best advice, no doubt.''

". . . will be twenty-five percent fatter. If you pull off Part Two—which I personally doubt you have a chance in hell of doing—you'll get another raise and have a check almost the size of mine. I've been *told* to give you any assignment you want.''

"Sounds good to me.''

"But if you fuck it up,'' continued Marv, his voice cheerful again, "I've also been told to can you.''

"For you, it works either way, doesn't it?'' I said. "Nice positioning, Marv.''

Marv in no way denied the accusation of office politics. "Thank you.''

"And I can imagine which you'd rather do, give me a raise and a trip around the world or can me.''

"I'd rather keep working here,'' said Marv. "Beyond that, I don't have an opinion. The game, Holmes, is afoot and the ball, to coin a phrase, is in your court.'' He hung up.

I stared at my computer screen. After a while, I even turned on the computer. I leafed through my notes on Fairview and realized I had no reason to look at them. I noticed Joy's picture on my desk and started telling her my troubles. I had just reached the part where the mean

Mr. Lusker bear puts two 9mm bullets in Daddy's paycheck—standard killing practice for paychecks, I explained—when the phone rang.

"Someone," said Rose.

"Just someone?" I asked. "No name?"

"I asked for a name," said Rose. "He said you'd talk
to him."

I remembered the parade of brokers and bankers. "I
don't talk to people without names."

"He said you would."

"He was wrong, Rose, tragically wrong," I said. "Take
a message."

I went back to my fairy tale, trying to explain to Joy's
picture how I wound up in a publish-or-perish situation,
unlike Marv, extremely poor positioning. Finally, I decided a good night's sleep might cure brain fade, shut off
the computer and started home.

On my way out, I picked up my accumulated messages
at Rose's desk and stuffed them unread in my coat pocket.
I told Rose to use one of Mr. Lusker's guns to shoot him
twice in the head if she got a chance before five o'clock
and took the elevator down to the ground-floor garage,
already planning a mindless evening, a good dinner,
brandy, TV, a hot bath, maybe one of Joy's coloring
books.

I emerged from the elevator and started toward my car,
the only sounds around me my footsteps on the concrete
floor and traffic noises from Wilshire Boulevard. Ahead of
me, I noticed a man in a business suit leaning in the passenger side of a car. After several seconds, I realized I
owned the car.

"*Hey!*" I shouted, my voice echoing off the concrete.
"*What do you think you're doing?*"

The man stood up and glanced in my direction.

"*That's right!*" I yelled, breaking into a trot toward
him. "*You!*"

Before I took two steps, the man bolted, hopping the
low wall that separated the garage from the sidewalk and

running. I ran to the wall and leaned out just as the man turned the corner at the end of the block.

"*Jerk!*"

I started back toward my car. The closer I got, the sicker I felt. Both doors stood open, their door panels popped loose and drooping away from the metal. I reached the driver's door and looked inside. The interior looked like a junkyard version of a Toyota, seats slashed and pulled apart, carpet ripped up from the floorboards, glove compartment open, its contents littering the floor, even the headliner cut diagonally and pulled down from the roof.

"Shit!"

I remembered Sergeant Gahr's description of the Fairviews' house and decided my car just got the same treatment, every nook and cranny probed. Why, I had no idea.

I got in, leaned across the front seat and jerked closed the passenger door. When I sat up behind the wheel, a spring, protruding through the slashed seat like a booby trap, goosed me.

The spring was the last straw. I lost control. I cursed once, twice, then a flood of obscenities. When I ran out of obscenities, I started on names, everyone I considered even remotely responsible for both the damage to my car and my general situation in life—Harold Shithead Lusker, Marvin Asshole Walters, Leon Faggot Fairview, Horton Sharkbait Queller, Gerald Dumbshit Jeeter. He, in particular, infuriated me. I drove home with the slashed headliner flapping in the moving air around me, its sound like a slow-speed tape of someone laughing.

By the time I got to my apartment building and parked beside Barbara's Datsun, I felt more in control, still angry but able to talk. I took the elevator up to the apartment and walked to the front door, planning how to break the news about the Toyota. I started to unlock the door, discovered it already unlocked and walked in.

"Barbo," I called, "I've got some good news and some bad news. The good news is we get new upholstery for the

Toyot—'' I stopped, hand on the doorknob. The living
room, a demolition zone, matched the Toyota, drawers
pulled out and dumped, couch and chairs ripped apart,
pictures pulled off the walls, their frames broken and their
paper backing slit. Mr. Bear lay in the center of the room,
eviscerated, cotton spilling from his abdomen. I heard
sounds from the direction of the bedroom.

I ran across the living room to the bedroom door, glass
crunching under my shoes, stepping on Mr. Bear. With
vague images of the Fairviews' suffocated and strip-
searched bodies in my mind, I pushed open the bedroom
door. Barbara, hugging Joy, sat on the edge of the slashed
mattress, crying, surrounded by rubble. When the door
opened, she started, saw me and lost control completely,
bawling, *"My things, Jerry!"*

I sat on the bed and put my arm around Barbara's shoulders. She collapsed against me, relying on me for emotional support for the first time in years. She cried. Joy
cried. I found myself choked up and about to cry.

"Barb, honey," I said, "tell me what happened."

Sobbing, she told me. She finished work, picked up Joy
from the daycare center and arrived home a few minutes
ahead of me. She found the front door wide open. She
thought I was home and walked in, scolding me for leaving the door open. Instead of me, she found the apartment
turned upside down, a rubbish heap. Her first reaction was
panic. When she realized whoever did it was no longer in
the apartment, she broke down. "All our things, Jerry!
Who would *do* something terrible like this?"

"I think it has to do with a story I'm working on."

"A story!" said Barbara, indignant that anything so
trivial could cause the destruction of her wonderful things.
"Is a story for that shitty magazine *this*"—she gestured
around at the destruction—"important?"

"Evidently to someone."

"To *you*, Jerry! Is it this important to you?"

Though I recognized Barbara simply wanted someplace
to dump her anger and picked me and *Global Capitalism*

as the handiest dumpster, I nevertheless thought about the question. The story had something to do with whether I kept my job at *Global Capitalism*. It also had something to do with whether I worked in journalism at all. To that extent, I considered it reasonably important. Intrinsically, the story had to do with murder and money, interesting enough subjects, but important? Important stories—international trade balances, wars, revolutions, assassinations—would get larger headlines than what happened to Horton Queller's computer program. As a form of high-finance gossip, the story had some value. The increased newsstand sales of *Global Capitalism*'s March issue testified to that. Even as a cautionary tale about the excesses of greed, the story might be worth something, the modern American equivalent of an Ancient Greek writer warning his countrymen against hubris, too much pride. Americans, the planet's premier materialists, needed as many warnings as possible about the consequences of too much greed. On the other hand, just another warning, especially a warning tucked away between the pages of an obscure business and financial magazine, only amounted to one more drop in a bucket already overflowing with bloody ink.

"It's not important," I said, deciding to head off an unnecessary argument. "Have you called the police?"

Barbara shook her head.

"I'll do it."

I picked up Joy and carried her into the living room. Joy saw Mr. Bear in the middle of the room and pointed at him from my arms. "He's dead."

"We could all be dead," said Barbara, behind me.

The comment, obvious, annoyed me, as though I were somehow responsible for the destruction around us and failing to live up to that responsibility. That argument too I decided to skip.

"We'll get a new Mr. Bear, Sweetheart," I said to Joy.

"Mean Luthker Bear did it."

"Only indirectly," I said and put Joy down beside the

phone on the breakfast counter. Instead of calling the Los Angeles police, I decided to call Sergeant Gahr in Orange County. She knew the situation as well as anyone and could tell me what, if anything, to do.

Waiting for the switchboard to find Sergeant Gahr, I watched Barbara paw through the apartment rubble, her initial reactions of panic and confusion giving way to anger. She held up twisted picture frames and discarded them into a throwaway pile. She tried to restuff a chair. She talked to herself. Watching her, I knew the feeling, the same anger I felt in the car. Whether we could ever get past any of it, I had no idea.

Sergeant Gahr came on the line.

"Ah, Mr. Jeeter, what can I do for you?"

"Listen, for one."

Sergeant Gahr listened, occasionally making sympathetic noises. Generally, she agreed with me. The Los Angeles police would probably find nothing of use in either my car or the apartment rubble. She nevertheless suggested I call them on the off chance whoever searched the apartment left something behind. "Tell me something, Mr. Jeeter."

"Sure."

"Why do these people think you have Queller's computer program?"

"Maybe they wanted something else."

"For example?"

"My notes," I suggested. "Maybe they thought I could lead them to Fairview."

"And can you?"

"I told you this afternoon, Sergeant, I don't know where he is."

"Perhaps they believe you conned Fairview out of the disk," said Sergeant Gahr.

"Is that what you believe?"

"I don't believe anything, Mr. Jeeter," she said. "Not yet, anyway. But you *are* a business reporter."

"Is that a felony?"

"No, but it positions you to exploit something like Queller's computer program, doesn't it? You know the right people."

"By the looks of this place," I said, uncomfortable with Sergeant Gahr's suggestion I had any involvement beyond writing about Queller's program, "I know the wrong people."

"Mr. Jeeter, I'm going to give you my home phone number. If anything else happens, please call me immediately."

"Hang on a sec," I said. "Let me get some paper."

I reached in my coat pocket and took out the pile of pink message slips from the office. The top slip caught my attention.

It's as simple as a phone call.
(Jerry, this is the no-name call)
R.

The no-name call? After a second, I remembered Rose interrupting my paralysis at the office with a phone call from someone who refused to give a name, someone who told Rose I would talk to him.

"Mr. Jeeter?"

I got a pencil. "Okay, I'm ready."

Sergeant Gahr gave me her home number. I wrote it on the no-name message slip.

"There *is* one other thing, Mr. Jeeter."

"What's that?"

"If I were these people and I still don't have what I wanted, whether it was your notes or Queller's program, and if I thought you could help me get what I wanted, I might decide to come and talk to you personally."

Chapter Twelve

Barbara and I packed Joy and a few things into both cars and drove to her mother's house in San Fernando Valley. Throughout the drive, Sergeant Gahr's comment haunted me, making me spend more time looking in mirrors than watching where I was going. Twice, I almost rear-ended cars ahead of me. I kept thinking about the Fairviews, my imaginary version of their dead bodies probably worse than the reality. As far as I was concerned, the situation was beyond any mere story for *Global Capitalism*. If people wanted to run around killing other people for a piece of plastic and a bunch of digital data, they could count me out. If Mr. Lusker wanted me to run around writing about it, *he* could count me out.

By the time I got to the office the next morning and pushed aside the glass door into the reception area, I knew I no longer worked at *Global Capitalism*.

Rose, reading a copy of *Forbes,* glanced up. "We're a little tardy today, aren't we?"

"Is Marv in?" I snapped.

"And surly, too," she said. "Not yet. Dentist."

"I hope it hurts." I glanced at Mr. Lusker's door. "What about him?"

Rose shook her head. "Big function at the estate. Balloons and everything. Investors too. We can always use more investors."

"More hot air," I said, adding another item to the list

146

of reasons Mr. Lusker wanted Part Two, a hot series to generate excitement about the magazine and pry loose investor dollars for expansion. "When Marv gets in, buzz me. Tell everyone else to suck eggs."

"We're not at all in a sparkling mood this morning, are we?"

"Definitely not," I said and went to my office. Before I could have any second thoughts, I took the stack of unanswered phone messages out of my coat pocket, placed them on the desk in front of me, got an outside line and started calling, working my way through bankers, brokers and investors. I told them all the same thing. I had no idea how to contact Leon Fairview. I knew nothing about Queller's program. I acknowledged writing the first installment of the series but told them someone else would write Part Two. That point, I stressed. I was off the story. When anyone pressed me for the name of the person writing Part Two, I gave out Marv's name. I hoped all my callbacks would send a message of my own. Somewhere out there in moneyland, whoever hired the people who demolished my car and apartment might be listening. I wanted my message to say forget all about Jeeter.

Near the bottom of the stack of messages, I ran across the short message from the no-name caller and reread it.

It's as simple as a phone call.
(Jerry, this is the no-name call)
R.

I shrugged and punched out the number. Mystery man or not, I wanted as many people as possible to know I no longer had anything to do with Queller or Fairview.

A man answered. "Hello?"

"This is Jerry Jeeter," I said. "I'm a writer with *Global Capitalism.* You left a simple-as-a-phone-call message at my office yesterday. This is the phone call."

The man laughed slightly, amused at either my phrasing

or my aggressive tone of voice. "Mr. Jeeter, I enjoyed your article on the disappearance of Horton Queller."

"It appears to be popular."

"I can imagine," he said. "The financial community seems to be more interested in him dead than alive."

"Frankly, I'm not interested in him at all," I said. "The guy was an egotistical yuppie shit. He's turned my life into a complete mess. But that's going to stop. The next article in the series—"

"I found your style interesting," he interrupted, as though I called to hear literary criticism. "A bit idiosyncratic, but interesting."

"The style in the next one will be different," I said. "I can guarantee that."

"I especially liked your zero-sum theory. It seemed to me accurate for the most part, though faulty in one or two aspects."

"Listen, whoever you are, I'm not returning this call to get editorial feedback. I don't need stroking and I don't need anyone blowing smoke up my ass."

"Smoke?" he said. "I am not blowing smoke at all, Mr. Jeeter. I was merely going to comment that most of life amounts to a zero-sum game."

"Okay, you've commented. So it's a tautology," I said, more irritated the longer the conversation lasted. "Big fucking deal. Everyone's been reading whatever they want into that zero-sum crap. Frankly, I don't even know what I meant anymore."

"I can imagine that too," he said, amused. "Taken as a whole, the zero-sum argument generally works, but the details change within the particular universe. There can in fact be winners and losers. Are you familiar with the mathematics of quantum mechanics—Niels Bohr, Heisenberg, Pauli, Dirac, the random universe?"

"No," I said, deciding I had a nut on the line. "And I don't give a flying fuck about any of it. I don't know anything about Niels Bohr or Heisenberg or anyone else and I absolutely don't know anything about Leon Fairview. I interviewed him for the article. He disappeared. That's it. No more Leon, at least as far as I'm concerned. Got that? Because that's the whole point of this bullshit, isn't it? Zero-sum, quantum mechanics, winners and losers—and eventually you'll get around to showing me how I can be a big winner in my little universe, right? So let's keep it simple. I don't know anything about Leon Fairview. I don't have a copy of Horton Queller's program. If I did have a copy of the program, I wouldn't know the first thing about how to make a zillion dollars off it . . ."

"I doubt that."

". . . and most of all, I don't know and I don't care where Leon Fairview is. Furthermore, I don't know how to get in touch with him. Now, is all that simple enough for you?"

"Quite simple," said the man, still amused. "Hang on a second and I'll let you talk to him."

"Him?" I said, too steamed up to understand what the man meant. "Him who?"

I heard the phone change hands.

"Mr. Jeeter?" I recognized Fairview's voice immediately.

"Where—"

"I'm with a friend, Mr. Jeeter. I want you to do me a favor."

"Leon, I'm trying to do myself a favor right now," I said. "I'm trying to get as far away from you as possible. If you've got any brains, you'll do the same thing."

"Pardon me?"

"You'll trash that computer program of Queller's or, better yet, take out an ad in the *Wall Street Journal* and publish it. That way everyone's got it, no one benefits and you don't wind up like your parents. Ask your mathematician buddy about it. He seems to know all about zero-sum games."

Fairview hesitated, taking a breath before he spoke. "My mother—"

"Your mother is dead as a doornail, Leon," I said,

intentionally insensitive to help make my point. "And you're next. These people are serious, professional killers. They tore up my car and my apartment. They killed your parents and sank the 'End Run.' They want Queller's program. I'd give it to them. I'd give it to everyone. *Give,* Leon, not sell. If you give Queller's program to the whole world, you might have a chance of coming out of this with your ass in one piece."

"Just a minute, please," said Fairview and covered the phone to talk to the other man, the content of their conversation indistinguishable but their tone, an argument, clear.

Finally, I heard the man shout, *"Just do it, Leon!"*

Fairview came back on the line. "I can't just give it away, Mr. Jeeter. My parents are already—that's already happened. Nothing I do will change that."

"That's real feeling of you, Leon," I said. "But you're still here. You can do something about staying here. If you don't, you'll wind up exactly like your parents."

"I can't do anything, Mr. Jeeter."

"Can't?" I said. "Is someone coercing you?"

"No."

"You're sure no one's forcing you to do something that isn't good for you?"

"No," said Fairview, more or less convincingly. "He's just a friend."

"With friends like that," I said, "you're just a short walk from getting two nine-millimeter bullets in your brain. Believe me, Leon, this is not just about money anymore. *You,* of all people, should know that."

He consulted with his friend again, then talked to me. "You just want me to give them the program so people will stop bothering you."

"You got that right," I said. "And they'll stop bothering you, too, if *bothering* is the right word. Stop trying to kill you is more like it."

"The favor—"

"No," I said, any sympathy I felt for Fairview vanishing. "Whatever it is, the answer's no."

"All I want you to do is write about this."

"You and everyone else," I said. "No, N-O. I don't know why you want me to write about it . . ."

"Because—"

". . . and I don't care. It's not going to happen. Someone might write about it but not me. Mrs. Jeeter didn't raise a kid dumb enough to put his family in danger for a byline."

"Mr. Jeeter—"

"Leon, read my lips," I said, "fuck off."

I hung up, angry.

The phone rang almost immediately.

I snapped the handset off the cradle, expecting Rose with a callback from Fairview. "Rose, just tell him to fuck himself and hang up."

"Marv?" she said. "I really don't think that's a wise idea."

"He's back."

"Two minutes ago. I think you got your wish."

"What wish?"

"It looks painful."

I hung up and left my office, marching down the corridor to Marv's office and barging in. I started to say something and noticed Marv's face. He looked as though the man who demolished my apartment worked on his face, the left side puffy and swollen, the mouth drooping, one eye half-closed.

"Imbacted withdom dooth," he explained.

"Good," I said. "You won't be able to say no."

"Do wat?"

"To taking me off the Fairview story."

Marv started in his chair as though a dentist had just probed a nerve. "You gan't do dat."

"Watch me."

"Heeter—"

"Don't 'Heeter' me, Marv," I said, simultaneously annoyed and amused at the effect of the Novocain on Marv's pronunciation. "My car got ripped apart yesterday while I was in here working. I went home and whoever did it gave my apartment the same treatment. Everything was totaled. If my wife and daughter had been there, they'd be totaled, too. Just so we don't have any misunderstandings, Marv, *totaled* in this context means *dead*. This thing isn't just a story anymore, it's a life-threatening disease. I just talked to Fairview on the phone . . ."

Marv started again, another nerve touched. "You dalked to him?"

". . . and told him to go fuck himself."

"You actually dalked to Bearview?"

"He's nuts, Marv. Maybe I thought I owed him something once because of what my story did to his family but no more. I've got my own family to worry about. Mr. Lusker was right about Fairview. The guy's a social parasite who doesn't give a shit about anybody but himself. Someone off-ed his parents and he's still out there trying to make a zillion dollars from Queller's program. That's nuts. What I care about is my family, even if it's not much of one anymore. So you're putting somebody else on this story or nobody on this story. I don't give a shit what you do as long as I'm off it."

"Heeter," said Marv, "I gan't do dat."

"Sure you can, Marv. In fact, you just did."

"Midder L wants you do let dim know how do bind Bearview."

"I wish I could bind him," I said, intentionally misunderstanding. "To a post. At least that way he'd stay out of trouble *and* out of my hair."

"Bind him! Bind him!" insisted Marv, trying to correct me by repeating his mistake until I got it right. "You've got a bhone number? Give it to anyone dat asks."

"It's really difficult to talk to you sometimes, Marv."

"Nobacain," he said.

"No, your brain. I can understand what you want just fine. You want me to give out Fairview's phone number so everybody in the western world will go after him and who cares how it comes out, this magazine will get a story. That's bullshit! Even if I were still on the story—which I'm not—I wouldn't go around giving out sources for my articles. Journalistically, it's considered bad form; in some circles, even unethical. You do remember that from the days when you had ethics?''

"Snot a source," said Marv. "Sonly a bhone number."

"Same thing," I responded, shaking my head. "Source, phone number—I can't give it out."

"Dink about it, Heeter," said Marv, anger adding to the Novocain distortion of his pronunciation. "You gotta gid do feed."

"I've got a kid to keep alive, you mean. I'll worry about feeding her later."

"Heeter—"

I shook my head and turned toward the door. "Sorry."

I left Marv in pain and went back to my office, closing the door. My phone kept ringing, the second line, Marv insisting I talk to him. I let it ring. Aside from the difficulty I would have talking to Marv on the phone when his pronunciation sounded like a dropout from a night class in "English as a Second Language," the substance of any conversation would only get me angrier. I had no intention of revealing Fairview's phone number to the world. I sat at my desk and deliberately tore up the message slip with the number on it, tearing the tiny pieces into tinier pieces until I was sure Scotch tape would never put Humpty-Dumpty together again. I scattered the pieces around the wastebasket.

When I finally calmed down, I unplugged the ringing phone at its base and tried to think. With less to gain than Caesar, I had just crossed the Rubicon. If I refused to give out Fairview's phone number, Part Two ground to a halt. More important, my involvement stopped. Marv's suggestion I give out the phone number offended me. The pressure from everyone to write Part Two, even from Fairview, offended me. Most of all, working at *Global Capitalism* for even another day offended me.

I booted the computer, date-stamped a fresh document and typed a salutation.

To Whom It May Concern:

I stopped and looked at the words on the screen, trying to think of my first sentence. How did I go about writing a letter of resignation? Did I state my real reasons? Did I trump up something phony for public consumption like "personal reasons"? I remembered Queller's resignation letter from Bollington Associates, short and to the point. If a two-word letter of resignation was good enough for a Queller, it was good enough for us peasants. I cleaned up Queller's diction and wrote my own version of a two-word resignation letter.

I quit.

I printed out a copy of the letter and signed it. Before I thought too much about what I was doing—a bad habit under any circumstances—I put the letter in an envelope, sealed it and took it back down the corridor to Marv.

On the phone when I walked in, Marv looked up at me, commenting into the phone, "Gold on, sir. He's here now."

I tossed the envelope on his desk.

Marv held the phone to his ear with his shoulder and opened the letter. He read it and commented into the phone. "He dinks he's guitting, sir."

"I don't *think* I'm quitting, Marv," I corrected. "I *am* quitting."

"He's not guitting, sir," said Marv, his expression, in spite of the swelling, weary. He began tearing up my letter.

"I can print more," I said.

Marv held the phone out to me.

I took it. "Sir—"

"Jerry," said Mr. Lusker, "come out to the estate."

"I can't, sir."

"And why not?"

"I don't work here anymore, sir," I explained, surprised by my own nerve. "I just quit."

Mr. Lusker laughed briefly. "Nonsense. I'll expect you before noon."

"Sir—" The line went dead.

I handed the phone back to Marv. "I'm not going."

"Sure you are," said Marv, his first correctly articulated sentence that morning, the Novocain evidently wearing off.

"No way."

"Sheeter," he said, still marginally under the influence, "you'll go out there and talk to the man. Talking to the man isn't going to hurt you, even if it is starting to hurt me."

"I don't see why I should do that, Marv."

"Okay," said Marv. "You want something in it for you. Here's the deal, Jeeter—it hurts just saying your name—"

"I can imagine."

"You go out there and talk to Mr. L and if you still want to quit after you talk to him, I'll make sure you get a good letter of recommendation, signed by him."

I thought about the deal. I would definitely need all the help I could get finding another job. A good letter of recommendation from Mr. Lusker would go a long way toward making that possible. Even if Mr. Lusker ultimately refused to sign the letter, Marv would sign it on *Global Capitalism* stationery. By itself, talking could do little damage. After all, I no longer worked for the magazine. I was immune to Mr. Lusker's manipulations.

Chapter Thirteen

Balloons, vertically striped, horizontally striped, one diagonally striped like a fat woman at a beauty contest, dotted the sky above Palos Verdes. I drove up the hill toward Mr. Lusker's estate and watched the balloons in the distance, their baskets tiny specks carrying tinier specks. On my previous visits to the estate, both Christmas parties, I felt uncomfortable, preferring not to be reminded that some people spent more on a small party than I earned in a month. This time, approaching the main gate—an arc of wrought-iron spelled out *Lusker* in script between two stone gate posts—I felt relaxed, comfortable, as though unemployment gave me a new perspective on life, somehow immunizing me against envy.

Unemployment also gave me a new perspective on Fairview. If I was out of my depth trying to associate with Mr. Lusker's wealthy friends, Fairview seemed to me even more out of his depth trying to pull off a deal for Queller's program. No matter how much his new partner, the man on the phone, knew about quantum mechanics, he could never match Queller's detailed understanding of the financial community. Fairview's odds on success were poor, about the same as his odds on survival. More important, none of it had anything to do with me. None of it was my problem or my responsibility. If Mr. Lusker got someone else to write about Fairview, I could read the piece and carp from the sidelines, a comfortable role and perhaps one of the reasons I originally picked journalism as a career. The sidelines were always safer, less committed, than actually playing the game.

I announced myself at a call box on a post and watched the double gates swing open in front of me. I started up the quarter-mile drive toward the house, a three-story monstrosity in white with wide entrance steps and a columned facade. The first time I came to the house, I felt an urge to pay admission, as though I were entering a preserved national monument. This time, balloons spread out across the sky behind the house, the place looked festive, a celebration at the national monument, perhaps a birthday party for Adam Smith.

I parked my demolished Toyota among the Mercedes and walked across the parking area toward the house, gravel crunching underfoot. Ahead of me, the top of a white balloon appeared from behind the house, looming like a creature from a science fiction movie, inflating. I walked up the steps to the front door and pressed the bell.

The Luskers' Mexican maid answered, a small brown woman in a black dress and white apron, her expression, after a glance at my sport coat, disapproving. She led me past a staircase out of *Gone With the Wind*—two elegantly dressed women descended it—past a long buffet stacked with fruits, imported cheeses and dips toward a set of double doors. She stopped at the doors to point out across the lawn.

Mr. Lusker stood beside the basket of the white balloon giving instructions to one of three rope handlers. Between us, people chatted in small groups on the lawn, most of them dressed in business suits and holding cocktail glasses. Unlike almost everyone else, Mr. Lusker had on a white down jacket and jeans, dressing as he pleased for his own party. He saw me, broke off the conversation and waved for me to hurry.

I crossed the lawn, conversations in several languages around me. I recognized French and Italian, both gradually replaced by the hiss of the balloon's propane heater.

"Good afternoon, sir!" I shouted above the sound of the heater.

Mr. Lusker, his usually neat fringe of gray hair pushed in several directions by the wind, nodded toward the wicker basket of the balloon. "Get in, Jeeter!"

"Sir?"

"Get in, dammit!" he shouted. "We're about to lift off!"

"I—"

"Just get in!" he insisted. "Don't argue!"

I stepped on a stool and climbed over the padded rim of the wicker basket. Mr. Lusker followed me, more agile than I expected.

"Sir—"

He waved me to silence. "In a minute, Jeeter!"

Simultaneously, Mr. Lusker released several sandbags on the basket, nodded to the rope handlers and turned a knob on the propane heater. The heater ignited above us, a blowtorch sound that drowned out any hope of conversation. The balloon, slowly, lifted off, the basket underneath me changing from stable to precarious.

"We're away, Jeeter!" shouted Mr. Lusker, grinning, holding the heater knob.

I looked around at the inside of the basket. "Are there any parachutes in—"

"I can't hear a word you're saying, Jeeter!" yelled Mr. Lusker. *"Wait until we gain some altitude!"*

Altitude. I disliked the word. I peered over the edge of the basket. Ropes dangled below us. The lawn, guests, house and pool receded. I looked around the basket for seat belts, found none and held on to a thick rope with both hands.

"Sir—"

Mr. Lusker grinned at me again. *"Hell of an experience, isn't it, Jeeter?"*

"Yes, sir," I shouted. *"But is it a safe experience?"*

"I can't hear you, Jeeter!"

Part of the Palos Verdes peninsula took shape below us,

houses and vegetation stopping at the coastline. We were moving, I noticed, toward the ocean. The sky, gray to the west, hinted at another storm.

"*Sir—*"

Mr. Lusker, balloonist, ignored me.

We drifted and rose, passing the lowest balloon, the balloon with a diagonal stripe. A man and woman occupied its basket. I recognized the woman, Madeline Mundell. She waved. I started to wave back. Wind rocked our basket. I clung to the rope.

"*Sir—*"

Mr. Lusker turned down the heater. The blowtorch noise diminished to a low hiss. We floated toward the ocean.

Mr. Lusker surveyed the world around him, chin out. "Not bad, eh, Jeeter?"

"I can understand your enthusiasm, sir."

"This is what it's all about," he said and glanced at me. "Freedom."

I felt trapped in a basket. "Yes, sir."

He noticed me clinging to the rope. "You don't really have to do that, you know."

"It makes me feel . . ." I looked down at the receding peninsula. ". . . secure."

Mr. Lusker laughed, enjoying my timidity. "Balloons are very stable, Jeeter, very safe."

Wind jostled us. "If you say so, sir."

"There are fewer accidents per mile traveled in balloons than in any other type of aircraft. Even if the heater conked out on us . . ."

"Does that happen often?"

". . . we could simply drift back down."

I looked over the side again at the approaching ocean. "And land where?"

"We have enough altitude to make it back to land with this wind pattern. Enjoy yourself, Jeeter. Most people consider this fun."

I began to wonder about the sanity of most people. "Sir, you wanted to talk to me."

Mr. Lusker shook his head, disappointed with me for not sharing his spirit of adventure. "Jeeter, you're a wimp."

I nodded. "Probably so, sir."

"I give you a free afternoon with a paid-up hooker for that April Fool's column of yours," he said, gesturing toward the diagonally striped balloon, "and you wimp out. Now I give you a ride in a perfectly safe balloon, something most people would be thrilled about, and you stand there looking like you're about to shit in your pants."

"I am, sir," I said and looked at the diagonally striped balloon. "What do you mean, hooker?"

"She's very good at it," said Mr. Lusker, again enjoying my reaction. "Very discreet, very polished, *very* sophisticated. Nothing ever gets back to inappropriate people."

"Like wives."

Mr. Lusker nodded. "She does have one bad habit."

"Prostitution?" I suggested.

"That's her business, Jeeter, not a bad habit. She's a bit greedy. I'm almost willing to bet she tried to work you for a buck or two even with her fee paid."

I remembered my "interview" with Madeline Mundell. Just before Barbara interrupted, Madeline moved the conversation to the idea of love in the afternoon, inquiring whether I had any cash on me and suggesting a place we could go. At the time, I thought she liked me for myself.

"Paid for, you say?"

"Five bills," said Mr. Lusker. "Quality never comes cheap."

I stared across the gulf of empty air at the other balloon. "Five hundred dollars for an afternoon—I think I'm in the wrong business."

"I think we're both in the wrong business," said Mr. Lusker and laughed once. "The business I'd like to be in is the balloon business, the freedom business." Enthusiastic about the idea, he grabbed two of the basket ropes and shook them, teetering the basket. *"Damn,* this is good up here!"

"At least you can afford to be in any business you want."

"Not yet, Jeeter," he said, "but soon. That is, if you keep up the good work."

Still holding the rope with both hands, I turned my attention to Mr. Lusker. "Then I guess your balloon's grounded, sir, because I just resigned."

"Hogwash," snorted Mr. Lusker and turned the heater knob. The heater came to life. Briefly, the blowtorch noise hissed my comment. "You have work to do, Jeeter. A man doesn't resign in the middle of a job."

"I do."

Mr. Lusker glanced at me, annoyed. "What do you want, Jeeter? More money?"

"Sir, my car was torn up and my apartment completely destroyed, probably by the same men who killed Leon Fairview's parents. They searched everything. They destroyed everything, just like the Fairviews' house. If I'd been there or my wife and daughter, we'd all be dead. This story isn't worth that kind of grief."

"I understand your point of view, Jeeter," he said, nodding, looking as though the destruction of everything I owned amounted to no more than a slight disagreement among friends. "Sometimes life gets rough."

"Rough!" I protested. "Rough I can take! This is life and death!"

"Combat pay."

"Pardon me?"

"I'll replace everything the men damaged and give you a substantial bonus—say, twenty thousand dollars. Call it combat pay."

The offer, unprecedented at *Global Capitalism,* surprised me. An extra twenty thousand dollars would pay all my outstanding bills and give Barbara and me a nest egg. On the other hand, dead, I would probably have little use for a nest egg. "No, sir."

"Thirty."

"Sir," I said. "It's not the money."

He twisted the heater knob again, a burst to help us maintain altitude. "What then?"

"I have a thing about death," I said, "especially my own."

He studied me a moment, his hand on the heater knob. "It's the responsibility, isn't it?"

"Responsibility?" The idea, unexpected, unsettled me. "What does that have to do—"

"You feel like the Fairviews are dead because of your first article and there's a possibility someone may kill Leon Fairview if you do what's necessary to make Part Two happen."

"What do you mean by 'do what's necessary'?"

"Release Fairview's phone number."

"You talked to Marv."

"At length."

"Sir, I just can't do that. It's like revealing a source."

"Jeeter, I want you to *think* for a change," said Mr. Lusker, pulling another rope and spilling hot air from the balloon to change our altitude and move us toward the ocean, "instead of letting your liberal guilt get out of hand. Fairview *wants* you to give out his number."

"He didn't say that."

"How else is he going to contact his customers?"

"That's his problem."

"Jeeter, dammit! Why are you being so . . . *obstinate?*"

"I thought we were talking about revealing sources," I said. "Journalistic integrity."

Mr. Lusker laughed, a short, mocking laugh. "Jeeter, give me a break."

"I'm serious, sir."

He looked at me again, thinking. "All right, let's assume you're serious."

"I am."

"If I can show you how you can pursue this story without compromising your precious journalistic integrity, will you do it?''

I heard it coming, one of Mr. Lusker's famous deals. He never made deals unless he held all the cards in the game. Still, I saw no way he could convince me to release Fairview's phone number. Without the phone number, no one would contact Fairview. If no one contacted Fairview, the story Mr. Lusker wanted would never happen. His deal sounded like a safe bet and a way to gracefully bow out of having anything to do with the story. I might even be able to keep my job.

"Okay."

"You'll do the story," said Mr. Lusker, nailing down the exact terms of our agreement.

"Sure," I said. "It'll be complete fiction, of course. I'll just make up the whole damn thing and you can print it."

"Fiction? What—"

"Sir, I'm not releasing Fairview's phone number and, without that, no one can find him. If no one can find him, nothing happens. If nothing happens, I'm going to *have* to write fiction."

"Impeccable logic, Jeeter," he said and twisted the heater knob briefly, a minor course adjustment. "Wrong, but impeccable."

"How's it wrong?"

"We do have a deal?"

"Sure."

Mr. Lusker unzipped the pocket of his jacket, withdrew a slip of paper and handed it to me.

I looked at the familiar seven-digit number on the paper. "How—"

"Call-accounting, Jeeter," said Mr. Lusker, reminding me of the sophisticated phone system at the office. "You called Fairview from *Global Capitalism*. I just told Marv to check out the numbers you called this morning. Most of them were brokerage houses. One was something else, a man. Marv tried to talk to him, but he hung up. Your reaction to the number just now confirms it." He smiled. "Clever, this modern technology."

"Mr. Lusker, you can't—"

"Of course I can," said Mr. Lusker and spilled more air from the balloon, changing our altitude and our course, moving us back toward the estate. "And that's precisely what I'm going to do as soon as we touch down. I told Marv to hold off until I had this little chat with you. As soon as I call him, he's going to start down that list of brokers' numbers—they're all interested in finding Fairview—and give out the good news, as well as the phone number."

"Sir, Fairview might be *killed* because of this!"

I half expected him to shrug and answer with his editorial tag line, *That's capitalism.* Instead, he shrugged and said, "It's not your call, Jeeter. It's Fairview's. He knows better than you do what this could cost him. He's already got two examples."

"His parents."

"He made his choice. Legally, morally, ethically, you're not responsible for *any* of it, just journalistically. All you have to do now is write about it, not indulge your guilt for causing it. I'll take all that difficult responsibility right off your little shoulders."

I felt like shoving Mr. Lusker out of his balloon. "I won't do it. For all I care, you can do it yourself, but not me."

"There isn't time for anyone else to get up to speed on this story. Besides, Jeeter, we had a deal."

"Fuck our deal," I said. "I resigned."

"And just what do you plan to do for a living?"

"I'll get a job."

"Delivering papers, no doubt."

"Whatever."

"I seriously wonder whether you'll get a job," said Mr. Lusker, as annoyed as I had ever seen him. "At least in journalism."

"Marv said he'd write me a letter of recommendation."

"Marv does what I tell him to do."

"Okay, pull all the strings you can pull. I don't need a letter of recommendation. I'll just tell anyone who asks exactly what happened."

"And I'm sure they'll take your word for it," he said, releasing more air. The balloon began to descend. "You mentioned writing fiction. By the time I'm finished, you'll have a first-rate reputation as a fiction writer. I'll look like I was taken in—no, Marv was taken in. That plays better."

"Probably not with Marv."

"He'll do it," said Mr. Lusker, as certain of Marv's cooperation as the safety of balloon flight. "You'll look like someone who trumped up a fictitious story because he was an insecure hack who wanted to be an important journalist. The world is full of assholes like that. Every editor sees them. They'll believe my version and you'll never play the word processor again."

I said nothing. I stood in the balloon and held on to the rope with both hands, enraged. Mr. Lusker's carrot, a $30,000 bonus, and Mr. Lusker's stick, the end of my career in journalism, only amounted to secondary considerations. What left me standing in the balloon turning scarlet with anger and prevented me from speaking was the man's arrogance. I kept asking myself what gave him the right to play with me or Fairview or anyone. I kept coming up with one answer: money. Money gave him freedom and enslaved me. Money let him treat me or anyone he chose like pieces on a game board. Money kept his wife faithful while he cheated on her with hookers or bought hookers for his friends or employees. Most of all, due to some warped sense of American values, money gave him credibility. He could lie about my performance at *Global Capitalism* and everyone would instantly believe him.

Even at the time, I recognized my reactions as clichés, a catalog of obvious differences between the wealthy few and the paycheck-to-paycheck many, the sort of pat phrases

I heard in college from tenth-rate Marxist academics. At bottom, what really bothered me more than any intellectualized sense of economic injustice was how I felt living my life on the wrong side of the economic equation— namely, powerless. I envied Mr. Lusker the power, the money, the Madeline Mundells. I even envied him his damn hot air balloon, his symbol of freedom. And, at the same time, I loathed it all.

I barely noticed our landing. Men grabbed ropes below us and secured them. The basket touched down, bounced once and settled. Mr. Lusker, ignoring me, climbed out of the basket and started across the lawn toward the house, presumably to call Marv.

I got out of the basket and walked slowly across the lawn. A waiter, patrolling the area, stopped in front of me with a tray of margaritas. I took two, downed one, returned the empty glass and snagged a third. I stood on the grass with a drink in each hand and watched the balloon with the diagonal stripe descend. I wondered whether Madeline Mundell accepted rain checks. I downed a second margarita. If I got drunk enough, I might have the nerve to walk up to her and find out.

A man in a business suit appeared in front of me and held out his hand.

"Axel Spitzer," he said, pronouncing it "Spy-tzer."

I recognized both Spitzer's name and his face. Like Mr. Lusker, he published magazines, most of them European, a few American. Spitzer Group America published *Spinnaker,* a sailing magazine, *International Holiday,* a travel magazine and *Housewife,* a middle America book with lead stories on quilting. Even in Europe, his magazines carried a reputation as stolid, dull information books for stolid, dull people. Spitzer himself looked normal enough, a middle-aged man with graying blond hair and the build of a former athlete, soccer perhaps.

"Jerry Jeeter," I said, juggling margaritas to shake hands.

"I could not help noticing you were in the balloon with Harold."

I nodded. "Business."

"Ah, so you publish, Mr. Jeeter."

"Sometimes," I answered, thinking of Part Two. "Sometimes not."

He nodded agreement and took a margarita off a passing tray. I deposited my empty glass and got a fourth drink.

Spitzer looked around at the crowd. "It is a wise philosophy sometimes not to publish."

"Sometimes it's a matter of survival."

"I agree. We once tried to publish a magazine concerning telecommunications in Europe."

"Didn't connect, huh?"

He looked at me a moment, got the joke and laughed. "Exactly right. Telecommunications is a boring subject."

"Call-accounting," I said. "Now there's an interesting subject. Why don't you and I start an entire magazine devoted to the dangers of call-accounting."

"Most people do not care much for telephones."

"Back to carrier pigeons, I say."

"Birds?" he said, as though weighing the possibility of publishing another special-interest magazine. "We were very small when we put out the telephone magazine. It almost killed us."

I nodded. "I know the feeling."

"You are interested in *Global Capitalism*, Mr. Jeeter?"

"Not very."

"I too am only not very interested," he said and looked into his margarita glass. "These drinks do something to my English."

"They do something to everybody's English," I said, downing my third, looking for a waiter, finally throwing my glass on the lawn. "Enough of them and you start speaking Spanish."

He looked at the people on the lawn. "There are others here more interested than I. They believe the magazine is—what is the American idiom? On a roll?"

"It's all smoke and mirrors," I said. "That's another American idiom."

He nodded. "I know it and perhaps you are right. It is a common tactic to increase the interest of investors. But the people here"—he used his margarita to point out two or three people on the lawn—"Antink of *Le Monde Financier* from Paris, Cruthers-Smyth of *World Financial Outlook* in London and that small woman trying to get attention by waving her arms around like a little girl, that is Mercuriali from *Il Ciacchierone* in Milano. It is a magazine for silly little teenage girls but Mercuriali wants to grow up someday and be important, so she too is interested. These people are not fools whom we have here. It must be *real* smoke and *real* mirrors, if you understand what I mean."

I looked around at the people. "Everyone here's in publishing?"

Spitzer nodded. "Yes, the Americans too. I do not know many of them. We are new in this market."

"I'm on my way out of this market," I said, considering the idea of circulating among the publishing moguls and looking for a job.

Spitzer sipped his margarita. "These are very good things, these drinks. It is the first time I have tasted one. I have drunk five."

"Tequila," I said, already beginning to feel my own three drinks and sipping my fourth. "It sneaks up on you."

"It is Mexican?"

"Right," I said and told him about authentic Mexican tequila with a worm in the bottom of each bottle.

He had difficulty with the word *worm*. When he finally got the concept, he peered into his glass as though expecting to find one. "It is good nevertheless."

"I've got an idea, Axel," I said, halfway through my fourth margarita. "Why don't we get blitzed and forget all these assholes."

"*Blitz,*" he said. "It means lightning in German."

"That's what tequila means in Spanish."

"Wirklich? I mean, really?" He shook his head, noticing the effects of his drinks. "I am blue."

I looked at his complexion. "You look okay. Do you need a paramedic or something?"

"Drunk," he explained. "Blue means drunk in German."

"Tequila means that in Spanish, too."

Spitzer frowned, trying to reconcile the two meanings, lightning and drunk. "An unusual word."

"Why don't we get out of here, Axel?" I suggested. "I'll show you the dark underbelly of L.A. L.A.'s got a lot of dark underbelly. We'll paint the town blue."

"Red," he corrected. "I know that one."

"Red, blue—if we get drunk enough the color won't matter. After that, we'll finish off the evening by coming back here and shooting Mr. Lusker twice in the gizzard. That's standard killing procedure for gizzards."

"Gizzard," echoed Spitzer. "Lizard. Blizzard. I know these words."

"Or maybe we'll go shoot Leon Fairview and get it over with," I said. "After all, someone's got to do it."

"Recht!" he said, agreeing, though to what he probably had no idea.

I took Spitzer's elbow and started to guide him toward the house. "We'll take your Mercedes."

Spitzer resisted, pulling away from me. "I cannot go. I must stay and make some business."

"You're not in much shape to make business—whoopee, maybe—but not business. Besides, business can wait. We're talking painting the town blue here."

Spitzer's eyes looked momentarily large and round. He ran his fingers through his hair and took a deep breath. "This tequila is demolish me."

"Definitely."

"Ich muss cafe haben," he said and echoed himself in English. "I must have coffee."

I pointed him toward the house. "The buffet."

Spitzer weaved up the grassy slope toward the house. I

finished my fourth margarita and watched the rest of the balloons land. One by one, they approached the house and settled to the ground. By the time the last balloon touched down, I was close to Spitzer's condition. I watched Madeline Mundell cross the lawn and fantasized. She noticed me watching, smiled and nodded a greeting. Knowing she was a hooker only made her more appealing to me. Cheating on your wife by having an affair meant acting irresponsibly. A fling with a prepaid hooker, especially one with Madeline's flanks and a reputation for discretion, appealed to my blossoming urge toward self-destruction.

Gradually, everyone outside moved inside. I followed. Instead of eating, I found another margarita, inspected the bottom of the glass for worms and drank it. When the line diminished at the buffet table, Mr. Lusker reappeared and stood on the bench for the grand piano, a chicken drumstick in one hand like a conductor, asking everyone to please quiet down.

"I have a few announcements of interest to the publishing community, ladies and gentlemen," he said and paused for the final murmur to die down. "First, I will be open throughout the rest of the day and evening to talk about *Global Capitalism*. That's the reason you're all here and I would be happy to discuss any aspect of the magazine with you. Our circulation—and I just checked these figures with our editor—is running well over one hundred and twenty thousand with new subscriptions up over twenty-five percent from last year."

The group applauded politely, a tepid reaction I interpreted as expressing their concern that any increase in circulation also meant an increase in the cost of buying in.

"Thank you," said Mr. Lusker, "but I'm not *entirely* responsible for this jump in our numbers." He looked around the crowd, spotted me and beamed. "Jerry"—he waved the chicken leg at me—"come up here."

I stared at him, unable to believe he actually meant me.

"Don't be shy," said Mr. Lusker. "You've done a great

job so far and you should get some recognition for it in the publishing community.''

Someone pushed me from behind. Almost involuntarily, I started toward Mr. Lusker, glancing back. Madeline Mundell stood in the crowd just behind me. The crowd ahead of me parted. I reached the piano bench.

Mr. Lusker stood on the bench and rested his free hand on my shoulder. ''This, ladies and gentlemen, is Jerry Jeeter. Jerry did the cover story for the issue of *Global Capitalism* currently on the stands, the story about Horton Queller, the options trader. As all of you who have read the story know, Jerry did a fine job. He worked up the story from almost nothing and it is hot indeed, a prizewinner if I ever saw one. Our sales jumped immediately when the story appeared.'' Mr. Lusker smiled down at me, a benign smile as though I were a favorite son. ''We're extremely proud of Jerry and what he's contributed to the magazine.''

''I'll bet,'' I said.

Mr. Lusker gave me a brief censuring frown and returned his attention to his audience, smiling. ''And Jerry's not finished yet.''

''That,'' I mumbled, ''I *wouldn't* bet on.''

''In the next issue of *Global Capitalism,* Jerry will tell the rest of the story of Horton Queller. I know precisely what Jerry has in mind for Part Two of this story . . .''

''Clue me in.''

''. . . and it's a knockout!'' He looked around the room. ''For our foreign friends, that means we are relying completely on Jerry to push our circulation above one hundred and fifty thousand for the next issue, and we have complete confidence his story will do it!''

More tepid applause and mental arithmetic.

''Indeed,'' continued Mr. Lusker, ''Jerry has completely convinced us of the veracity of his story and I'm forced to back him up completely on it.''

''What story?'' I asked.

''I'm reluctant to steal any of Jerry's fire,'' said Mr.

Lusker, slowing his speech slightly to indicate he was about to make an important point, "but we're all professionals here and I'm sure I can rely on all of you to keep this information to yourselves until the April issue of *Global Capitalism* with Jerry's article hits the stands. In the April issue, Jerry will show that Horton Queller is *not* in fact dead."

No applause. No noise whatsoever, even from me. Somehow I managed to block out what Mr. Lusker said, probably from inability to believe my ears. I looked around at the crowd. Everyone stood staring at me, drinks in hand, looking as though I had just beamed into their midst from outer space. I heard someone in the back of the crowd say, "Jesus Christ!"

Applause broke out, this time loud. Everyone in the room, all of them interested in *Global Capitalism* as an investment, had read my piece on Queller. The idea of Queller alive captured their imaginations completely. To publishers constantly searching out talent for their own magazines, having me in front of them was something like having Woodward or Bernstein in the room at the height of the Watergate scandal.

"But—" I said.

Mr. Lusker cut me off, quieting the crowd with his chicken drumstick. "Thank you. I know you want to hear more about it but you're just going to have to read all about it in next month's *Global Capitalism*. I've instructed Jerry not to talk about the story to anyone. You can understand why. I'm sorry. We may be colleagues but we're also, some of us, competitors. Thank you very much for your attention."

Mr. Lusker stepped down from the piano bench and gave me one of the most vicious looks I have ever received from anyone, commenting, "Try to get a job after the shit hits the fan on this one, asshole."

Stunned, I stood beside the piano bench as Mr. Lusker walked away. He set me up. Slowly, through the alcohol, I realized how completely my ass had just been kicked. Mr. Lusker finally believed I wanted nothing to do with Part Two. He decided it was time to hang me out to dry and let me strangle on the clothesline. If I tried to hustle a job from anyone in the room, they would all tell me to come and see them once Part Two came out. If I tried to insist on starting with them before Part Two appeared, they would immediately know the truth; namely, that no Part Two existed and that I wanted out of the *Global Capitalism* office before the dam broke. Later, when the dam did break, everyone would consider me responsible and no one would hire me.

"You are a writer," said Axel Spitzer in front of me again with a margarita in each hand. He offered me one.

"Was a writer," I corrected, taking the drink and draining the glass. I gave him back the empty glass. "Past tense."

"Yes," he said. "I can see the past tense."

"You can?"

"You will be editor."

"You don't need one, do you?"

"One what?"

"An editor," I said. "Or a writer. Or even a janitor."

"You do not speak German, no?"

"Yes."

"Hm?"

"Yes, I don't speak German."

He shook his head as though too many margaritas or too many negatives were interfering with his understanding. "Our editors in Germany speak German."

"Figures."

"Perhaps here," he suggested. "Perhaps you become an editor here."

I thought about working on a sailing magazine, a travel magazine, a magazine for quilting housewives. "I think I'll pump gas instead. Listen, Axel, it's been nice but I'm on my way out of here. This place is starting to turn my stomach."

"Me too," he said, the sick expression on his face looking as though he meant it literally. "I go with."

"No, that's okay," I said. "I can make it without a copilot."

"Copilot," he said and laughed. "I did not copilot a

balloon today. To me it seems a stupid way to go around the air in a balloon. Where do you go now?''

I shrugged, wondering how many cardboard boxes Rose could find for me to use cleaning out my desk. "Back to the office, I suppose."

"The office," he said. "I wish to see the office."

"I'm sure Mr. Lusker can arrange—"

"I go with," he said, taking my elbow and pushing me toward the front door.

"Axel—"

"We take my car," he said. "Safer."

Before I could protest, Spitzer had me halfway to the front door. Mr. Lusker, talking to the short Italian woman, saw me leaving and caught up with us at the door.

"Jeeter," said Mr. Lusker, more or less blocking my exit, "you still have a choice."

"Fuck off, sir."

Spitzer looked at me. "You talk to your employer that way?"

"Harold and I are great friends," I said. "Nowadays, I talk to him any way I please."

Spitzer shook his head. "Americans."

"Where are you going, Jeeter?"

"What's it to you?"

"I expect copy on the file server tomorrow," said Mr. Lusker. "Do it and you're a big hero. You'll be able to name your price with any publisher in this room."

"Fuck them too."

Mr. Lusker inspected me, thought better of saying anything in front of Spitzer and got out of our way. "Sober up and think about it. It's your call, Jeeter. Make it."

"Come on, Axel," I said. "I'll show you the *Global Capitalism* offices. We can stop by Marv Walter's office and beat him up."

Chapter Fourteen

"This," said Spitzer, pouring us both drinks in the back seat of his white Mercedes and passing one to me, "is German tequila."

I downed half a glassful, choked and exhaled, my eyes large.

Spitzer smiled. "Schnapps."

"It just about schnapped me into outer space."

"To space," said Spitzer and held up his glass in a toast, "the final frontier."

I laughed. "You're a trekkie?"

He nodded. "I watch the reruns every time I come here. I always like to look at the future. It is more *optimistisch.*"

"You're slurring your speech, Axel," I said. "Why don't you lay off the sauce a few minutes and talk to me about something."

"Where is *Global Capitalism?*"

"Up shit creek, maybe," I said. "At least I hope so."

"The address."

I gave him the Wilshire Boulevard address. He said something in German to the chauffeur and returned his attention to me. "What Harold say about the circulation of *Global Capitalism*, it is true?"

I shrugged. "Probably. He doesn't lie about that sort of thing. People can check it too easily. Tell me something, Axel. Why are you here today? Free booze?"

Spitzer shook his head, refilling my schnapps glass and his own. "I come to buy *Global Capitalism.*"

"You mean invest."

"We must diversify the American group and look at the future. Sailboats and travel and *Hausfrauen* do not the empire make." He looked at me. "Is that correct?"

"You got me," I said. "I've never made an empire. Let's back up a second so I can get this straight. Are you here to invest in *Global Capitalism* or buy it?"

"Buy, buy. That's why we come," he said, making his large-eyed expression. He put down the schnapps bottle and tumbler, leaned back against the seat and fell asleep, mumbling, "I buy her."

I put down my own glass and touched the window button beside me. The window slid down. Air rushed in. I put my face in the stream of air and breathed, trying to sober up. With fewer drinks than Spitzer, I managed to stay awake. I sat back beside his snoring body and watched the traffic slip by outside. *Global Capitalism* was for sale. The idea explained all of Mr. Lusker's behavior, an explanation I found substantially more convincing than Marv's notion of boosting newsstand sales and adding subscribers. Mr. Lusker wanted Part Two because it generated excitement about the magazine among potential purchasers. He wanted the magazine to seem hot, an up-and-coming competitor to *Fortune, Forbes* and *Inc.* For Mr. Lusker, everything, even his willingness to endanger Leon Fairview's life, focused on one goal, upping the sale price of the magazine. The idea infuriated me.

Spitzer's driver dropped me in front of the *Global Capitalism* offices. Using sign language, I told him to take the comatose Spitzer back to Mr. Lusker's estate, then commandeered the schnapps bottle and went up to the office. In the elevator, swigging schnapps, I looked around at the familiar paneling, the familiar metal doors, the out-of-date elevator license with *Oops* scrawled across it in red ink. I tried to feel sentimental, my last journey to the salt mines of *Global Capitalism.* Even half-drunk, I felt very little, except perhaps relief.

Crossing from the elevator to the office door, I saw Rose at her desk juggling phone calls, the phone to her ear, the eraser end of a pencil at work on the console. Rose, at least, I would miss. I pushed open the glass door.

Rose looked up from the phones. "I thought you were supposed to have some German with you."

"News does travel fast," I said. "Tell Mr. Lusker the German decided to take a nap instead of buy *Global Capitalism.*"

"Buy?" said Rose, alert. "Was that the operative word?"

I nodded. "You're all on the auction block, everyone except me, of course. I don't work here anymore so I suppose Mr. Lusker will have to reduce the sale price by forty-nine cents to adjust for the loss. Which brings up another question. Do you have any cardboard boxes hidden away for the traditional desk-cleaning ceremony?"

"You did say buy," persisted Rose, "not invest."

"I did indeed. At this very moment, the great patriot has a houseful of foreigners, trying to work them up into a feeding frenzy to buy"—I waved the schnapps bottle around at the walls, the offices, the sick philodendron in the corner—"this third-rate piece of garbage called a magazine."

"Interesting," said Rose and noticed the bottle. "What's that?"

"German tequila," I said and held out the bottle. "Want some?"

She put her nose over the mouth of the bottle, sniffed once and made a face. "I've had my medicine today, thank you."

"Boxes?"

She nodded. "By the way, Marv says you're supposed to—"

"Fuck Marv," I said and started toward my office with

the schnapps bottle. "Who gives a flying holy rat's ass what shithead Marv has to say about anything?"

In my office, I put the schnapps bottle within easy reach and sat down behind my desk, opening the waist-level drawer and beginning to remove objects, a pitiful collection of dead pens, broken rubber bands and desiccated ink pads.

"Not much to show for three years on the job," I commented, hoping for something more interesting, more unexpected, a defaced smile button perhaps.

The longer I worked, the angrier I got. I drank, pawed through drawers and mumbled. Once, I found Mr. Lusker's signature on an old memo and scribbled over it, holding the pen like an ice pick. That he knew from the beginning he intended to sell the magazine got me angriest. He put me at risk, he put my family at risk. Anyone he thought he needed to help him sell the magazine, he put at risk.

"And That's Capitalism!" I shouted, the phrase floating through my mind, mocking me, angering me.

I took my college award for "Most Valuable Staff Member" off the wall and put it on the desk beside Joy's picture.

"Well, sweetheart," I said, going through drawers and glancing at Joy's picture, "the Mr. Lusker bear finally ate Daddy."

"Boxes, Daddy?" asked Rose from the doorway.

I waved my entire arm in the general direction of the floor. "Just put them there. You know something, Rosie Bear, you're cute."

"I know," she said. "I'm also married."

"So am I," I said. "Sort of."

"You're also close to faced."

"Drunk and unemployed," I said. "What will become of me?"

"Just don't barf."

"But this is my last chance to barf in the office, Rosie Bear. Would you deny me that?"

"Yes."

"Harold Lusker is a shithead," I stated.

"Is that a new bumper sticker? If so, I'd like one."

"Harold Lusker is a walleyed sapsucker."

"I've got a great idea, Jerry."

"What's that?"

"Coffee."

"No," I said and swigged from the schnapps bottle.

"You won't even be able to copilot the elevator if you keep this up, much less drive."

" 'Sokay," I said. "I left my vehicular at the sapsucker's."

"Jerry," said Rose, her voice earnest, "I know this is a bad time to discuss reality . . ."

"Reality, schmee-ality."

". . . but . . ."

"What *is* reality anyway, Rosie Bear?"

". . . why is it such a big deal to . . ."

" 'All that we see or seem is but a dream within a dream,' " I quoted.

". . . just do what Harold wants?"

"Poe," I said. "Harold Poe, a great writer. Macabre. Like reality."

"Dammit, Jerry," said Rose, angry with me. *"Why are you doing this to yourself?"*

"It's a dirty job," I said, "but somebody's got to do it."

"Just write the damn piece Harold wants and forget about it!"

"Write," I said and looked at my computer. I reached over and flipped the power switch. "Now there's an idea."

"A good one, too."

The monitor lit up. The computer beeped, ready. I positioned my fingers more or less in the general vicinity of the keyboard and looked up at Rose. "Write what?"

"The story."

I shook my head. "No can do, Rosetta Bear."

"Why?"

"No story." I noticed Rose confiscating my schnapps bottle and frowned. "Give me that."

"Marv says your principles are getting in the way."

"Marv wouldn't know a principle if one called him into its office."

"Jerry, why can't you just do the story?"

"I told you," I said, grabbing a handful of air in a move for the schnapps, "no story."

"Make one up," suggested Rose. "Write a really bad story—*that* I know you can do—and he'll get what he wants and he won't print it and everything will be fixed."

"Write," I said, as though the activity were new and intriguing. I stared at the blank page on the screen. "Now there's an idea. I could write some piece of trash he'd never publish. If Mr. Sapsucker Bear can go around making up facts, so can I. I can make up facts with the best of them. In college, I once made up an entire story about the football team without a fact in it. How does that sound for an idea, Rosie?"

"It sounded good when I suggested it," said Rose. "It still sounds good."

"How about this?" I typed a couple of quick sentences.

Rose read over my shoulder. " 'Horton Queeler—' You misspelled *Queller*."

"He's dead," I said. "He won't mind."

" 'Horton Queller was alive. The financial whiz-kid and wunderkind of Wall Street—' Isn't that redundant, whiz-kid and wunderkind?"

"Everyone's a critic."

" '. . . whiz-kid and wunderkind of Wall Street—the man who made his firm $300 million last year and was thought by every bear in the Wall Street woods to be food for the fishes—abruptly, unexpectedly, came back from the dead.' " Rose looked at me. "Is he?"

"Is he what?"

"Back from the dead—I mean, alive."

"Mr. Sapsucker says so."

"But is he?"

"Rosie, the guy is stone dead," I said and made a cookie monster with my hand, its mouth munching, "eaten alive by the sharks he hung out with. Sharks of a feather, as they say."

"Then why did you say he's alive?"

"You're missing the point."

"Assume I'm stupid."

"Ahh, but you're not, Rosie. You're one of the most intellectually intelligent people I know."

"True," she said. "But assume I'm stupid anyway."

"Because the Sapsucker says he's alive." I told Rose about Mr. Lusker's time-release public humiliation of me at the estate. "He just said it to put me on the pot—I mean, spot. Either I write the story he wants or I never work again."

Rose thought a moment, frowning. "Sometimes I think Harold's not a nice person."

"How about all the time?"

"If he did that to me," she said, "I'd be very angry."

"No shit."

"And if he did that to me," she continued, "I might be tempted to give him exactly what he said he wanted."

I frowned. "Hm?"

"I might be tempted to write the story exactly the way he said it happened. I might leave the story on the file server. I might do that knowing he probably couldn't resist showing the story to people interested in buying his magazine. I might do that knowing that when it all turned out to be fiction, I would be long gone and the story would never get published to hurt me and Harold would be the one with egg on his face."

The idea sobered me, sort of. I imagined Mr. Lusker trumpeting a totally fictional story as upcoming in the next issue of *Global Capitalism.* I imagined his lame attempts at an explanation when every word of it turned out to be fabrication. I could even hedge against any accusations of bad journalism by labeling it "Fact Check to Come," a practice we occasionally used in the office when a story

got written before anyone knew anything to write. To protect myself, I could run off a date-stamped copy on a floppy
disk and mail it to myself. I could tell people an over-
zealous publisher stepped over the line with what was only
a draft of an article and that forced me to quit. Mr. Lusker
would wind up eating a very large crow and I would—
maybe—wind up with another job. Even if Mr. Lusker
failed to take the bait, I could use the story and
overzealous-publisher explanation to counter his state-
ments in front of the publishers at the estate.

"Rosie bear," I said, "sometimes I think *you're* not a
nice person."

Rose took my schnapps bottle and left. I looked at the
computer screen. If Mr. Lusker wanted Queller brought
back from the dead, I would bring him back. I remembered the man who answered the phone for Fairview, the
quantum mechanic. I decided he could play Queller. He
knew enough about mathematics.

I pulled up the original story, Part One, and reread it,
familiarizing myself with details to reconcile both articles.
I deleted the sentences I wrote for Rose and sketched in a
brief background paragraph for anyone who failed to read
the first article, potential purchasers of *Global Capitalism,*
for example. I picked up the story from the break-in at
Fairview's apartment, this time handling it from the fictional Queller's point of view and making dippy Fairview
the fall guy.

Working cleared my head. Queller, I asserted, hired two
men to drag him out of Fairview's apartment. This accounted for his failure to yell for help. Queller's plan—I
thought about it a second, fabricating the most convoluted
plan I could imagine that fit the facts—was to convince
Fairview he was abducted in order to make Fairview sound
convincing when he told his story to the press, namely, to
someone like me. Queller supported Fairview for years
and knew him well. He knew Fairview would immediately
try to sell the algorithm, Fairview's only shot at a con-

tinuing life of leisure. I suggested Queller probably talked to Fairview in advance about how to conduct the sale, the type of magazine that would reach the most potential customers, the type of writer to prepare the most effective ad copy—all of it merely hypothetical at the time but in fact part of Queller's attempt to educate Fairview. Queller trained Fairview then motivated him with a catastrophe, Queller's own ability to predict human behavior under stress giving him confidence about which way Fairview would jump.

I showed Queller outside Fairview's apartment after the rigged abduction getting into a black BMW. I used a flashback to show the same people a month earlier at the Newport marina boarding a boat with a drunken derelict. I described them dressing the derelict in jeans and cowboy boots, killing him, putting Queller's I.D. in the pocket, hacking off the derelict's head and hands—identifying parts—and using the parts to chum for sharks. When the sharks showed up, I showed them dumping the body overboard.

I paused and reread the paragraph, wondering how my fictional bad guys could be sure the derelict's body would survive long enough to be identified as Queller. If anything, throwing it into an ocean full of sharks guaranteed the opposite. I rewrote the paragraph, showing them soaking the jeans in shark repellant and dumping the body close to shore. Sharks ate the arms, nibbled at the torso, chomped the head, bit off one leg, tasted shark repellant on the jeans and went away. The body washed ashore.

"That doesn't make sense," I said, sober enough to be critical. "Too uncertain."

I deleted the paragraph and started on a third version. This time, I tied a rope around the corpse's torso and dangled it over the side, chumming the water with assorted body parts. I let the sharks take a few bites, then dragged the decapitated thing back on board, put Queller's I.D. in the pocket of the one-legged jeans, moved the boat away from the sharks and dumped the body near the surf. That got the shark-eaten and unrecognizable corpse on shore in reasonably good condition, the I.D. intact.

The next part was easy. I jumped forward in time and reprised my interview with Fairview, detailing the impact of my first article, namely, a line of customers for Queller's computer program stretching from New York to Tokyo.

Next, I killed off Fairview's parents. I had Queller do that too. Finding a rationale for his actions stumped me at first. I got up and paced, wandered out into the corridor and drifted toward the front of the office, thinking. I reached Rose's desk.

"I've got a problem."

"I know," said Rose and nodded toward a large Styrofoam cup on the edge of her desk, coffee. "That will help solve it."

I peeled off the plastic cap and sipped the coffee. "Why would Queller kill Fairview's parents?"

Rose, startled by the question, looked at me. "Did he?"

"Of course not," I said. I told her what I had written so far. "Fiction, Rose. Think fiction. I'm trying to make all the details fit."

Rose looked baffled. "That's a tough one."

"I know," I said, sipping coffee.

"Maybe for the same reason all these people"—she gestured at a stack of pink message slips—"were calling you."

I drank more coffee and thought about the suggestion. "To find Fairview?"

Rose nodded. "The way you're telling it, Fairview didn't know Queller was still alive. Maybe Fairview hid too well. Your Queller still needed him as a front man and maybe Fairview had the only copy of the computer program."

"Not bad, except the last part," I said. "My version of Queller wouldn't be dumb enough to actually give Fairview a usable copy of the program. The rest of it works okay, the front-man idea."

"If your version of Queller is so smart," objected Rose,

enjoying the game, "how come the Fairviews' house got searched so completely. And your apartment. You said they went through everything with a fine-toothed comb."

"A fine-toothed bulldozer," I corrected and shrugged. "I can always make Queller a little dumber. After all, everybody makes mistakes."

"A mistake's weak."

"A mistake's the best I can do," I said. "Besides, a good mistake or miscalculation in the middle of all this deft catastrophe psychology and manipulation makes it all sound real. Verisimilitude, Rose. All the best novelists worry about it."

Marv's door opened. Willie Lien, *Global Capitalism's* art director, came out carrying several large sheets of bristol board, pasteups of something. He gave me a peculiar look and disappeared down the corridor without speaking, my new status as a nonperson confirmed.

Marv's head appeared in the doorway. "Jeeter, in here."

I started back toward my office with the coffee cup. "Not now, Marv. First of all, you can't give a nonemployee orders. Second, I'm working."

"Working?" he snapped, ignoring my first-of-all. "On what? I talked to Mr. L."

"I'm rewriting my letter of resignation," I answered and kept going, heading off any attempt by Marv to stick his nose in a nonemployee's business.

Back in my office, I wrote up Queller's unsuccessful attempts to contact Fairview. I used Rose's front-man idea. My Queller still needed Fairview as a front man, someone to deal with the growing line of customers but let him stay dead. To account for the search of Fairview's parents' house and my apartment, I decided Queller mistakenly gave Fairview a usable copy of his program and wanted to control every copy as well as find Fairview. I showed Queller's two men killing off the Fairviews, suffocating Mrs. Fairview with a pillow, a dramatic scene with gagging sound effects from the disconnected Mr. Fairview. I followed the men to the "End Run" to search for the

computer disk and showed them scuttling the boat to simultaneously get rid of any evidence of the search and
give Fairview one less place to hide.

"So far," I said, rereading the copy, "so good."

The next problem proved more intractable. Somehow, I
had to let Queller find Fairview. I drank the last of the
cold coffee and had Queller contact Wolf Wolverton, tell
Wolverton about the boat and convince him Fairview was
in danger. Wolverton gave Queller the location. I remembered my own attempt to find Fairview through Wolverton
and had Wolverton tell Queller about it. That accounted
for the it's-as-simple-as-a-phone-call message to me at the
office. Simultaneously, I showed Queller's leg-breakers
searching my apartment, an example of poor coordination
that gave the whole sequence the ring of truth, another
daub of realistic screwup on my portrait of Queller.

I skipped the lovers' reunion. I did wonder about it. If
my fabricated reunion actually occurred in real life, how
would it happen? Would Queller and Fairview embrace,
kiss, fondle and one or the other of them drop his drawers?
I had no idea nor did I need to know. Irrelevant, definitely
irrelevant. Besides, I had my audience to consider. The
piece was supposed to be a fictionalized version of a
Global Capitalism story, not gay porn.

My next problem proved more complicated than I expected. I decided my fictional Queller, reunited with Fairview, would need to obscure the trail to Fairview's
doorstep in order to prevent anyone else following it and
finding him. I thought about my own efforts to find Fairview. Anyone looking for him would follow something
like the same route. My Queller needed to tie up loose
ends if he ever hoped to reach Tahiti incognito. I decided
several people had to go—first, Lindbergh Pemberton. I
wrote a scene blowing up Lindy's Landing, a spectacular
explosion that burned the human monument alive. I liked
the scene. Bumping off Pemberton was almost justified by
the money he gouged out of me.

I got rid of Wolf Wolverton easily. I remembered his

angry reaction to me during our last phone conversation and the skeet shooting trophy in his office. I also remembered the diversionary story I gave Mark Weisel and his enthusiastic reaction to the idea. I decided to kill off everyone I disliked. I had Weisel write an exposé on Wolverton's preference for hands-on coaching and Wolverton—his career in shambles, provoked by my fictional and manipulative Queller—kill Weisel and commit suicide. A shotgun seemed to me the appropriate instrument for a macho skeet shooter like Wolverton.

"Not bad," I said, genuinely liking the idea, fantasy retribution.

With most of the known details reconciled to my fiction and the trail to Queller's doorstep cut, I sat back and re-read the story, polishing a word here and there for effect. Fiction writers always polish for effect. Hemingway polished endlessly for effect. I could do no less. I looked at my story and it was a good story, a damn good story, and I wrote it true, damn true; that is, true to life, even if it was made up. But . . .

"I still need an ending," I said. "Endings, Ernest, are hard, damn hard."

On the slim chance Mr. Lusker went completely nuts and actually published the story, I decided someone had to kill off Queller, another zero-sum game and a tidy ending. Fiction writers like tidy endings. I considered having Queller's leg-breakers rebel and kill him for the floppy disk.

"Too obvious."

I considered having Fairview learn Queller's leg-breakers killed his parents and kill Queller for revenge.

"Better," I said, "but out of character. The guy's a wimp. He'd probably go hide somewhere and pee on himself."

I considered having Queller die in a dramatic shoot-out with the police.

"No," I said, rejecting the idea. "The man isn't stupid. He'd just give up."

I considered the ending I once heard attributed to a bored mystery writer—*And they all shot each other.*

"Too simple," I decided and called Rose, my coauthor. "I'm running out of avenging angels, Rose."

"I'm sorry to hear that," she said. "Everyone should have a lifetime supply."

"Can I have my schnapps back?" I asked. "That might help."

"No."

"I need inspiration."

"The muse is failing you," she said. "Pity."

"I need someone to kill Queller, creatively speaking." I outlined the options.

"Jerry," she said, "this is fun and everything, but the phones are going nuts at the moment and I'm afraid you'll just have to kill him off all by yourself."

I thought. "Not bad."

"Hm?"

"Thanks, Rose."

"Any time," she said, bewildered.

I introduced myself into the story, the intrepid reporter whose car was thrashed, apartment demolished and family endangered, who, threatened, nevertheless pursued truth. Occasionally laughing aloud at the characterization, I wrote about an angry version of myself, a man dedicated to making the rich and privileged uncomfortable, a man driven by a vision of journalism as the last, best hope of free men.

I reread the characterization, found it a bit too much, deleted it and wrote a toned-down version. I reread the toned-down version, decided it sounded bland and restored the seeker-of-truth version. If Mr. Lusker wanted me to be a hero in the eyes of the publishing world, I would give him what he wanted.

The thoughtful reporter considered the logic of Queller's position. With impeccable logic of his own, the reporter realized Queller had only one alternative if he hoped to wind up in Tahiti without extradition papers following him on the next plane, that is, kill Fairview. Queller had to rig Fairview's death to look as though the men who killed Fairview's parents found Fairview, killed him and took the computer program. The logical reporter, able to put himself into the mind of even a Horton Queller, understood this and recognized his own ethical obligation to prevent the crime. He called the police. The police, believing Queller dead, refused to listen, considering the reporter a crank. The reporter saw only one option. Checking a reverse telephone directory in his office, the reporter got the address associated with Fairview's phone number and drove south, taking with him a Mauser once used in an aborted plot to kill Adolf Hitler.

The reporter arrived at Queller's hideout and confronted him in a Mexican standoff, asking about Fairview. Queller tried to dismiss the reporter's concerns. The reporter, his own logic more persuasive than Queller's lies, refused to listen. The two men stood face to face, both armed, both dangerous. Queller, hoping to corrupt the journalist, offered money, a bribe larger than anything the journalist could ever hope to earn on his own.

"How much?" I said. "A million dollars would be nice."

The journalist, loyal only to the truth and the public's right to know—scorning mere money as a canker on the face of civilization—refused the million dollars. With the journalist's refusal to be corrupted, Queller realized the journalist too must die and raised a gun to fire. The journalist's Mauser fired twice, two deft shots in Queller's head, standard killing procedure with a 9mm weapon. Queller died instantly, humanely. The reporter called the police. At last, the police listened.

I sat back and reread the ending. Some of it—actually most of it—sounded arch, self-conscious. Though I liked myself as the incorruptible defender of truth, justice and the American way, not to mention free men everywhere, I doubted Mr. Lusker would buy it. On the other hand, he only wanted the story to drum up enthusiasm among people who knew nothing about me. I remembered the April Fool's editorial. As much as I disliked admitting it, Mr. Lusker did have a sense of humor. He might laugh and show the story around. I could rely on everyone else to misread the story as truth, putting him in even more of a bind when he tried to explain it as a joke.

I titled the story "Death of a Whiz-kid," labeled it "Fact Check To Come," printed out a copy to show Barbara, saved an extra copy on a date-stamped floppy disk for insurance and saved the story itself to the file server, locking it under the password BIGDEAL. Mr. Lusker knew the password or would eventually remember it from Part One. I liked the password even more for Part Two. It expressed my opinion of the entire situation.

"And that," I said, folding the printout of Part Two and slipping it into my coat pocket with the floppy disk, "is that."

My head, I noticed on the way out of the office with my cardboard box full of junk, ached, the beginning of a hangover.

Chapter Fifteen

I took a cab back to Mr. Lusker's estate, a long and expensive ride to pick up my car. The hangover made it seem longer, drearier. I sat in the backseat of the cab with the cardboard box and watched L.A. move past in the haze, a dusty collection of tired buildings. Ahead of us, the sky darkened, the storm I saw from Mr. Lusker's balloon, last of the season, preparing to wash away the Santa Ana dust.

I thought about the story I had just spent most of the afternoon writing. The longer I thought, the less I believed my time bomb would explode. I took the story out of my coat pocket and reread it. Parts of it still made me laugh, especially the Mexican standoff ending with myself as the intrepid journalist. Whether or not Mr. Lusker believed a word of it—unlike some of his employees, Mr. Lusker had no track record as an idiot—I enjoyed writing it. Half-drunk and angry, it seemed like a good idea, therapy I probably needed.

The cab dropped me at Mr. Lusker's front gate. I paid the driver and walked over to the call box on the post, expecting simply to identify myself, get the gate open, pick up my car and leave. I needed a hot bath as much as Los Angeles needed rain. Instead of opening the gate, the Luskers' maid asked me to wait. Too weary to protest, I waited.

Mr. Lusker's tinny voice replaced the maid's. "Jeeter, is that you?"

"No, it's the '60 Minutes' crew doing an exposé on publishers who float their empires on hot air."

Mr. Lusker ignored the comment. "We have to talk."

"No, we don't," I said. "I have to get my car. Then I have to go home. Then I have to take a long, hot bath."

"Come up to the house."

"For another session of show-and-tell?" I said, remembering Mr. Lusker displaying me to the assembled multitude. "No, thank you. Just open the gate."

The electric lock gave a metallic clank. The wrought-iron gates parted. I walked up the drive toward the house carrying my cardboard box. The last of the balloons, deflating on the far side of the house, seemed an appropriate enough image for my life in general.

I reached the parking area, put the cardboard box in the backseat of the Toyota and got in, avoiding the spring sticking up through the upholstery. The car's gutted interior also seemed like an appropriate symbol, my life torn apart and cut up. I put the key in the ignition. Mr. Lusker appeared at the driver's side window.

"Just hold it a second, Jeeter."

"You hold it," I said. "I'm too tired to hold anything."

"Tell me about the explosion."

"What explosion?"

"At the boat landing."

"Lindy's Landing?"

He nodded.

I sighed, wondering how many seconds elapsed after I saved Part Two at the office before Mr. Lusker accessed the file server with his computer at home, retrieved the story and read it. Electrons, like bad news, evidently traveled faster than cabs.

"What about it?" I asked. "The fuel stop blew up. All very dramatic—flames, explosion, billowing clouds of black burning fuel—just the ticket for the evening news. Cooked the old geezer like a fried egg. It served him right for being an asshole. What's the big deal? Wasn't it dramatic enough or logical enough for your''—I nodded toward the house—"customers?''

"I understand you're upset, Jeeter, but—''

"*Upset's* not the word," I said. "*Revolted*—that's a good one. *Disgusted*—that's another good one. But"—I gave a perfunctory smile—"that's capitalism, right?''

"I do appreciate your feelings in this matter . . .''

"Bullshit.''

". . . but there are other considerations.''

"What?'' I nodded toward the house again. "They weren't impressed?''

A faint smile surfaced on Mr. Lusker's face. "Oh, they were quite impressed.''

"Then what's the problem? Keep the people with the money happy and everything's okay, right? That's capitalism, too.''

"The problem, Jeeter,'' said Mr. Lusker, looking both annoyed and puzzled, "is that I don't understand what the explosion *means.*''

I sighed again, this time a long and impatient sigh. "It *means* Queller was burning bridges, getting rid of anyone who could lead back to him. That's so damn obvious it doesn't need to be spelled out. The same thing's true with Wolverton.''

"Wolverton?'' said Mr. Lusker, his frown deepening. "The coach?''

"The coach. He's a link to Queller, too. He has to go. Staying with the known facts, it's difficult to say how much Queller had to do with that. Maybe he just provoked Wolverton. In any case, Queller has to get rid of all these people. How else can he sail off to Tahiti and live happily ever after?''

Mr. Lusker's frown vanished. He beamed at me. "This story is going to make one *hell* of a splash, Jeeter!''

"I'm glad you think so,'' I said, bewildered. "You're actually going to use it?''

"Of *course* I'm going to use it! How could I *not* use it? Just make sure you get everything *absolutely* right."

"It's as *absolutely* right as it's going to get," I said and started the car. "Do you mind getting out of the way? I don't need a lawsuit for running over your foot to add to my other troubles."

Mr. Lusker stepped back, smiling, his eyes on the sky and the approaching storm, talking to the air above my car. "You've really done it this time, Jeeter."

"Have I?" I said and backed out. "So what else is new?"

I drove toward the gate watching Mr. Lusker in the rear-view mirror. He walked toward the house, slowly at first, then broke into a trot, taking the steps up to his front door two at a time. He disappeared into the house.

"Asshole," I said and stepped on the gas, wanting to get as far away as possible from the estate and Mr. Lusker. The gate posts flicked past.

I got on the freeway and started for the San Fernando Valley. Driving, I kept thinking about the conversation with Mr. Lusker and remembering his image in the rearview mirror. I felt as though I had just dealt him the card he needed in a high-stakes game. I remembered him bounding up the steps to his house. When Mr. Lusker bounds, someone should worry.

The closer I got to the Valley, the less I felt like spending another night under my mother-in-law's roof. I needed time to think, to feel, to sort out my life. Realistically, I could probably still get a job in journalism. Shopping newspapers, circulated free on doorsteps, always needed someone to write about a new store in the mall. Or advertising copy—I could write that. I could use the ad I wrote for Fairview as a sample of my work, an ad with multimillion-dollar sales potential. Or public relations, the graveyard of dead journalists—that had potential. I could sit around all day writing double-spaced press releases extolling the virtues of a second-rate product and the visionary entrepreneur who invented it. That I wanted to do none of these things hardly mattered.

Finally, I decided I would get a better night's sleep on the slashed mattress at the apartment than on a whole mattress at my mother-in-law's with Barbara pointedly ignoring me. I pulled off the freeway and called Barbara.

When I told her about quitting, she remained silent a moment. "And?"

"And what?"

"What are you going to do now?"

"Get something to eat, get some sleep and try to clean up the apartment."

"For a living, Jerry," she asked. "What are you going to do for a living?"

"Think about it tomorrow."

Walking back to my car from the pay phone, I noticed a black BMW parked down the street with someone in it. When I pulled away from the curb, the BMW followed.

I changed lanes. The BMW changed lanes. I turned corners. The BMW turned corners. I settled into traffic on Verdugo. The BMW stayed with me. Abruptly, glancing in the mirror to catch the BMW out of position, I made two quick turns, parked on a side street and shut off the headlights. I waited. No one followed.

"More paranoia," I concluded. "They probably made more than one black BMW."

I turned the car around and got back on Verdugo, checking the cars around me. Satisfied no BMWs lurked in traffic, I began to notice my stomach. Food, I decided, would help clear my head, preferably junk food, the cure for depression. A sign for a pizzeria caught my eye. I slowed, pulled in and parked, leaving the Toyota unlocked and hoping someone would steal it.

Inside, I took a table in the bar beside a bad mural of a gondola in moonlight, ordered a small pepperoni pizza from the Mexican waitress and looked around at the patrons, my eyes adjusting to the dim light. Three people sat at the bar, a middle-aged couple drinking wine and a man eating bread sticks and drinking beer. All three watched a TV on the wall behind the bar, their faces illuminated by the screen, supplicants at the altar of news. I joined the worshipers.

International affairs, national affairs, weather and . . .

". . . a dramatic story this evening from Newport Beach. Christine Chang reports."

The picture cut to a slow panorama of Newport Bay with Christine Chang's meticulous English doing a voice-over. "At this quiet marina today came the death of a well-known local personality, Lindbergh J. Pemberton, the third, owner of Lindy's Landing, a Newport landmark for over forty years."

The camera panned to Christine Chang herself holding a microphone, a pile of charred wood and collapsed metal behind her, the burned-out wreckage of Lindy's Landing.

"At approximately three forty-five this afternoon, authorities say, this harbor reverberated with the explosion of a fuel pump on this dock. Mr. Pemberton, known to locals as Lindy, was coiling rope on the dock at the time. Authorities are still trying to ascertain the exact cause of the explosion that ripped metal, splintered wood and killed Mr. Pemberton instantly, his body pulverized by the explosion, cooked by the flames and thrown into the bay behind me." The camera panned to a tight spot of water in the bay, then returned to the reporter.

"You gotta pulverize 'em before you cook 'em," said the man at the bar, as though he were watching Julia Child discuss cooking abalone.

Someone else in the room laughed.

"Shh," I said.

"So far," continued Christine Chang, "authorities believe the explosion was accidental."

The picture changed to a fireman discussing possible causes of the explosion, then returned to the reporter. "From Newport Beach, this is Christine Chang."

I remembered Mr. Lusker's questions at the estate about the explosion. I remembered his delighted bounds up the steps to his front door. At the time, I thought his questions had to do with my story. In fact, he meant the actual explosion, something he evidently heard on the news or from Marv, a news addict.

I stared at the TV, now showing the Lakers dribbling, and echoed Mr. Lusker's question at the estate: "But what does it *mean?*"

"Shh," said the man at the bar.

"Coincidence?" I asked. "I doubt that."

"Shh," said the man, more insistent, needing his sports fix. "Lakers."

"But what does it *mean?*"

"Sudden death," answered the man at the bar, gesturing toward the TV. "That's what it means. Now shut up!"

"Sudden death," I echoed, got up, bought some quarters from the bartender and found a pay phone on the wall near the rest rooms. I got a phone number from the Orange County Directory Assistance and pumped quarters into the phone for the toll call.

"Cage," answered a different teenage voice.

"Coach Wolverton, please."

"He ain't here."

"How can I get in touch with him?"

"Touch," said the voice. "You ain't one of his faggot buddies?"

"No, I'm a reporter."

"You Weasel?"

"Weisel," I corrected. "Mark Weisel."

"Whatever," said the boy. "You sure reamed the wolf."

"I did?"

"Them stories in the paper," he said and laughed again. "Anyways, he ain't here no more. They suspended him."

"Who? The school board?"

"I was you, dude, I'd watch my ass," he said. "The wolf's pissed. Bye." He hung up.

I called Wolverton's home number. His resonant voice

on the answering machine told me to leave my name and number. I did.

I called Mark Weisel's inside number at the *Times*. I kept thinking of the incinerated picture of Lindy's Landing on the news and remembering the fictional incineration I wrote that afternoon. The least I could do for the real Weisel was let him know Wolverton might be out of control. The phone rang three times, clicked once and rang again.

"City desk."

"I thought this was Mark Weisel's number."

"Weisel's in no shape to take calls," said the man, evidently assuming anyone who called on an inside line belonged to the paper. "What do you need?"

"What happened to Mark?"

"Some nut walked in and wasted him."

"Wasted?" I said. "As in killed?"

"Blew him right out of his swivel chair," clarified the man. "Shotguns are real messy."

"Is he—"

"As a doornail. Point-blank slam dunk all over the wall."

"You're a little cold about this."

"News in the news room," he said, indifferent. "We try to stay objective. Besides, the guy was a prick."

"The man who shot him—"

"Wolverton," supplied the voice. "Walked in here as calm as you please, blasted the Weasel, reloaded and did himself."

"Did himself?"

"Sucked his shotgun."

"Did he say anything?"

"It's a little hard to talk after you suck a shotgun."

"Before," I said. "Did he say anything before he killed himself?"

"Like what?" asked the voice. *"Sic semper tyranus?"*

"Like why he did it."

"You ought to read the paper once in a while," he said.

"That piece Weisel did on the him pretty well explains it. The guy got suspended from his job. My guess is they were about to can him. His life was falling apart. I'd say that gave him a reason or two. On the other hand, maybe he just didn't like Weisel's prose style. I felt like shooting him myself for that, arrogant asshole. Whatever the reason, I'd say the man was definitely pissed. Who is this, anyway?"

My head spun from the information, Wolverton walking into Weisel's office and killing him, committing suicide, using a shotgun.

"You still there?" asked the voice.

"Uh—"

"Who is this?"

"Jerr—a friend," I said and I hung up.

I reached into my coat pocket for another quarter and felt the printout of my story on Queller. The human monument, Wolverton, Weisel—I shivered. I had other calls to make. I decided they could wait until I calmed down.

I walked back into the bar. My pizza, dark circles of pepperoni dotting the tomato sauce like shotgun wounds, waited at the table. I sat down in front of it and looked at the pepperoni, my appetite vanishing.

"But what does it *mean?*" I asked the pizza.

"Shh," said someone.

I stared at the pizza a long time, blocked, unable to make meaningful connections. After a while, I sensed someone standing beside the table.

"Can I have a beer?" I asked. "No, make that a schnapps. Do you have any schnapps?"

"I doubt an Italian restaurant has schnapps," said a man's voice. "But you can ask."

I looked up. A short man in an expensive suit stood beside the table, his face familiar, as though I had once seen it in a murky newspaper photograph or a line drawing portrait in the *Wall Street Journal.*

"I thought we should talk," said the man and held out his hand, introducing himself. "Horton Queller."

Chapter Sixteen

Queller sat opposite me at the table. In person, he looked older than thirty-four, more like a middle-aged man with lingering traces of youth. The lines around the eyes looked middle-aged, the curly brown hair, boyish.

He watched me a few moments, letting me adjust to his presence—or existence—and probably hoping for a reaction. Finally, he smiled. "Surprised, Jeeter?"

"I don't know," I said, feeling less than completely in touch with reality. "But I don't seem to know much these days."

The smile increased minutely. "I thought journalists knew everything."

"Some think they do."

He glanced at the pizza. "Do you mind?"

"I didn't know dead men ate."

"This one does," he said and picked up a slice of pizza. "Following you out to the valley and back, I didn't get a chance to eat."

He bit off the tip of the pizza and chewed. "Hot."

"So's Lindbergh Pemberton."

"I heard about that in the car," he said, chewing. "I think Leon knew him."

"And you didn't?"

"Never met the man."

"You never met him," I said, "but you torched his office. Or you had someone do it."

About to take a second bite of pizza, Queller hesitated and looked at me. "Me? Where do you get that?"

"Cutting the trail," I said. "Someone might go through Pemberton's boat records and find out Leon owned a boat with Wolverton, contact Wolverton, find Fairview and ultimately find you."

Queller took the bite, chewed and thought. "I can understand why you might see the situation that way. The logic of it fits."

"Is there another way to see it?"

"The truth," said Queller. "I recognize most journalists can't be bothered with that, but I'm sure you're the exception."

"I doubt I even know what the word means anymore."

Queller flagged down a waitress and ordered two beers, then looked at me. "Do you even want to hear the truth, Jeeter?"

"Sure," I said. "Why not?"

"Someone—I honestly don't know who—is indeed following the same trail you followed to find Leon. It could be anyone. Your 'cutting the trail' expression is apt. That's precisely what they're doing. They murdered Leon's parents. They probably murdered this Pemberton. The sooner Leon and I leave the area, the safer it will be for everyone, you included."

"Why are these hypothetical people doing it?"

"To protect themselves, of course. The situational logic is obvious."

"From what I've seen," I said, watching Queller finish off one slice of pizza and start on a second, "these men are professionals. They don't leave much evidence lying around. They don't need to protect themselves by going back and committing gratuitous crimes."

"Economically," he said between bites, "they need to protect themselves. I knew a Zen master years ago, Jeeter. Interesting man. He found the California preoccupation with Eastern cults amusing. He once jokingly suggested forming a cult of his own to teach Occidentals about the mysteries of life. He proposed a series of exercises in life for his students. One of the exercises involved grasping knitting needles in each hand. Each hand would use its needle to inflict as much damage on the other hand as possible while defending itself from the other knitting needle. When he suggested the exercise, I laughed and at the same time realized economics worked in exactly the same way, a delicate balance between defense and offense, but all of it controlled by the same overall rules."

"A game."

Queller nodded. "But a game is possible to model mathematically, predictively. With enough information about the knitting needle game, it would be possible to predict the exact place in space and time where initiative shifts from one hand to the other."

"Like your options algorithm."

"Both the program itself and, for purposes of this conversation, the situation surrounding it, use the knitting needle principle. The overall situation is like the Zen student with a knitting needle in each hand. Anyone trying to obtain the program is only one hand, forced by the situation to defend itself against the other hand while gaining its objective."

"I'm sure you believe all this intellectualized sleight of hand."

"Actually, I prefer 'the invisible hand,' " said Queller, quoting Adam Smith on the economic forces behind free markets. "It controls our behavior whether or not we acknowledge its existence." He smiled. "Like God."

"What about Wolverton?" I asked. "What's Adam Smith got to say about him?"

Queller shrugged. "What about him?"

I told Queller about Mark Weisel's exposé of Wolverton's extracurricular activities, Wolverton's rampage in Weisel's office and his suicide.

Queller finished his second slice of pizza. "Interesting. With his career in ruins—his livelihood gone—he probably felt as though he no longer existed, economically speaking, or existed only as Weisel portrayed him, a contradictory image of himself he found unacceptable, a profound cognitive dissonance he resolved by ceasing to exist as an economic unit.''

I laughed. ''You certainly keep things simple, don't you? I'm sure you encouraged the resolution of his cognitive dissonance.''

''Not at all. *I* certainly didn't put that reporter onto the story.''

I felt a twinge of guilt. ''Okay. We'll let that one go for now. What about the derelict?''

The waitress arrived with our beers. Queller sipped his. ''What derelict?''

''The body with your I.D. on it.''

''Bought it,'' said Queller and selected a third slice of pizza. ''If you're not going to have any of this, I'll eat it. It's good.''

''You *bought* it!''

''Of course.'' He bit into his third pizza slice, chewed and looked at me. ''Anything's for sale, Jeeter, even bodies. You looked surprised. Medical schools buy bodies all the time.''

''You're not a medical school,'' I said. ''And you don't just walk into Neiman-Marcus and buy a body.''

''On the contrary, several years ago, Neiman-Marcus advertised a set of his and hers Egyptian mummies in their Christmas catalog.''

''And that's what you did?'' I asked. ''Buy his-and-hers mummies from Neiman-Marcus?''

''Of course not. I paid two men fifteen thousand dollars and they delivered a body three days later. I have no idea where it came from. I took the body out on a boat . . .''

''The 'End Run?' ''

''. . . and cut it up.''

''That must have been fun.''

He gave me an irritated glance. ''I disliked doing it but found it necessary under the logic of the situation.''

''The invisible hand got a little bloody.''

He ignored the comment. "I used some of the blood and parts to attract sharks."

"Saying 'parts' sounds worse than telling me which parts."

"Would you like to know which parts?"

"I'll pass. So you hacked away on the corpse and took what was left of it out on a boat and dangled it over the side until the sharks chewed on it. That might have even been fun in a grizzly sort of way, like marlin fishing."

"I've never enjoyed fishing," said Queller.

"Okay, so it wasn't fun. You moved the boat away from the sharks and dumped that hunk of meat over the side with your I.D. in the pocket of the jeans."

Queller nodded. "Very good, Jeeter. But none of it was fun."

"Whatever you say. Then—"

"I threw up. I took showers until I thought my skin would come off. I woke up at night sweating with the image of that . . . *thing* in my mind. I have never done anything even remotely like that in my life. I have never even cleaned a fish. It sickened me, Jeeter." He held up both hands like a surgeon about to enter an operating room. "Do you have any idea how much dried blood you can accumulate under your fingernails?"

Absently, I reached for a slice of pizza, noticed the tomato sauce and changed my mind, sipping my beer instead. "There's probably some criminal act in all that, body-napping, burial at sea without a permit—"

"Littering," suggested Queller. "Are these details you mock important?"

"Details are always important," I said. "Life's details."

"I was protecting my own life—and Leon's. I did what was necessary under the circumstances."

"To avoid ceasing to exist as an economic unit," I said.

Queller understood my sarcasm but agreed. "That's exactly correct, Jeeter, no matter how unfeeling you consider it."

"And if it came down to a choice between your own wonderful economic unit and Fairview's, you'd make the obvious choice."

"Wouldn't you?"

"I don't know."

"I do know. You would make the same choice any sane man would make."

"Which brings up another question."

He ignored the comment. "In any case, the choice never came up."

"Where is Leon, by the way?"

"Safe," he said, "if that's your question. Waiting for me to think for him, as usual."

"So tell me about your plan to protect Leon."

"I knew I intended to sell the algorithm. I also have a good understanding of what it can be worth to the right people."

"A billion dollars?"

Queller laughed. "How did you arrive at that peculiar figure?"

"A multiple of what it can earn."

"Jeeter, anyone could duplicate my program from scratch for a fraction of a billion dollars. I will be happy to realize twenty to thirty million, the fifteen million I should have earned last year from Ralph Bollington and a surcharge for the aggravation this situation has cost me."

"Not to mention the cost of bodies."

"I had no other choice."

"I'm sure you think so."

"How else could I handle it and survive, Jeeter? I needed to protect myself. That much was obvious. For the kind of money my program is capable of generating, ninety-nine percent of the people on the planet would kill their mothers. Such people are not going to worry much about me. I needed to take care of myself."

"And Leon," I said. "You had to take care of your front man."

He nodded.

The longer I listened to Queller, the more sense he made. That worried me. For all his intellectual air, as though he could predict with precision the consequences of chaotic events—something I had no doubt he believed—his explanation nevertheless seemed possible, a situation he initiated getting out of hand and making him more a victim of events than the Machiavellian villain behind them, my characterization of him in the fictional Part Two. At the same time, I could also imagine Queller, certifiably bright and an expert on chaos, arranging everything to look like chaos.

"Okay, assuming for the moment all this crap of yours is true . . ."

"It is, Jeeter."

". . . what do you want from me? You wouldn't be here eating my pizza if you didn't want something."

Queller looked at me a moment, phrasing his response carefully. "I want to stay dead."

Under either explanation of events—Queller as perpetrator, Queller as victim—I understood his reasoning. "And you think I might blow it for you with the next installment of my series in *Global Capitalism*."

"I'm certain you will."

"Unless we have this conversation."

"That's right. I want to wind up dead at the end of your article," he said. "I don't care how you do it. I want the trail cut, as you put it, publicly and forever."

"That's it?"

"That's all I want from you, Jeeter," he said and sipped his beer. "The rest of it will take care of itself."

"Or you'll take care of it."

He shrugged. "Same thing."

I reached in my coat pocket and took out the hard copy of my story, unfolded it and passed it to him across the table.

He took the pages. "What's this?"

"Read it," I said. "You'll like it."

Queller read, at first serious, eventually laughing once

or twice. Watching him, I had no idea whether he laughed because something in my fictional account struck him as surprisingly accurate or surprisingly inept. Turning to the last page, he glanced at me a moment. "This is very interesting."

"I thought you'd like it."

Queller read the last page. For two months, he seemed to me no more than an abstraction, an idea that caused events, not a person. I watched him read, studying him, trying to get some sense of his reality as a human being. In spite of the extraordinary events surrounding him, Queller seemed to me no different than any other Wall Street yuppie. Expensive suit, expensive hairstyle, a mild air of self-importance, he seemed to me essentially a traditional young-man-on-the-make with no outward signs of his extraordinary ability. He obviously recognized the tactical advantage of blending into his surroundings.

Yet, underneath the pin-stripe camouflage, Queller was undoubtedly extraordinary, better than anyone at the game they all played. I remembered the *Wall Street Journal* profile of him. Several people who knew him in school characterized him as an observer, someone who watched everyone's behavior carefully, even measured it with stopwatches. His Ph.D. dissertation, mathematical modeling of chaotic behavior, and his time as a university teacher showed him again as more an observer than a participant. I remembered a comment of Queller's from the *Journal* profile about having only one thing left to do after developing his theories, namely, try them, as though dealing in a billion dollars worth of options positions were of no more importance to him than filling a classmate's dorm room with balloons.

Nevertheless, he played the game. Even after he knew his theories worked, he played. Hooked on the action, the money, the feeling that what he was doing somehow mattered, he considered the game important. Playing it changed him. Underneath everything—the mathematical brilliance and the psychological insight—Queller found himself acting out values as conventional as his pin-striped suit. Watching him across the table, I shied away from one thought, how well I understood him.

Queller finished reading and set aside the sheets of paper. "Very good, Jeeter. I see why you resisted my version of events. You had your own interesting but completely false interpretation to cloud your judgement."

"If it clouded my judgment."

"I think Leon would be annoyed by your suggestion I planned to kill him off." He laughed. "I did like the part about you shooting me in a Mexican standoff. You would certainly win such a duel. I have never handled a gun in my life. And the gun you killed me with—I particularly liked that—a gun used in an assassination attempt on Adolf Hitler. Very colorful. I must be important to have someone kill me with such an important gun."

"It actually exists," I said, self-conscious about the melodramatic detail. "The magazine's publisher is an avid gun collector."

"I'm glad something in your little fantasy actually exists. Have you ever considered writing fiction?"

"That is fiction," I said. "I wrote it as a joke."

"On me?"

"On my publisher."

"The balloonist," said Queller, amused. "The Malcolm Forbes of Los Angeles."

"He would probably resent the characterization," I said. "Anyway, call it a joke. Call it a letter of resignation. Whatever you call it, I knew at the time I wrote it that none of it was true. I just made it up. Believe me, I had a couple of shaky moments when I heard about the explosion at Lindy's Landing. I may have written that story but for a few minutes I felt like Kafka was writing the script for my life. Anyway, it was a joke. Besides, I was drunk."

"You did get one part right."

"What was that?"

"I educated Leon," he said. "I kept telling him what I *ought* to do. I ought to sell the program. I ought to get some magazine to do a story on me and leak the existence of the program. I ought to—''

''Advertise.''

He nodded. ''Exactly. I even told him the type of magazine and the type of writer I needed. Not you, of course, but someone like you. I wanted him to be convincing when I disappeared.''

''You hired the men to do that?''

''Yes,'' he acknowledged. ''It took me forever to get a few simple ideas through Leon's mulish head.''

''You don't seem to think too much of Fairview.''

''Leon's attractive,'' said Queller. ''Not bright. Which is not a good reason to kill him, if that's what you're thinking.''

''What is a good reason to kill him?'' I asked, pushing Queller. ''To cut the trail?''

He ignored the question. ''Jeeter, I *am* fond of Leon. I just don't expect much of him. In any case, Leon is irrelevant to what I want from you and I believe in telling people what I want. What I want from you is''—he gestured toward the sheets of paper on the table—''something like that. Without the Mexican standoff ending, of course. You might write it so your readers begin to believe I am indeed alive—all the factual suggestions are already in place—then have it turn out that Leon simply resurrected me to add credibility when he sold the algorithm. That sounds convincing.''

''How will Fairview feel about being the fall guy?''

''Leon will do as I say,'' said Queller, dismissing the question with a wave. ''He wants to be with me.''

''In Tahiti.''

''Wherever.''

I remembered my original impression of Fairview from the interview on the ''End Run,'' an impression Mr. Lusker convinced me to disregard as unrealistic. ''Because he's in love with you?''

''Exactly.''

"I thought you believed the invisible hand controlled everything, economics," I said, "not love."

"And so it does," responded Queller. "It's always seemed to me that people believe they are in love when they get what they want from the other person. If what they want is a free ride in life and they get it, they are in love. The free ride I can offer Leon makes for deep and abiding love."

"But you don't intend to take him with you to Tahiti."

"Of course I'll take Leon," said Queller, as though he were discussing a favorite house pet and needed a container to ship him air freight. "I'll take him wherever I go. I told you. I'm fond of Leon."

"Okay, so now I know what you want," I said. "So what?"

"What's in it for you, right?" He smiled. "Fame?"

"I've seen my name in print before."

"But this is a story about the great Horton Queller," said Queller, his tone mocking his own importance, "the whiz-kid no one noticed until he disappeared."

"Even writing about so obviously important a subject, I doubt the Pulitzer committee will break down my door to give me a prize. And speaking of breaking things, you hired the men who ransacked my apartment, right?"

"As you said in your little fiction," answered Queller, "I had difficulty finding Leon. I thought you might know more than I did."

"The chaos got out of hand," I said. "Like it did at Fairview's parents."

"I had nothing whatsoever to do with the death of Leon's parents. So mere fame is an insufficient motivation for you. Pity. Financial security? How does that sound, Jeeter?"

"Everyone likes being comfortable."

"Perhaps more than comfortable. Freedom's a key concept here."

I thought of Mr. Lusker in his balloon, *Global Capitalism* about to let him enjoy Queller's key concept. I decided to find out how much Queller thought I was worth. "The key concept here is money, maybe a trust account on Grand Cayman Island."

"Very good, Jeeter," he said, impressed. "You do your homework."

"I try."

"I wasn't aware anyone knew about my activities on Grand Cayman."

"If all you want is protection, why don't you just call a cop?"

"Why would I want to call the police?"

"Tell them your story. Considering who you are, you can make it credible. Money always makes people credible. Tell them someone's trying to find you and kill you to get their hands on your computer program. They'll check it out and realize it's true. You'll get protection."

"For how long?"

"As long as it takes."

"A lifetime?" Queller shook his head. "I doubt it. And that's what it would take. Think about the amount of money involved here, Jeeter. Police are cheap to buy. Even if the police prove as stalwart and incorruptible as"—he gestured at Part Two on the table—"you depict yourself in that fiction, they can't protect me forever. As long as I am alive, I will never, never be left alone. Eventually, some-day . . ."

"In Tahiti."

". . . they will find me and kill me—*if* they know I am alive."

"Why kill you?" I asked. "All they want is your damn computer program. Give it to them. They'll have what they want and go away."

"The knitting needles, Jeeter. I'm not afraid of people who *don't* have the program. I'm afraid of anyone I sell it to. They will need to be sure the competition never gets a copy."

"And you intend to sell it to everyone."

"Of course. As you pointed out in your first article,

selling it to everyone is a zero-sum game. At that point, no one will care about me. I can sit back and laugh at the fools and not worry. But to do it, I need to be dead, publicly dead.''

"And that's what you really want," I asked, "to laugh at the fools."

"Jeeter, these men owe me. It's as simple as that. I made hundreds of millions of dollars for them. I showed them how the game is played. I did something wonderful and their greed stopped them from seeing it. They wanted *more.*"

"Everyone wants more," I said. "That's a fundamental assumption of economics."

"The greed of these men is insatiable."

"Yours isn't trivial."

"The word *greed* is meaningless to me. *Money,* yes— that's how the game is scored." He shook his head. "But not *greed.* I wanted to do something worth doing. I wanted to prove the order in catastrophe and make some kind of a statement."

"Be important."

"Yes, dammit! That much, they owe me. The money I take away from them—twenty, fifty, one hundred million dollars—is only to get their attention. I don't expect someone who earns forty thousand dollars a year to understand . . .''

"Thirty-five," I corrected.

". . . but it is the only thing these fools understand or respect and it is the only way to laugh at them, take away what they value most.''

"A joke."

"A joke the size of their greed," he said and looked past me at the air. "A joke they'll never get but a perfect joke nonetheless. All of them are swine, Jeeter.''

I watched Queller's face as he spoke. He hated everyone he knew on Wall Street, perhaps even the idea of Wall Street as an abstraction. He loathed how it seduced him and changed him. He loathed Adam Smith's invisible hand pushing him to seek the admiration of people he despised, twisting his feelings into shapes even he failed to recognize. At first, he probably believed his own unmatched career on the Street would express his contempt and let him laugh at people he considered fools. Finally, playing the game, he changed. He came to see his own achievement as merely a grandiose expression of values he considered shallow, a contradiction he both embodied and scorned. To resolve the contradiction, he resigned from Bollington Associates and started his own zero-sum game, his joke, trying to force everyone he despised to look at themselves for what they were, most of all, forcing Horton Queller to look at Horton Queller.

"You're a complicated man," I said.

He took a deep breath and calmed down, still looking past me at the air. "Sometimes I doubt it's worth my trouble."

"It's not," I said. "It won't get you what you want."

"Perhaps not," he said.

"But it's all you're about anymore, isn't it? Without it, you're just like Wolverton."

Queller looked at me. For a brief second, he knew I understood him completely and too well.

The moment passed. "And what will it cost me to get what I want, Jeeter?"

"Too much."

"Dead, Jeeter," he said. "That's what I want."

"I understand that."

He reached inside his coat and took out a small booklet, tossing it into the center of the table as though it were a discarded napkin.

I looked at it. "What's this?"

"As you said to me about your fiction, you'll enjoy it."

I opened the booklet. My name on the first page caught my attention. After that, my mind rejected what it saw. I squinted. "What—"

"Anything's for sale, Jeeter, and I believe in paying for what I want. That passbook—a trust account on Grand

Cayman Island—should answer all the questions you need answered.''

I finally focused on the page. Even able to read the single entry in the passbook, a million dollars, I failed to believe it. I looked at the passbook, front, back, blank pages after the single entry on the first page.

"You're bribing me."

"And quite well, too."

I tossed the passbook on the table. "This isn't real."

"It definitely *is* real, Jeeter. You're wondering how you can trust a dead man. When you write the article I want, how do you know I won't revoke the trust and take away the money."

"I hadn't really gotten that far, yet," I said, "but it's not a bad question."

"With that passbook in your hands, the account is irrevocable, provided the escrow terms are met."

"What escrow terms?"

"An article must appear in *Global Capitalism* portraying me as dead. The money won't be released until that event occurs. If the event fails to occur within the next sixty days, the money reverts to . . . another account."

"With your money, you could probably get a passbook just like this one printed up," I said. "Which would be a lot cheaper than actually parting with a million dollars."

Queller shook his head. "Not just like that one. That one's genuine. Feel free to call the bank. Give them the account number. I arranged to have them read you the terms of the trust. It's all quite real."

I looked at the passbook on the table. Even if the passbook were real, even if I accepted the bribe, how would I explain to the world my sudden good fortune or, for that matter, how would I explain it to the Internal Revenue Service or my wife. On the other hand, with enough motivation, I could usually explain anything. I thought about the odds against my ever again being in a position to be bribed with a million dollars.

"This *is* real?" I asked.

"Very."

In theory, I could do what Queller wanted done. I could make up with Mr. Lusker and write the story. The dance might take fancy footwork, but it seemed possible. With a million-dollar bonus, I could live comfortably while I scolded myself for my lack of integrity.

"Take it, Jeeter," urged Queller. "It's as simple as that."

I shook my head. "It's not."

Queller became irritated, his voice petulant. "Just take the damn passbook, Jeeter. Do it."

"Do you always get what you want?"

"Always."

"Maybe not."

"Not enough money?" He said and laughed. "What? Your integrity's worth more? Don't be greedy, Jeeter. It's enough. Greed is unbecoming in a serious journalist."

I started to reach for the passbook. More than anything, Queller's condescending tone of voice stopped my hand, as though he were dealing with a reluctant employee. He already thought he owned me. Listening to him, I felt as though I were joining the list of people he scorned. I withdrew my hand.

I sat back in my chair, took a breath and looked at him. "High finance goes through me like too many beers. I've got to pee."

"Think, you mean."

"That too," I said, standing up. "I'll be back."

"I'm sure you will."

I walked to the rear of the restaurant, my stomach upset, my head foggy, feeling as though three days had passed since I sat down and ordered pizza. I found the men's room and stood at the urinal, peeing and thinking. Nothing about the situation seemed real, especially the million dollars. Queller was right. People who earned $35,000 a year were genetically incapable of understanding people who tossed a million dollars across a pizzeria table as a bribe.

I zipped my fly, washed my hands and went back into the restaurant, both my bladder and my mind less burdened. When I reached the bar, the table was empty, Queller gone. I noticed the check for the pizza on a plastic tray.

''Stiffed for the check,'' I said and picked it off the tray. The passbook lay on the tray like a tip.

Chapter Seventeen

I paid the check and went out to my car. I looked around the restaurant parking lot for Queller but saw no sign of either him or the BMW. Not that I expected to find him. Except for the Grand Cayman passbook in my coat pocket, my entire conversation with him could have been a figment of my imagination, a hallucination produced by too much stress. Horton Queller, after all, was dead. Everyone knew that. They read it in the article I wrote.

I drove home, distracted, confused, glancing frequently in the mirrors for BMWs. The storm finally arrived, initially a light mist on the windshield. Too preoccupied to worry about mere weather, I failed to turn on the windshield wipers. Gradually, the outside world blurred, stoplights, taillights and shopwindows becoming smeared patches of light on the glass. Once, I clicked on the interior light and glanced at the passbook, half expecting to find it blank. It still contained a million dollars. I looked up and found myself staring at headlights, money again threatening to kill me. I swerved, felt a *whoomp* of air as an oncoming truck jostled the car and got back on the right side of the road.

I waited until I got to the parking garage under my apartment to look at the passbook again, studied it all the way across the garage to the elevator, checked it again in the elevator and, finally, inside my demolished apartment, propped the passbook against a broken vase on the

217

coffee table, poured vodka into a tumbler full of ice and sat on the couch, sipping my drink and watching the passbook as though I expected it to do something, vanish perhaps.

"This is nuts," I said and nodded, agreeing with myself. "Absolutely nuts."

I stared at the passbook some more. All Queller wanted for his money—for his million dollars in a Cayman Island account—was to stay dead. If I wrote the article, became a hero at *Global Capitalism* for boosting circulation and simultaneously fulfilled my promise as the magazine's superstar reporter—in short, if I did exactly what everyone wanted me to do—I would never again have to do anything anyone wanted me to do.

I refilled the vodka glass and walked over to the computer at the desk in the corner. I plugged the cord from the modem into the telephone wall jack, booted up the computer and brought up the telecommunications software. I told the computer to call the *Global Capitalism* data line. It called and connected.

On line with the office file server, I found my subdirectory and started to pull up Part Two. A prompt appeared on my screen.

Enter Password:

I typed in BIGDEAL. An error message appeared.

Error: Incorrect Password

I tried again. The error message reappeared. I tried a third time, looking at the keyboard and carefully spelling out the password hunt-and-peck style.

Error: Incorrect Password

I noticed a READ.ME file in the directory and pulled it up.

Jeeter,

In case you get any bright ideas about erasing anything to play little pay-back games, I changed the password on your ''Death of a Whiz-Kid'' piece. With a
little editing—in particular, that ending; you must have
been drunk or thought I was stupid when you wrote it—
it runs as is.

H.L.

I tried to erase the file. Another error message appeared, informing me the file was marked ''read-only,'' a
procedure usually used to prevent accidental erasures.
Even if I drove to the office and did something drastic to
get rid of the file—erase the entire office file server, for
example—Mr. Lusker probably had a backup of my story
on his home computer.

I shut off the computer and walked back to the couch.
I sat down and stared at the Cayman Island passbook,
remembering Mr. Lusker at the estate. He trotted back to
his house, called the office and found the story. He remembered the BIGDEAL password from Part One and read
the story. He decided most of the story, except the ending,
explained the known facts and probably began circulating
an abridged copy of it among potential buyers of the magazine, hoping to generate enthusiasm and up the sale price.
At the same time, he relocked the document with a different password to keep me from meddling.

''Asshole,'' I said.

Mr. Lusker's actions put me in an awkward position. I
could still do what Queller wanted. Doing it would take
some creative lying but Mr. Lusker would eventually let
me rewrite the piece. For his purposes—selling *Global
Capitalism*—any ending would work. I remembered the
bored-mystery-writer ending, *And they all shot each other.*
I could have Fairview and Queller shoot each other. I could
tell Queller in advance how the story ended and he could
pick up two more bodies at Neiman-Marcus.

''No,'' I said, rejecting the ending as implausible, a

product of my generally stunned condition. "That won't work."

I could have Fairview shoot Queller and run off by himself to Tahiti. That way, Queller would only have to buy one body.

"No good," I said, shaking my head. "Bullets leave too much of a corpse for identification."

I could have both Fairview and Queller vanish, presumed murdered by someone looking for Queller's computer program.

"That," I said, thinking, "has possibilities—presumed murdered doesn't require any bodies."

No matter what ending I ultimately decided to use, I had to do something. That much was clear. If I sat on my hands, Mr. Lusker would run the story more or less as I wrote it, probably editing it to leave Queller alive at the end; for me, a fate worse than death, that is, bankruptcy. The Cayman Island passbook would empty automatically. The story would be picked apart by every journalist from New York to Tokyo. My reputation would go from nonexistent to infamous. *Cheater Jeeter* would become a synonym for slipshod journalism. I would wind up broke, out of work, scorned and despised. My wife would leave me. My daughter would grow up thinking of her father as a fraud, a con man, a spineless and contemptible human being. My friends, if I still had any, would spit on me. I would find myself staring into the bottom of an empty schnapps or tequila bottle and suck a shotgun like Wolverton, a contradiction resolved.

All of which meant I had to do something.

"But what, dammit?"

I walked to the breakfast counter, took out the slip of paper Mr. Lusker gave me in the balloon with Fairview's phone number on it and called the number.

Queller answered.

"This is Jeeter," I said. "I've got a problem."

I told Queller about Mr. Lusker and the story, including Mr. Lusker's reasons for wanting the story.

"Interesting," said Queller. "And you believe these other publishers have already seen your fiction."

"Some version of it," I said. "Yes."

"You believe he probably omitted the ending?" asked Queller, thinking.

"I would in his position," I said. "His note said he thought I was drunk when I wrote it. Which I sort of was."

Queller thought some more. "It still works, Jeeter. Use the scenario I gave you."

"What scenario?"

"Leon resurrected me, a figment of his imagination, just to make the sale of my algorithm credible."

I considered the suggestion. The explanation might convince Mr. Lusker. I could explain my original ending as a product of alcohol and frustration. The scenario still caused Queller a few problems. "If Leon's alive at the end of the story, you've got the same problem you're trying to avoid. They'll look for Leon and find you."

"Kill him."

"Pardon me?"

"Kill off Leon."

I heard Fairview's voice in the background. *"Hortie!"*

Queller explained to Fairview, a fictional killing. "It's the only way. We'll fake it like I did the last time."

"But *dying,* Hortie—"

"Do you have anyone here you care about, Leon?" asked Queller, trying to convince Fairview to die gracefully.

"Just you."

"And I'll be there," said Queller. "So what's the problem? As Jeeter keeps saying, it cuts the trail. We'll be safe. Even *you* can understand that."

"Hortie, I wish you'd *stop* that," protested Fairview. "I'm not stupid."

"Of course you're not, Leon," said Queller, his voice sounding as though he had held the same conversation more times than he cared to remember.

"It's just that you're very smart," said Fairview.

Queller laughed. "Oh, is that it? Anyway, Leon, it's simple. I've done it before."

"You might try 'Trust me,' " I suggested.

Queller ignored me. "Everything will seem perfect in every detail, Leon."

Perfect in every detail—the phrase bothered me. Some subtle cast to Queller's voice bothered me, as though he already knew how to make everything perfect in every detail. When Queller himself disappeared, nothing was perfect, especially the shark-eaten torso.

"Queller."

"What?" snapped Queller, irritated by the distraction from his attempt to calm Fairview.

"It won't work."

"Why don't you leave that part to me, Jeeter?" he said, his voice indicating I had just joined the line of idiots led by Fairview. "I'll handle stage management."

"But—"

"Just do your part, Jeeter. You're being well paid." He hung up.

I tried to call back. Busy, the phone evidently off the hook.

I carried the phone back to the couch and sat down. I looked at the million-dollar passbook. Going over every possible scenario, I could think of only one way Queller could stage-manage the events at the end of my story and make reality perfect in every detail. He wanted more for his money than just a story in a magazine.

I tapped out 911 on the telephone.

A woman answered. "What agency do you need, sir?"

"Police."

The line clicked. A man replaced the woman. "L.A.P.D."

"I'd like to report a murder," I said and hesitated, the word *murder* premature. "I mean a murder about to take place."

"Name?"

"Mine or the victim's?"

"Yours first."

I gave my name. "The victim or potential victim or whatever he is—"

"You sound confused, sir," said the man. "Why don't you slow down and take it step by step. Where is this alleged homicide going to take place?"

"Where?" I said. "I . . . don't know."

"In Los Angeles?"

"No," I said. "At least I don't think so. I don't know."

"All right," said the man, his initial gravity giving way to tolerant aggravation. "Do we know *when* the homicide is going to take place?"

"Soon, I think."

"Soon," he said. "All right. Let's move right along to who."

"Leon Fairview."

"That's the name of the person you think will be the victim of this homicide somewhere sometime?"

"Yes."

"But Mr. Fairview is alive at this moment."

"That's correct."

"How can we contact Mr. Fairview?"

I gave the officer the phone number.

"Area code?"

"Seven one four."

"Orange County," he commented, as though I had just missed the grand prize on a quiz show by a single question. "That's out of our jurisdiction, sir."

"I understand, but—"

"Why don't you give someone down in Orange County a call. But frankly, sir, assuming you have any basis in fact for this call—"

"I do."

"I'm sure you think so," he continued. "Assuming we're talking reality her, I doubt the authorities in Orange County will be able to help you unless you can come up with more details."

"Details," I said. "What kind of details?"

"When, for example," he suggested. "Or where."

"But—"

"I have another call, sir." He hung up.

I felt as though I had just been written off as a nut. Thinking about the conversation—no when, no where—I probably deserved it. If I called a police agency in Orange County, I would get the same nut-case treatment. The where, at least, I could give them.

I took the elevator down to my car and drove toward the *Global Capitalism* office. Drinking half the day, together with the general wear and tear on my nerves, left me bone tired. I rolled down the window to stay alert. Rain blew in, soaking me. I parked on Wilshire Boulevard and went up to the office using my unreturned key to get in. I flicked on the office lights and walked back to the magazine's library. I finally found the bookcase full of directories, its bottom shelf phone books, the last few phone books reverse directories for Los Angeles and Orange Counties. I looked up Queller's number. The directory, recent, showed the address as somewhere on the Balboa Peninsula and the name as *Q. Horton*.

I called the Newport Beach police from the library phone and asked for Sergeant Gahr.

"She's gone home for the evening," said a male voice. "What do you need?"

"I need Sergeant Gahr," I said, wishing I still had the pick message slip from Fairview with Sergeant Gahr's phone number on it. "Or her home phone number. She gave it to me once but I accidentally tore it up."

"Is this an emergency?"

"Definitely."

"Perhaps I can help."

"The phone number—"

"We don't give out home phone numbers."

I started telling the story. The more I talked, the more inept I sounded, disappearances, sharks, murders, mil-

lions of dollars at stake, magazine articles, real and imagined, all of it jumbled into an urgent, incoherent mess.
"Believe me, officer, this is not a nut call."

"I understand, sir," he said, patronizing me. "Perhaps
if you could come in and tell us about it in person—"

"There isn't or might not be enough time."

"Sir, we receive many unsubstantiated calls from people who entertain themselves by having police cars drive
to someone's house. Since this homicide you speak of is
not currently in progress—"

"It *might* be in progress," I said. "I don't *know* whether
it's in progress."

"Neither do we until we verify what you have to say."

"So verify it."

"You'll have to come in and talk to us, Mr. Jeeter."
He hung up.

I called the house on the Balboa Peninsula. The line
was still busy.

I left the library and walked down the corridor to my
office. I sat at my desk in the dark and tried to think. By
the time I drove to Newport Beach and convinced the police to listen, Fairview might be dead, the last detail perfect in Queller's plan and my own version of events an
apparent delusion. I looked at the silhouette of my computer on the desk and remembered the afternoon spent
rationalizing every detail of Queller's story to fit a fictional
reality. Perhaps other alternatives existed. Perhaps thinking through the events for my fictionalized version of
Queller's demise blinded me from seeing any of those alternatives. Whatever the cause, sound logic or profound
myopia, I saw only one logical resolution to the situation.

I left my office and walked through the empty building
to Mr. Lusker's office, flicking on lights as I went. I
crossed Mr. Lusker's office and picked up a ballooning
trophy on his desk, five pounds of metal and wood. I
walked over to the glass case on the wall and threw the
trophy at it. The office filled with the sound of shattering
glass. I used the trophy to clear away jagged shards of

glass from the wooden frame, reached into the gun case and took the Mauser off its display pegs. I found the release mechanism for the ammunition clip and popped the clip into my palm. I could see the shiny brass cases of the bullets. I jammed the clip back into the gun, jacked a shell into the chamber and hefted the Mauser in my hand. It weighed more than I expected. I put it in my belt and buttoned my coat. My stomach felt terrible, vodka, nerves and uncertainty making me nauseous. Ulcers were the least of my problems.

I drove south. Rain, heavy, slowed me, blurring stoplights and neon, giving the world the surreal look of a deluded reality. Once, changing lanes on the freeway to pass a creeping truck, I almost spun out. The Toyota, after a long sideways skid across two lanes of wet pavement, abruptly righted itself, throwing the Mauser off the passenger seat. I saw the Mauser in midair and grabbed for it, missed and heard it hit the floorboard with a thud. I imagined myself shot through the heart at seventy miles an hour, my problems solved, no more Queller, no more unemployment, no more racing through rainy nights for reasons I only vaguely understood.

I settled down behind the wheel and asked myself questions, the first question—so what?—the most important. So what if Fairview wound up dead? Who was Fairview to me? If I turned around, went home, made myself a stiff drink and took it to bed, what possible difference could it make to me or anyone? If Fairview's body made every detail perfect for Queller and Queller wound up laughing in Tahiti, so what? If I simply did what Queller wanted and cashed my paycheck, again, so what?

Good questions, no answers. I drove, a loaded Mauser on the front seat floorboards and my own irrational behavior utterly unjustified in my mind. I felt muddled, mixed up and confused. I drove nonetheless, leaving Los Angeles County and starting into Orange County for who knew what vague reasons. Rain beat on the roof of the car, obliterated images on the windshield and gave the steering a planing, out-of-control feel, as though the world were slipping away beneath me.

Maybe I thought of myself as a little boy doing the right thing to please grown-ups or the wrong thing to get their attention. Maybe I wanted to feel like the hero of my own life, an adolescent fantasy with me at center stage. Maybe, like Wolverton, my life a shambles of contradictions and all of them my own doing, I wanted to take another step toward oblivion and resolution of the contradictions. On the other hand, maybe I just wanted an opportunity to shoot Horton Queller for being an asshole, the embodiment of everything the adult in me envied and despised—arrogance, wealth, power. Child, adolescent, adult—whatever made me step off the sidelines—I no longer knew. I remember driving, merging onto the Newport Freeway and fighting a heavy gust of wind to stay on the road. I remember both hands on the wheel, the Mauser on the floorboards and my foot to the floor.

"Asshole," I remember saying, though who I meant eluded me.

I reached the end of the freeway, found the Balboa Peninsula and drove down it, hunched over the wheel and peering through the windshield at street numbers. I passed the street where someone killed Leon Fairview's parents. I passed the donut shop where I met Leona Fairview before she led me to the "End Run." I passed the street that led to the car ferry and a ride across Newport Bay to what was left of Lindy's Landing. Finally, I passed the football field of Balboa High School, once Wolverton's domain. The trip, a dark and rainy instant replay of my life during the previous two months, unsettled me even more. I had even less idea why any of the events I wrote about happened than why I was doing whatever it was I thought I was doing. Events simply occurred, my autobiography written in the passive voice.

Eventually I neared the end of the peninsula. The houses became larger and more expensive, an upscale neighborhood with boat slips. I slowed, checking house numbers. I missed the house completely on the first pass, probably some subtle, Freudian resistance to walking into situations where people carried loaded guns and killed each other. On the second pass, I saw the black BMW.

I parked behind it, got out, put the Mauser in my coat pocket to keep it dry and walked to the house. Rain, blowing in off the ocean, soaked me, plastering my hair to my forehead and my shirt to my chest. A high adobe wall blocked my view of the house. The few windows I could see from the street were dark, giving the house a generally deserted look. On the wall beside the gate, I saw a call box, walked over to it and pushed the button.

Nothing happened. No lights, no crackle from the call box.

I tried again, holding down the button. Even in the rain, I could hear the distant sound of the bell inside. A light went on. I released the button.

The call box came alive. "Yeah?"

I recognized Queller's voice. "This is Jeeter."

An electric lock on the gate buzzed immediately. I pushed open the gate and walked across a Mexican tile patio toward the front door. The door opened before I reached it. Queller, in shirt sleeves, looked at me from the doorway, his expression amused.

"Jeeter," he said, his tone ironic, as though he knew perfectly well the answer to his next question. "What brings you out on this rainy night? Selling magazine subscriptions?"

"Fairview," I said and glanced past him toward the interior of the house. "Do I get to come in?"

Queller stepped aside and pushed the door completely open.

I walked past him into the foyer, an area that carried on the Mexican theme of the patio, red tile floor, thick timbers protruding from stucco walls, rough wooden cabinets and *equipál* style furniture, wicker with taut leather seats.

I looked around. "Where's Fairview?"

"Obviously not here at the moment," said Queller.

"Or ever again?"

Queller smiled and shook his head. "Jeeter, you are definitely something else. You're beginning to believe your own fictionalizing."

"Where is he?"

Queller glanced at my coat pocket. "And do you have the famous Adolf Hitler gun with you? We mustn't forget that. Otherwise, reality wouldn't match your story."

"Where's Leon?"

"I haven't the slightest idea."

"Floating in Newport Bay?"

"On a night like this?" said Queller. "Hardly. Leon does enjoy swimming but not in this weather. Unless you are completely over the edge, come into the living room. We'll talk."

Queller walked ahead of me, stepping down into the living room and walking past a set of facing leather couches toward the fireplace. He took a brandy glass off the fireplace mantel, turned his back to the fire and stood with the glass, waiting for me.

I followed him, taking the single step down into the living room and positioning myself facing him at the opposite end of the coffee table between the couches.

Queller nodded toward one of the couches. "Have a seat."

"I'll stand."

"What is it you need from me to get over this foolishness, Jeeter?"

"Not smoke and mirrors," I said. "The truth might help."

"And would you recognize the truth if you heard it?"

"Try me."

"I already told you all there is to tell of the truth," he said and sipped his brandy. "I told you this evening at the restaurant. By the way, I'd offer you a drink but you've probably had too much already."

"I'm not drunk."

"Then I'll keep you sober. It's difficult enough dealing with sober lunatics."

"I'm not nuts either."

He shrugged. "Our opinions probably differ on the point."

"Where's Leon?"

Queller sighed. "We needed some things, Jeeter. I sent Leon to the store. It's as simple as that."

"On a night like this?"

"You wanted the truth." Queller shrugged. "You don't believe it when you hear it. Where does that leave us? Leon will be back."

"I'll wait."

"Wait as long as you like. Leon is *not* dead, Jeeter. I don't believe you covered that point adequately in your story. Was he or was he not dead in your story?"

"It was ambiguous."

"Well, *now* you have the answer. No more ambiguity. Leon is definitely alive and well. You might get out your little notebook and jot that down."

"Convince me."

"That, I'm afraid, is impossible. You are truly deluded, Jeeter, a figment of your own imagination."

"As I said, convince me."

Queller looked irritated, also worried, as though he were beginning to think he did have a lunatic in his living room. *"Why* are you doing this, Jeeter? I simply don't understand. Do you *want* your story to be true so much that you are acting out its events in spite of yourself? Is this some lunatic form of self-fulfilling prophecy, a third-rate hack who wants to be important so he turns his pitiful efforts into reality to justify his own existence?"

"Maybe the logic of the situation just fits. Maybe writing that story forced me to think everything through."

"Logic!" said Queller, as though the word coming from my mouth were an abomination. "You rationalized a set of events and now you *need* to make them fit. Your 'logic'

is just another form of self-justification, Jeeter. Ask your-self *why* you are doing this, *why* you are here."

"I know why I'm here."

"Really?" said Queller and laughed once, contempt on his face. "I seriously doubt that. Be honest with yourself. Can you state precisely the reason you just drove fifty miles through a rain storm to arrive at my front door with your famous Mauser in your coat pocket?"

I became aware of the weight of the Mauser in my pocket and the weight of my doubts. "To prevent you from killing Fairview."

"Good God, Jeeter! You are completely out of your mind! I love the man."

"You treat him like a house pet."

"Is that a capital offense?"

"No, but—"

"And you're right. I do sometimes treat Leon poorly. Unless—"

"Unless what?"

"Do you have some interest in Leon?"

"Interest?" I failed to understand what he meant.

"Do you want Leon?"

I still failed to understand. "For what?"

"No," he said, recognizing my reaction as honest. "You intend to shoot me for being arrogant, not as a rival for Leon's affections. Believe me, Jeeter, if you go around shooting people for being arrogant, you will run out of ammunition long before the job is done. And if you ac-tually believe all this rubbish about Leon—"

"I do," I said. "How else can you make everything 'perfect in every detail?' "

Irritation flickered across Queller's face, though irrita-tion at what was impossible to tell, perhaps at me for making the suggestion or at himself for using a phrase that brought me to his door. "If you actually believe this non-sense, why not call the police."

"I tried."

"And they thought you were a nut."

"Not exactly."

"That's exactly what they thought, isn't it, Jeeter? You called the police. You told them your version of events— these are people with no involvement in the situation whatsoever—and they wrote you down as a nut."

I sensed how little of my resolve remained, how much uncertainty and doubt. "We'll wait for Leon."

"No," said Queller and shook his head. "I don't believe we will wait for Leon. You clearly have a screw or two loose. I'm extremely uncomfortable around you. I don't want you waiting here."

"We'll wait."

"You'll force me?"

"If necessary," I said. "You can call the police yourself and get rid of me."

"Dead men don't call the police and I intend to remain dead."

"How?" I said. "That's what I'm here to find out. How do you intend to remain dead?"

Queller dismissed the question. "You know the answer, Jeeter. Certainly *not* by killing Leon. If something I said on the phone gave you the wrong impression, I'm sorry. Even the suggestion I might kill Leon is complete insanity—*your* delusion, not mine. But, if I were constructing such a scenario, you've just given me the perfect way to do it."

"Me?" I said. "What do I have to do with—"

"You've already left your footprints everywhere."

I frowned. "What are you talking—"

"Your delusion is on record with the police. They tape-record all incoming phone calls. If, deluded and out of control, you came here to turn your fantasies into reality, finding Leon alive would spoil your plan."

"What are you saying?" I asked, unsettled by the implications of Queller's statement.

"It's clear enough. A lunatic with a gun who wants people dead to fit a story he had *already* written might try to kill Leon. The police might find two bodies here, check into everything—including the story you wrote beforehand—and conclude only you had anything to do with what happened. They might decide that I was also only a figment of your imagination. All of this would make the papers and accomplish exactly the purpose I intend." He smiled and sipped his brandy. "Like the idea, Jeeter? As fiction, that is."

The idea, convincing, scared me. "Not much."

"But the logic of it," he said, reinforcing his point, "you do appreciate that?"

"Appreciate is probably the wrong word."

"You're the writer. You pick the word. But, on the chance I might be tempted to turn my own fiction into reality, I suggest you go elsewhere to thumb through your thesaurus."

I put my hand in my coat pocket, my index finger through the trigger loop of the Mauser. I cocked the weapon with my thumb. "I think I'll wait for Leon."

Queller heard the sound of the cocking Mauser and looked at my pocket. "You actually do have that *thing* in there?"

"That's right."

"That worries me."

"It worries me too."

"You're completely out of control, Jeeter. Please give it to me."

"Not likely."

He lifted one eyebrow. "You intend to shoot me?"

"I—" I hesitated. I no more knew the answer to that question than I did to Queller's question about why I drove fifty miles through a rainy night to get to the house. "I don't know. Maybe."

"I think it's definitely time for you to leave, Jeeter," said Queller and moved to put his brandy glass back on the mantel.

At the same time, he did something peculiar. *Peculiar* is a vague word. Peculiar is the sort of word they train you in journalism classes to delete. Peculiar is still the only word I can think of to describe Queller's action. Time and again, I have analyzed those few seconds and tried to determine what cue I saw, something Queller did or failed to do. Perhaps it had to do with his arm when he put the brandy glass back on the mantel. Normally, when someone reaches up to a higher location to put down a glass, he lifts the glass to a position level with the place he intends to put it and slides the glass to rest rather than setting it down. Queller's movements—almost studied, as though forcing the gesture to look casual—moved his arm too far or too high. Somehow, I read the movement as an attempt to distract me.

Almost involuntarily, I stepped back. My heel hit the single step at the doorway to the living room. I tripped and fell backwards, landing on my elbow. The Mauser, caught in my coat pocket, fired, the bullet ripping through the material. Half of Queller's face vanished, blown off by the bullet. He staggered back against the mantel.

"Oh, Jesus!" I said.

Queller's right hand, grasping for support on the mantel, brushed the brandy glass, sending it to the tile in front of the fireplace. The glass seemed to fall to the tile in slow motion, liquid spilling from it in midair, the glass exploding against the tile, the brandy catching fire. Queller's left hand, jerking spasmodically, held an automatic. The weapon fired once, twice, the bullets ricocheting around the room.

Maybe it was the sound of the brandy glass shattering. Maybe it was Queller's hand jerking and firing the gun. Maybe it was just the sight of Queller still alive with half a face. Or maybe it was what I felt about Queller, my own complicated identification with him and what he represented to me.

Maybe, maybe, maybe.

Whatever maybe explained it, I fired a second time. What was left of Queller's face exploded like the brandy glass. He collapsed into the flames in front of the fireplace, twitching, jerking, his clothes beginning to burn.

At the same moment, I heard the front door open behind me.

"Hortie," said a voice. "I'm back. I got your favorite things."

Chapter Eighteen

I stood at my office window and stared down at Wilshire Boulevard, depressed, procrastinating. Late afternoon sunlight cast long autumn shadows on the sidewalk, the first hints of winter. I barely remembered summer. For six months, whenever I paused to think or relax, I remembered only a rainy night and what was left of Horton Queller's face, flesh torn away, bone exposed. I woke up nights sweating with Queller's destroyed face before my eyes. The images always stopped with the sound of the second shot, always the sound of the second shot. If I fired only once, I could have lived with it, an accident. The second shot, echoing through months of nightmares, haunted me.

The phone beeped behind me. I pulled my attention from the street below me and walked to my desk, sitting down to answer.

"Yeah?"

Marv's voice responded. "Jerry?"

"What, Marv?"

"You sound funny."

"Preoccupied."

"That seems to happen a lot these days," said Marv, leaking criticism.

"What do you need?"

"Your attention, for one thing," said Marv, repeating

the criticism. "I've got the December lead story together for your okay."

"You do it, Marv," I said, the idea of spending the rest of the afternoon picking nits out of the December cover story annoying me. "I'm sure you'll do a good job."

Marv hesitated.

I sighed. "Okay, tell me about it, Marv. You've wanted to say something for six months."

"This isn't my job, Jerry. That's all I've got to say. You did this to me last month, too. I can't work on the stuff I'm supposed to work on and edit the damn magazine, too. That's not my job anymore."

"You're saying I'm not pulling my weight."

"No offense, Jerry, but I *know* you're not pulling your weight. *I'm* pulling it. I'm working up the stuff I'm assigned and editing everybody else's stuff on top of it. I'm just a worker ant around here these days. It's not my job to pull the whole book together."

Marv, promoted horizontally to senior editor when I became editor-in-chief, had a point. "Okay, tomorrow morning at nine o'clock you'll get my full attention. Not today."

Marv hesitated again.

"What?" I snapped, irritated.

"It'll be the same story tomorrow. I'll wind up doing the whole damn thing myself because you're off someplace in outer space. Jerry, do you mind if I make a personal comment?"

"Probably," I said. "But go ahead."

"I think you need professional help."

"A shrink."

"Whatever it takes," said Marv. "You're supposed to be editing this magazine. You're supposed to have your fingers on everything. You don't. I know this is wasted breath. You'll rationalize everything and say I'm just pissed off about you getting my job and—"

"Marv—"

"Let me finish," said Marv, committed to the conversation and wanting to get everything out before he lost his steam or his nerve. "At first, I *was* pissed—no, I take that back. I'm still pissed, but that's not the point."

"What's the point?" I asked. "That I'm nuts?"

"Traumatized is a better word."

I saw Queller's exploded face. "I've got a reason to be traumatized."

"I agree," said Marv. "You went through a terrible experience. I wouldn't wish it on anyone. But they've got plenty of experts who deal with post traumatic stress syndrome nowadays. You can get help."

"I recognize you're trying to be a friend, Marv, but—"

"You got that wrong," said Marv, taking an unexpectedly honest tack. "I'm just trying to do a job and you're in the way. You're more of a problem than a solution. The troops are rebelling, too. You don't even see half the things that go on around here because people just skip you and bring the problems to me. I wind up doing both our jobs and not doing either one of them right because I don't have enough time. You lay stuff off on me to do and, if I don't do it, the magazine goes down the tubes, which I don't want to happen because I've got bills to pay. Maybe you don't care—that Pulitzer money probably gives you a little more freedom than us mere mortals—but this magazine needs a full-time editor. Somebody's got to do it and there aren't enough hours in the day for me to do my own job and yours too."

"You're right."

Marv hesitated again, caught off guard by my answer, then cheered up. "Okay, Jerry. Tomorrow, nine o'clock."

I hung up and looked around the office, its decor changed from Marv's days, the coin collection and sailboat pictures replaced by plaques Rose insisted I hang—a Loeb Award for distinguished business and financial journalism, a Pulitzer for investigative reporting—both due to my articles on Queller. In spite of the personalized look of the office, I simply occupied the room without doing the job it represented. Queller, the reason I had the job in the first place, kept me from doing it.

I picked up a stack of letters on my desk and started through them, hoping something would catch my attention. I stopped at a letter from the Columbia School of Journalism and opened it. A professor, compiling a university level journalism textbook, wanted to reprint my articles on Queller in a section of his book called "The Journalist Engagé," grouping them with pieces by Woodward and Berstein, Oriana Fallaci and Robert Scheer from his radical days with *Ramparts*. The letter praised my dedication to both reporting the truth and accepting responsibility for the consequences of my involvement in the events I reported. I had no idea what any of the words meant—*dedication, truth, responsibility*—academic abstractions, smoke.

The phone beeped again, the private line. I answered.

"Jerry, I must go back to Germany next week," said Axel. "I will be gone one month. We will not have problems here I hope."

"Just one, Axel," I said. "An employee who's not doing his work may not be here when you get back."

"An employee?"

"Me."

Axel cursed in German and said, "I come in."

I looked at the connecting door between our offices. "You don't need to. Marv can come back in as editor."

"Marv is a toad," said Axel.

"Toady," I corrected. "But he also knows how to edit this magazine and he'll get the job done."

"You can do the job."

"I can't, Axel. I just sit here and stare at the walls. I can't take your money and not do the job."

Axel thought. "It is still this Queller business?"

"I have to work it out."

"It is a terrible price you pay," said Axel, sympathetic. "But the responsibility is not yours."

I noticed the professor's letter on my desk, praising me

for accepting responsibility. For the millionth time, I remembered Queller and the rainy night in March when I killed him. When I asked myself why I did it, memory blurred. I understood the first shot. Somehow, I read Queller's movements correctly, the brandy glass in his right hand a distraction from the automatic in his left hand. I stepped backwards, tripped and fell. My elbow hit the tile. The weapon in my hand fired. Half of Queller's face disappeared. But the second shot, when I knew Queller was only an instant away from death or already dead and simply jerking from reflex—why did I fire a second time?

The police never gave the question a moment's thought. They questioned me. They questioned Fairview. Fairview, incoherent, gave them nothing close to a reasonable explanation. Even later, he had no idea what actually occurred. Everyone relied on my version of events, Jeeter the trained journalist, able to report what actually happened. The police released me and closed the case, the official conclusion "excusable homicide;" that is, self-defense.

Excusable homicide.

The phrase haunted me almost as much as Queller's destroyed face. Everyone excused me, as though killing Horton Queller amounted to no more than a social *faux pas*, something polite society overlooked. Even Mr. Lusker, who walked back to his house and used his computer to read the events before they occurred, excused me, publishing Part Two verbatim including my Mexican-standoff ending. The story served his interests, no matter what he believed in fact occurred.

Even reading the financial pages of the newspaper haunted me. I kept noticing combinations of transactions in Queller's style, options spreads with enormous volume and quick turnovers, as though his ghost were still executing trades. At first, I thought my own sensitivity to anything having to do with Queller made me see his ghost, the heightened awareness of a man who buys a new red Ford and sees new red Fords everywhere. After all, I knew better than anyone that Queller died before he could sell his program to anyone and the police never found his copy.

When the newspapers broke the story, they all talked about the missing program and mentioned that Fairview returned his only copy to Queller. Whoever killed Fairview's parents and sank the "End Run"—muscle hired by Queller or hired by any of a hundred firms on Wall Street—either believed Fairview could no longer lead them to the program or decided to let the situation cool down before they went after him again. By the time it did cool down, the last piece of Queller's escape plan was in place and no one any longer had a reason to find Fairview. That last piece, Queller's last joke, I stumbled over almost by accident.

When Part Two appeared in *Global Capitalism,* I called Queller's bank on Grand Cayman. The banker in Georgetown, his accent faintly British, verified completion of the trust terms with the publication of "Death of a Whiz-kid," then added, "We also sent out the disks, sir."

Disks?

According to the bank officer, Queller's instructions included sending copies of a computer disk left with the bank to one hundred financial institutions around the world—Queller's final joke and the resolution of his own economic contradictions. Queller intended to sell the program to as many people as possible, then vanish. When he set up the million-dollar trust account, his mind was on disappearing forever. He understood economics. Even if he sold the program to as many people as possible, a large group of have-nots, people without the program, would still be searching for a way to compete under the new rules of the game. In spite of Queller's best efforts to stay dead, he knew that someone, someday, might pick up the trail to Tahiti or wherever. He needed an insurance policy, a way to remove any incentive for anyone ever to find him. I told him how to do it.

When he read the zero-sum ending to Part One, Queller understood his only alternative. For him to be safe, everyone had to have the program. That way, no one had any incentive even to remember him, much less pick up his trail. The idea probably amused him, extracting tens of millions of dollars from the financial community in exchange for nothing, another zero-sum game and a last laugh before the man who wanted his achievements acknowledged saved himself by fading into anonymity. What I saw on the financial pages was indeed Queller's ghost, the rules of the game changing as the program diffused through the financial community, everyone trying to use it before everyone else, everyone scrambling to get some short-term advantage before no one had any advantage at all.

Queller's ghost lived on. Queller himself died. Why? Everyone believed my version of events, though I no longer knew what I believed. Perhaps Queller did manipulate everything. Perhaps he hired the men who killed Fairview's parents in order to recontact Fairview. Perhaps he had them blow up Pemberton's shed to cut the trail. Perhaps he prodded Wolverton into a murder-suicide and planned to kill both Fairview and me as part of a deranged joke on Wall Street. Perhaps.

On the other hand, perhaps Queller's version of events was true. Perhaps someone else killed Fairview's parents and Pemberton, people willing to pursue Queller to the ends of the earth and kill to get their hands on his computer program. Perhaps Wolverton and Weisel were only casualties of the pursuit. Perhaps Queller, standing at the fireplace with his brandy glass, genuinely believed I was insane and a danger to him. Perhaps he only wanted the automatic in his pocket to force me out of the house. Perhaps all of it amounted to no more than a misunderstanding between two men whose nerves were on edge—all of it except the second shot.

"Jerry," said Axel. "You are still there?"

I took a breath to clear my head. "I'm here."

"You are not responsible for the affair with Queller."

"Affair," I said. "Interesting word. If—"

"*If* is not a game to play. You cannot win such a game."

"I know," I said. "Axel, I really don't think I can work for *Global Capitalism* anymore."

"And you do what?"

"Think, read, maybe write."

"You come to Europe with me?"

"I appreciate the offer, Axel, but I don't think so. I need a real vacation. I need someplace very quiet. My nerves are shot."

"Where?"

"Grand Cayman Island, maybe," I said. "I have some business to take care of there."

"You have an account there for the prize money?"

"Something like that."

"It is a good choice, Jerry. Very quiet. Perhaps you will see Harold. I talked to him last week. He is flying a new balloon in the Caribbean with that thin woman."

"Madeline Mundell."

"I find her very attractive."

"Call her when she gets back," I suggested. "I'm sure she'll be interested. I'll give you my decision before you leave for Europe."

I got off the phone, realizing I already knew my decision. I called Rose and asked her to find me a cardboard box. I sat back and looked at the desk I wanted once upon a time. Joy's picture smiled at me from the corner of the desk, a cake with four candles in front of her, four fingers with frosting on them held in the air. Somewhere over the six months since I killed Queller, Barbara and I made a silent decision to stay together. We seldom talked. Our relationship remained polite, distant, passionless, a relationship without demands on my preoccupied feelings.

I looked at Joy's picture and imagined the cake with more candles on it. Emotionally, only Queller and Joy meant anything to me, past and future. Someday, when Joy outgrew bear stories, I wanted her to understand about her father and Queller.

I glanced at the computer beside my desk, reached over

and flipped the power switch, bringing up a blank document. I typed the first words of a long letter—''Dearest Joy''—and looked at her picture again. I thought about what I wanted her to understand and what I needed to understand myself, doubts, pain, confusion—why. Why I pulled the trigger twice. Who I thought I was killing.

I started the letter.

Envy? Resentment? Greed? Or, as the police finally decided, self-defense? Do any of these words accurately describe why I did it? Perhaps.